W9-AHR-892

# THE BLACK CHAMBER

Other Novels by David Chacko

*Price*

*Gage*

*Brick Alley*

# THE BLACK CHAMBER

A novel by

**DAVID CHACKO**

. . . . . . .

ST. MARTIN'S PRESS
NEW YORK

 For information, address St. Martin's Press, 175 Fifth Avenue, New York, N.Y. 10010.

Editor: Jared Kieling

Copyedited by Daniel Otis

LIBRARY OF CONGRESS
Library of Congress Cataloging-in-Publication Data

Chacko, David.
The black chamber : a novel of espionage / by David Chacko.
p. cm.
ISBN 0-312-01390-6 : $17.95
I. Title.
PS3553.H2B5 1988
813'.54—dc 19 87-27347
CIP

First Edition

10 9 8 7 6 5 4 3 2 1

*For Ruth and Al*

*Only those means of security are good,*
*are certain, are lasting, that depend*
*on yourself and your own vigor.*

—Machiavelli
The Prince

# THE BLACK CHAMBER

# PART ONE

# MARINER

# The Clay

THE weather had been dense, funky, for days. Rain dropped suddenly from black rapid clouds and left a wake of strangely invigorating calm. Lightning and thunder were commonplace. To the north and west tornadoes had been reported; they had leapfrogged the Federal City, as if repelled by other centers of chaos.

It was after ten o'clock by the time Warfield arrived at his house outside Laurel. There had been an emergency at headquarters having to do with an outfall of low-frequency signals that emanated from Cuba. No one had seen anything like it since the preinvasion days of Grenada. The barrage continued from five-fifteen to eight o'clock virtually unabated, directionally westward, and was not receipted for by any ground station.

Warfield would never have been involved in the scramble except that someone in K-2 was sure the groups were being encrypted by means of a book code. He had been requested to stand by to supply information on enemy assets in the area who were known to have used that archaic but effective procedure. When it was decided some hours later that the blind transmissions were instead encyphered on a one-time pad, which could have been used by anyone, Warfield was sent home.

No one apologized. His employer, the National Security Agency of the United States government, did not offer apologies. For all purposes but the one for which it labored—the collection and decyphering of intelligence—NSA did not exist. Warfield had known, accepted, and loved that paradox since he had given up his army rank almost fifteen years ago to become a very specialized kind of agent. Only lately had he begun to question that decision. For the first time in his professional life, Warfield felt genuine boredom. The feeling had nothing to do with the stop-and-go rhythms of mission time, or even the dead spaces between missions; it came from being misused.

But Warfield's mood might have had more to do with the heavy atmosphere at the end of the southern summer. When he opened the windows in the old house, the smell of earth and ozone penetrated every room. The air had texture and freight. Both the clock on his night stand and the one in the kitchen were seventeen minutes of outtage wrong. It was as if an intruder had entered the house, stolen time, left a smell, and lingered somewhere nearby.

He had checked the mail and uncapped a bottle of Pilsner Urquhell when the phone rang. It was a sharp scrap of electronic sound, and Warfield spoke into the receiver with the same kind of forced greeting because he felt that some unseen axis was turning in his life. He was right, and he would have known her voice if she had not spoken more than the first clipped syllable.

"Stephen. This is Bett. Whatever you do, don't hang up."

He said nothing. There are silences that hold the past like

a talisman, a worm in the blood; they speak of disorder, love as rubbish, and can only be broken by a plea.

"I need your help, Stephen."

"This line's not secure," he said automatically.

"Then I'll meet you. At the Lincoln. Please."

His response should have been automatic. Yes was easy. No the easiest. Anything else would be desperate, a capitulation. "How are you?"

"I want to come in," she said. "Please, Stephen."

"All right."

Five years ago, when they were sharing the entire floor of an old Georgian mansion off Columbia Road in a forgotten neighborhood north of Dupont Circle, he and Bettina had over a period of time watched the renovation of the Lincoln, which was directly across the street. It had been a shabby second-class hotel populated by whores of both sexes, welfare families, and far too many people who carried guitar cases. There had been a buffet cafeteria whose steam tables were open until midnight and a lobby of incredible Gilded Age decadence.

The lobby had been retained and refurbished, but the rest of the placc had been peeled back to the rafters. The work went on for weeks. Hard chutes appeared at every window and down them into dumpsters passed the entire contents of the hotel, flooring and furniture, plumbing and plaster, until nothing was left but the shell. Even that was stripped back to the original brick and stone, and one day the sandblasters removed identity itself, pulverizing the name Lincoln from the facade and finding an older, perhaps more honest one chiseled into the stone: The Clay.

The rediscovered name had the right kind of cachet to be

kept, and the rising price of apartments in the city guaranteed a successful conversion to condominiums. The Clay was now filled room to studio with mortagees. The cafeteria that had served nothing but roast beef and red potatoes had been replaced by a snack boutique that served nothing but croissants and imported coffee. Perhaps no one else in the city could recall the pile of living filth that had once borne the name of the man who preserved the Union.

Warfield sat with his back to the wall in a Breuer chair before a small table with his coffee and a microwaved croissant containing spinach and feta cheese. Bettina was not in sight. The croissant was not as bad as he had imagined.

He wondered how long he would wait for her in this place and what the minutes would mean. Her voice on the phone had entered him like something with wings, beating the dust from all the old places, never alighting. Coming back to this street with its token familiarity had given those feelings a center to circle round. Even the new things, like the JOB poster on the wall that depicted a ripe woman reclining among smoke clouds, had the power to incite memory. If he closed his eyes, he knew he would see Bettina. Like the poster bitch, she too had an unconventional nose and hips that seemed about to heave apart.

If he closed his eyes Warfield might have that dream of the past, but it could be dangerous. He did not think he had been followed in his car, or on foot from the curb space where he had parked. He had seen no watchers in the street. There were only two other customers in the coffee shop, none of whom had paid him less than normal inattention.

Still, he could not tell what might come from Bettina's end. She was in trouble and she was outside: an orphan. No government agency would offer her protection. Some might do her harm. She had embarrassed them all mortally—the State Department, the White House, and most of all the small and secret intelligence section called Turnkey for which she had worked.

It was true that Turnkey, which was a special unit within NSA, had not survived the flap. The total and public failure of Bettina's mission had given credence to every claim and complaint that had ever arisen from the various competing agencies, especially CIA. In the name of economies of scale their redundancy was noted, and within six months Turnkey had been radically downsized. Personnel were reassigned within NSA and without, some were retired in grade, while a few were simply let go. Even the section's files were ordered to be turned over, like booty, to Central Intelligence.

That of course had been done and not done, because it was actually impossible to eliminate, or co-opt, sin. A few extraordinarily sensitive files had been held back, while the rest, which were computerized, had been dummied. No one knew of their continued existence but the deputy assistant director of NSA and their keeper, Stephen Warfield. He was the only member of Turnkey to survive in place.

There were days, whole days, when Warfield felt like a priest trapped in the confessional, and there were other days when he realized that he was no more than a monk. He was Brother Silence, who had been given the care of the records on the morning the barbarians had first been sighted over the ridge. That the barbarians were of his own nation did not for practical purposes matter.

That he had been and could be as brutal and ruthless as the worst of them also did not matter. Monks were only on occasion saints. In the Far East, where Warfield had undergone much of his apprenticeship, monks were often the most skillful and dangerous kind of enemy. In Korea after the war, on Taiwan, and in Vietnam, Warfield had come to know, if not master, every principle of self-defense and its systems. They were all alike in that they venerated survival and the counterattack. The systems were complete and sustaining as long as the reasons for survival were never questioned. If you had to ask, you were, as all good monks knew, quite mad or quite dead.

Bettina had seemed to understand that from the start. Of course she had had prior training with the intelligence evaluation section of NSA, but in Warfield's experience that rarely produced anything more than a constrained paranoia that was just not good enough for the field. The world was not full of enemies; it was indifferent. Enemies were created, slowly or quickly, carefully or haphazardly, but always by deliberate policy. The successful agent began with that assumption. The failure saw its light only at the very end.

Bettina had begun with as fine a grasp of the life as Warfield had ever seen. She possessed a fatalism so fine-tuned and well hidden that it was hard to credit in a young American woman. He laid it to her background. Bettina's father was a German mathematician who had fled his country during the late thirties and lost virtually every friend and relative to the Holocaust and war. He married late, after the war, to another kind of waif, the daughter of a Southern politician who came to the District with her father and proceeded to disregard his every wish, including his choice of husbands.

So Bettina had grown up with a father whose antecedents had been obliterated and a mother who had been disowned. It might have made for a good and loving mixture had they not come to hate each other so much, to divorce and squabble over the child in the courts, laying every indiscretion and unkindness open to public scrutiny. From the age of eight Bettina saw herself as an object of contention and negotiation, a prize, but one whose value was determined by tensions that had no reference to her worth. She would always be partially confused and completely hesitant about the possibilities of love, even as she learned to exploit its levers. In fact it was her amazement at its appearance and her detachment in its face that made her so desirable. All men wanted to move her. Very few had.

Warfield thought with professional pride and some personal bitterness that it was possible none ever had. Even with that boy, the ersatz guerrilla. Even with himself. The first time he had seen her Warfield had said to himself that, well, all pretty women were pretty much alike, but he had known that he was lying. This one did not act like most of them, she did not carry herself like any of them, and she was not really pretty. She was animal handsome, animal in her carriage and gait, animal in the swift instinctive assessment of every object and organism that lit the field of her bright blue eyes. She looked at everything as if it were pure potential that must prove itself harmless, hers.

A grown man should not be made to feel that way, and when he does, he has almost certainly lost the edge his experience has lent him. Which was fine, almost perfect for the life. That it might be equally disastrous for the normal existence known as life was also given. Bettina had not been engineered for domesticity. Her mother, who in later years achieved something of a reputation as a hostess, had passed the girl in cotillion under the proud and lecherous eye of official Washington. By the age of sixteen Bettina had mastered the jargon of power that passed for polite conversation in the capital. Her virginity had been lost previously, impolitely, to a drunken aide to the Joint Chiefs of Staff. Her experiences of the city taught Bettina that all men were pretty much alike.

She had been married after college. He was a young lawyer in the Justice Department specializing in civil rights of others. It was a time when there was very little else, if you believed the newspapers, and he did. Ned Eglon made a name for himself in Jimmy Carter's administration, never imagining how quickly that kind of fame could turn to liability. When the Iranians changed the guard in the White House, Bettina's husband changed his priorities, his job, and their relationship. It seemed after all that what was important had everything to do with money. It was called consultancy, or lobbying. The clients were of all political persuasions, and the souls of young attorneys were among the cheapest things they bought.

It would not do to emphasize Bettina's moral objections to her husband's conversion in values, because few women minded very much what their husbands labored at or with; but she had always balanced her discontents, of which there were a number, against the good he might be accomplishing in his work. When that method of accounting was overwhelmed by mere dollars, some emotional adhesion was lost. Ambition, which was something they had shared in him, reasserted itself in her. In the space of thirty significant days, she took a separate vacation, a lover, and a job. When he protested all three steps, especially the last, Bettina left him.

NSA was glad to have her. The divorce was a good recommendation, as were her three languages and her political science major. In addition, she had grown up with a hobby in cryptology. Her father had put his mathematical skills at the disposal of the several intelligence organizations that had preceded the foundation of NSA, and he had kept his ties on a more informal basis through the Research Institute at Princeton, where he lived. Until his death in 1981, he had tutored Bettina in the arcane sciences.

It was Warfield's understanding that she had performed very well in W Group, which was an analysis section at the interface of electronic and communications intelligence. W Group was one of the few sections that came close to all-source capability—the privilege of seeing the whole picture that NSA's array of filters provided. Warfield knew that Bettina had carried out her assignments for Turnkey competently, and that once, in Germany, she had behaved with exceptional courage and skill that had saved the life of the agent known as Mariner, who was himself.

He would have felt that he owed her had they never been lovers. He would have come at her call in spite of the fact that she had destroyed the unit that had been the focus of his life for almost a decade. He would have put at risk the position and pride he had left because he had never understood what happened in El Salvador that could have caused Bettina to make the mistakes and misjudgments that amounted in their accumulation to a pattern of incompetence, or, in a different scenario, to the accusation of treason.

It had been a CIA operation—all of Central America was—and they had requested Bettina on loan for a one-time mission because their own personnel in the region were too well known or too easily identified. Regardless of directives to the contrary, the Agency's case men—even when they were women—still tended to look like they had just come down from New Haven for a spot of secret war. Bettina, on the other hand, had Spanish, prior training and experience, and most importantly, she did not seem to be an advertisement for the *Yanqui* elite. She had the kind of black ambrosial hair so common down toward Capricorn, the modest height, the slow intensity of speech and gesture. Her blue eyes, though startling, would become a woman named Consuela Holzmann, whose parentage was well mixed.

Although the interdepartmental cooperation was unusual, Warfield had not dwelled on the fact. There was nothing to be done. The administration had fixed on the region as a test of its resolve, and every resource was fair game. Theoretically, cooperation between CIA and NSA was close, sweet, brotherly. In practice, Langley hated the very idea of Turnkey because of what its existence said about them.

Warfield had not known the parameters of Bettina's assignment in Central America because he was not involved in the operation. Even though they were in love at the time—or in any case he was—Warfield did not ask for details that might breach security. He knew that Bettina was leaving on a Sunday. They spent the preceding two days lazing at the shore. Warfield would have given something important—he could not say what—to have known that those were the last hours they would spend together for an age.

He certainly did not have any indication that Bettina would go haywire. Neither had her CIA control, Merrycroft, an old Central American hand who was also known as United Fruit. He had come by the name because of his severe affectations and the number of governments he had helped purchase in the area from time to time. Guatemala, Cuba, Chile—Merrycroft had been present for all the big shows. His experience and determination, now that he was running his own circus, were unquestioned.

But the days of outriding submachine gunners with one or two suitcases filled with money had passed, and the new problem in Managua could not be easily cowboyed. Merrycroft had already spent his budget in bribes and the lives of two agents trying to prove what his government said was necessary to be proved: that the instability in the region was fostered by an international conspiracy and abetted by the red hand of the Sandinistas.

Seen in retrospect—and Warfield had seen it all that way when they questioned him for hours and days following the crash and Bettina's disappearance—the basic problem was that the revolutionaries whom Merrycroft sought to disconcert had taken the same courses and perhaps attended the same schools as he had. They were younger, they were smarter, and they did not in any way look upon the business at hand as a game. In addition they had a mentor who was an idealogue and a genius: It was Lenin who had said that the key to deception was to tell people what they wanted to hear.

So Merrycroft ran Bettina into a cell that had been infiltrated some months before by an agent who had been accidentally shredded through the zeal of one of the government hit squads. His death was thought to be the best kind of recommendation for someone bearing the same kind of cover. Bettina was said to have been sent by the Peruvian Shining Path to aid her brothers in El Salvador. She was apparently accepted by them as her predecessor had been.

For the next three months things turned hazy. Bettina either found the process of making contact with her control too dangerous, or she was being deliberately disdainful of Merrycroft. The drops that had been set up were not used. The only report she made was rendered in person when she suddenly appeared in broad daylight at the safe house in the capital to give the details of the cell's activity while she had been a member of it. The report was more like a catalogue of successful guerrilla sabotage in the area, and Bettina's attitude was thought too proprietary, as if she were proud of the effectiveness of her adopted unit.

Merrycroft almost pulled her out that day. He probably would have if there had been less pressure for results and any other operation that showed the least sign of promise. But Bettina's penetration was the sum of several million in appropriated funds, and she had indicated a willingness to return undercover. Moreover, she demanded it.

Reluctantly, her control agreed. He also set a deadline of thirty days to obtain the kind of proofs that were wanted, or Bettina would be withdrawn and the cell closed out. It was one of those conditions that are unfortunate because they require that the agent conform to the calendar instead of his instincts. Threatened with a closure, Bettina had to move fast. She had to force things or confront failure.

By that time, it might have been asked which side of the street she was working. In all agents there is a streak of romanticism and fantasy that attracts them to the life and sustains them; it is the bedrock onto which is built the training and techniques that are altogether realistic. The finished products are human beings whose imaginations are leashed by their cynicism. If the leash is somehow broken by boredom or, conversely, by a new attraction, the result is a dangerous phenomenon—the double.

Yet when Bettina brought the boy out, no one was thinking seriously about the possibility because they were overcome by the sheer bounty of the blessing. The deed had been done in one week less than the allotted time, and the specimen was exactly what had been ordered by the highest levels through every branch of the intelligence services of the United States of America. Some immediate adjustments were made for the public presentation—it was decided that Roderigo Diaz had been captured by the Treasury Police in a routine raid—but nothing stopped the sudden gushing rush to press. What had been discovered was nothing less than living evidence of the conspiracy—a guerrilla who had been trained in the Middle East, funneled through Cuba, armed in Nicaragua, and introduced to the struggle in El Salvador like a new strain of plague.

Two things helped seal the catastrophic outcome of the mission. The first was the tremendous haste that seized everyone concerned and caused Señor Diaz to be shifted out of the country on the first available transport so that he could be properly displayed and the maximum in propaganda extracted from his young hide. The second was the fact that no one had ever debriefed the boy or apparently asked after more than his health.

For that last oversight Bettina was to blame, since she guarded access to Diaz quite literally with her body. She said that he had come out voluntarily, that he had agreed to speak for publication, and that she would not be responsible if anyone disturbed his commitment. Bettina had the room next to his in the safe house, the seat next to him on the plane to Washington, and she had sworn she would appear very near his side for the blitzkrieg press conference that had been called to sanctify his revelations.

It was impossible to believe at this remove that so many people had been so very willing to put their prestige on the line for one lonesome guerrilla, but they had done it. The department heads, the various deputies, even the Cabinet officers. They all believed implicitly in the confession of Roderigo Diaz because it was precisely what they wanted to hear. The elementary steps in confirmation that would have been taken in every case as a matter of established procedure were forgotten if not rejected. Text had been thrown away in the interests of creed.

Warfield first heard about the event in London, where he was on assignment. He did not even know that the boy-guerrilla whose story was flung across the front pages of every newspaper in the world had been Bettina's protégé. He could not imagine how anyone had sponsored such an incredible and destructive farce, least of all the agent he had trained. When he found out that it was her, his shock turned to the deepest kind of anger and shame. At second hand, NSA and Stephen Warfield had participated in the greatest intelligence blunder since the Bay of Pigs.

Roderigo Diaz had indeed met the press. He had stood before the bright lights and the busy cameras like a swarthy sacrificial lamb, and when they had asked him to describe his revolutionary progress through the international terrorist underground to the bosom of El Salvador, he had blinked his eyes twice, as if awakening, and said: Who, me?

Roderigo Diaz then proceeded to deny the involvement of any and all outside influences in his country's struggle for independence except, of course, the forces of American imperialism. He denied that he had been in Syria, or Libya, or Cuba, or Nicaragua, or any country on earth whose name ended in A. He said that he would not tell the story that the Treasury Police and American intelligence had given him to tell. He said that he had been tortured and beaten.

He said a lot of other things too, but they didn't matter. In the space of five minutes Roderigo Diaz had destroyed the thesis by which official Washington lived, and there would be every manner of righteous reprisal taken. Diaz, who had laughed in their faces, would be delivered for good and all into the mercies of the Treasury Police. NSA would be subjected to a savage internal investigation that would result in the eradication of Section Turnkey. And Bettina . . .

They would have drawn and quartered her if she could have been found. But in the five minutes that Roderigo Diaz used to recant his testimony and martyr himself for the cause, Bettina had simply faded away. Her disappearance was nothing that any decent agent could have accomplished without the diversion of the decade for cover, and by the time the bureaucratic mind set itself toward revenge, she was long gone. Warfield had never seen her again, nor had anyone else in the intelligence community, though they had looked. They had opened Warfield's mind by means of interrogation until he was drained of every bit of knowledge about her, and then they brought on the pictures.

The black and white photographs displayed the evidence of how Diaz had been tortured. On the outside of the folder someone had inscribed the legend "Beauty and the Grease."

On the inside were the shots that had been taken surreptitiously by Merrycroft's people at the safe house where Bettina had brought the boy, and what they showed was that in the most essential parts he was not a boy but a man well-hung. Warfield had been damaged much more than he should have been by the sights revealed because the very last time he had seen Bettina it had been himself partnered in the acts.

Common things, like the birthmark high on her hip, were transformed into emblems of indelible ugliness. Her black hair against the enhanced whiteness of her skin gave her the look of a sinful clown. Her smoothness against him who was all dark clotted hair made Warfield think of every degenerate conjunction between human and beast. They did it like dogs, like contortionists, like gargoyles. They did it and did it for a very select audience who would hate them forever.

Warfield had hated Diaz until he knew the boy was painfully dead, and he had hated Bettina until his mind healed itself. Only then could he begin to look at the situation objectively. Furthermore, he had to ask himself if the things that Bettina had done, including the night in heaven, were anything more than had been required. The answer was: Feasibly no. Given the pressures of the situation, Bettina had perhaps acted professionally. Only if she had been part of the deception, as CIA and everyone else obviously assumed, was she guilty of anything more than bad judgment.

And he didn't know that she had been part of it. Bettina had run, but in the same circumstances Warfield might have done the same. From the moment Diaz retracted his story, her career was finished. Their affair was compromised. If she had stayed on, Bettina would have been subject to deliberate and random sessions of harassment that would have made the ones that Warfield experienced seem tame. The chance also existed that they might choose to make an example, the kind that could turn her into a human husk.

So Bettina, for whatever reasons, had run. Guilty or not, she was still running.

The Croissanterie's plate glass window fronted the street, and strong track lighting spilled out onto the pavement halfway to the curb. Anyone passing on foot was clearly visible. There was only one public entrance, a glass door framed in the everpresent light oak. It seemed to Warfield that the neighborhood must have changed decisively to allow such a fragile barrier to exist. The air conditioning worked almost without noise, creating the one constant discrepancy: inside, dryness made colors sharp and crisp; outside in the thick air they were candied and brash.

He saw her first for just a second, arrested in the transparent glass of the door as if within the borders of a photograph. It was such a strange way to see Bettina after all those long months, but the image did not last—she chose not to stop in the doorway. She kept walking. He barely had time to record the way she looked, especially the changes.

At the distance, Warfield could not tell what the years had done and what were elements of disguise, but he knew the woman was Bettina. Though she was cut off at the knees by a barrier of ferns, her stride had that same big-cat kick and roll, as if space were merely the distance between targets. Her hair, as dark and lovely as a nocturne, was styled differently, falling briskly across her forehead in a modish butch cut. Even the sleepy arrogance of her face had been altered simply but drastically by the removal of the dark mole that had hung near the corner of her mouth. Warfield found himself fixated for an instant by the absence of that blemish. How clever to have it excised. How much of her sensuality had been divested with it, leaving looks that were still dark but more wholesome, less distinctive.

He did not pay much attention to her clothing because it seemed nicely current, suited to the burgeoning status of the area, and also because he saw the telltale nearly at once. Bettina had a raincoat with her, one of those cheap plastic kinds that folded into a pocket or purse. She had it undone, which was natural considering the weather, but she also had it slung across her left shoulder.

The contact was off.

Bettina continued down the street at the same normal pace. She had not taken more than three seconds to pass the windows of the place. She had looked neither to the right or left, except for one brief instant when her eyes shifted onto Warfield seated at his little table. The look was perhaps more than she had intended. In that split second of fused emotion, all that was special in their relationship became incandescent again.

It might have made him careless. Warfield barely waited until she had time to clear the block before he went out into the street looking for whatever had warned Bettina off.

He found it almost immediately. Two men appeared in tandem from the service alley at the side of the Clay like puppets from the wing. The first wore a blue windbreaker, the second a green. There was nothing unusual about them if a man were looking for a pair of defensive halfbacks. They were a little more than the average height and the same in build, both taller though no broader than Warfield.

He did not know who they had followed to this place or how many of them there were. He did not know if they had spotted Bettina and tailed her out of the street, perhaps with another team. All that seemed clear was that the two were very serious about their work.

They stopped just short of fighting range, knowing the

proper distance. The man in the blue windbreaker, who was on the dark side of white and had a face as closed and blunt as a medieval helmet, pulled his left hand from behind his hip, displaying the short belled muzzle of a Colt .45, one of the new issue no longer than a man's hand. He gestured with it toward a dark green sedan parked at the curb.

"Get in the car, please, Mr. Warfield."

He had spoken without accent, almost without inflection. The second man said nothing and did not show a weapon. He was as black as human beings are ever made and as ugly as a stump. Although he opened his stance slightly toward the car, he did not take his eyes from Warfield for as much as an instant.

"You people know my name?"

The man in the blue windbreaker held all he needed to know in his gun hand, and he was not about to continue the conversation, but Warfield was counting on the fraction of a second's hesitation that a question always provides when he spun and threw the crane kick. It worked. He showed the man nothing but a fast pivoting profile and struck his forearm hard just as the weapon discharged. Warfield felt only a flare of heat off his hip. He followed through with a backfist that should have broken the man's nose and an elbow to the ribs. Then he whipped him by his gun hand headlong into the next car up the line at the curb.

The man had no time to correct his balance. His head struck the window of the brand-new sports car, rattling the glass, setting off the shock sensors of the car's alarm system and putting one of the wildest, weirdest sounds on earth into the street.

The noise was so loud and unexpected that Warfield hesitated a moment. He should have gone smoothly into his next move without thinking, dropping into a low-horse and turning, catching the black man coming in high. Instead he crouched late and spun right into the blow, which was probably the butt of another compact .45. Warfield took it high on the cheek and low on the forehead, losing his stance and pitching backward onto the pavement. He rolled and got to his hands and knees. In that position he thought he saw new movement up the street.

Maybe it was the glass of the door of the Croissanterie opening and probably a man was shouting, "Hey! What the hell's going on out here?" but Warfield did not know that or anything else for sure because of the whooping klaxon that was going off all around and the kick that lifted him off the ground onto his back and the next one that drove his balls up into his body and the last that smashed his head down onto the damp cement in front of the Clay.

# The Puzzle Palace

"ARE you sure it was Bettina?"

Jack Brindisi, NSA's deputy assistant director, posed the question through the bit of a full-bent pipe. He used the pipe and his glen-plaid suit in hopes that they would make him look more like an intellectual and less like a killer; but no one could escape the destiny of a very cruel mouth and a low, very flat voice that seemed to come from someone behind him. It was even flatter at four o'clock in the morning.

"I want you to be completely sure, Stephen."

"I'm as sure as I can be."

"No wish fulfillment here?"

Warfield shook his head, and it hurt. He had a possible concussion, an unbelievable rhythmic ache that fell just short of a hernia, and three cracked ribs. He had left the city one step ahead of the police and driven with his chin on the steering column to Fort Meade, where he had checked into the hospital. The staff, who were all NSA, had treated him and assigned him a room and bed, but perhaps not before they had notified the DAD.

"What about the talent?" said Brindisi. "There were two of them at least, you say. Who were they?"

"I don't know," said Warfield. "I never saw either of them before. But they knew what they were doing. If it hadn't been for that lucky alarm, they would have had me cold."

"To what purpose?"

"I'm guessing that they wanted me to lead them to Bettina," he said. "They probably didn't spot her in the street."

"Are we quite sure they weren't after you?"

"Jack, if they wanted me, they could have me any time. If they wanted you, or any other high-level officer, all they have to do is pull in the parking lot out front and take down license numbers. We've got the best reputation in the world for security—and the worst security systems. You know that."

The DAD did not react to the criticism. He had his good points of character, which included a respect for the truth and a certain tolerance for initiative among his people. Warfield was banking on that to give him the breathing room that he needed.

"So we gained nothing from this venture," said the DAD curtly. "We don't even know if we're dealing with the Opposition or the damned Competition."

"There isn't any competition these days, Jack. We're all on the same side, remember?"

The DAD gave Warfield the same brown-eyed no-refund stare that he put to congressional committees and mad dogs. He did not like to be reminded that NSA no longer had tactical capability. He liked to think of Turnkey's demise as a temporary thing that would last until the first unsuccessful black op landed CIA or FBI on the front pages again. The administration would then have to turn once more to the only intelligence branch that could penetrate an enemy on every level. Until that day Jack Brindisi would remain one bitter Italian-American whose Ph.D. did not subdue his taste for revenge.

"If it's home folks," he said, "we'll hear about it."

"Through channels?"

"Eventually."

That was true, if not quite reassuring. The DAD was all-source on nearly everything, and in time he could track down a whisper in a wind storm in Somaliland; but time could very well be short for Bettina.

"I don't think we can rule out Langley or the Bureau, Jack. Those two men knew my name."

"That doesn't prove anything," he said. "You've been around long enough to make all the files. You'd certainly be on any list of possible contacts."

"That may be true," said Warfield. "Or it might mean that they have me wired."

"We already have your car. I'll send a team out to clear your real estate."

The DAD tapped his pipe, which was still unlit, against the arm of thc plastic chair. "Do you think there's any chance that she'll contact you again?"

"Maybe," said Warfield. "If she hasn't been scared off. She said she wanted to come in."

"That shouldn't have been so hard to accomplish," said the DAD with irony. "Almost anyone would have been glad to have her in hand. You could have, Stephen, if you'd followed proper procedures."

"Did you really want fifteen U.S. marshalls there, Jack? Or maybe the National Guard?"

"That might have been preferable to complete confusion," he said succinctly. "I'd like very much to know what we're dealing with. Where has she been the last three years? What does she have that could interest anyone now?"

"Maybe it's tied to the Central American thing."

"How does it work—this Central American thing?"

"I don't know," said Warfield for the second time in five minutes.

"But you'd like to find out."

"Yes."

The deputy assistant director looked out the window into the light of false dawn as it teemed over the small city that housed NSA above and below ground. It was his. Though directors and their deputies might be rotated every two or three years, the DAD was by virtue of longevity and practical knowledge the de facto head of his country's most secret intelligence agency. He knew not only where the bodies were buried but how deep.

"You'd have no support in the field," said Brindisi finally. "Everything we can do in-house—I'll set up a three-man twenty-four-hour watch—but there will be nothing outside. If you're uncovered, we don't know you, because you resigned this morning. I'll want that document on my desk in an hour."

"You'll have it."

The deputy assistant director rose to his feet from the easy chair with his usual brusqueness. Before leaving the room, he smiled as if to assert his sometime huumanity. "I'm assuming that you're well enough to go ahead with this."

"You shouldn't show concern, Jack. It's not you."

"You're right," he said. "We've all got to behave in character. That's something you should keep in mind if you're going to be dealing with Bettina."

Before he left Fort George G. Meade, Warfield spent two hours at a desk on the fourth floor of the Operations Building. He concocted his pro forma resignation, knowing that it was necessary. NSA had to be able to plausibly deny Warfield's existence to the world. The unit called Turnkey had been born when CIA was under heavy fire from the Church committee during the mid-seventies. The agency had violated their charter, it was said, and congressional oversight was to be the rule of the day. CIA would no longer be able to mount clandestine operations without half of Washington knowing it in advance.

But the chief executive of a superpower must have some tactical espionage unit at his disposal. With the agency's charter amended to function like a strait jacket, a quick look around the intelligence services disclosed that one of them in fact had no charter at all. NSA had been formed by the executive order of President Truman. It was not subject to congressional scrutiny, and its budget was so large that a small war could have been hidden in it.

So Turnkey was created. Its personnel were recruited almost exclusively from elite units of the military. Backed by the monies and the intelligence processing capabilities of NSA, the section had conducted the most effective clandestine operations of the post-Watergate era, and they were most effective because they were completely unknown. Neither Congress nor the press could penetrate the security barrier of Fort Mcade. Once any member of Turnkey departed that protection, he handed in a back-dated resignation of his services to NSA.

It seemed almost like the old days as Warfield sealed the document and placed it inside the pneumatic tube that conveyed interdepartmental messages throughout the Puzzle Palace. Next he tapped into Vulcan, NSA's auxiliary computer. Though Vulcan did not have the speed of the massive Signal Intelligence machines, it was still one of the most powerful computers in or out of government. Its data base dwarfed that of any other agency, and with a lot of manipulation and a little cheating, Vulcan could access nearly all of those too.

Warfield was looking for the files of the men who had bulldozed him in the street outside the Clay. With only physical description and age as a guide, the process of culling was difficult. Vulcan called up a round two dozen possibles from domestic sources and triple that number from foreign. After forty-five minutes of examining some fairly poor hip-shot photography, Warfield thought he had a probable.

The subject's name was Roland Gasqué. Delete the mustache, and he would closely match the first man in the street, the one who had revealed his .45 palm gun and spoken in that flat unaccented American English. Gasqué had been born in Woonsocket, Rhode Island, of French-Canadian parents. When his father died, the mother returned to Canada with her teenage son. Though the dossier did not say so, there was little doubt that necessity would have made Gasqué bilingual. His English and French would probably both be correct, colloquial, and yet a bit stiff. He was also left-handed.

The rest of the file made good reading for anyone amazed by evil. Roland Gasqué was one of the few men who reversed a major trend of migration during the Vietnam War. Still an American citizen, he had come down from Canada to enlist in the U.S. Army at the age of eighteen. He had served two consecutive tours in Vietnam in the Quartermaster Corps and had risen all the way to Spec Five when he was implicated in the brutal murder of a prostitute. Admitting nothing but taking a less-than-honorable discharge, Gasqué had eventually hired back into Vietnam with a civilian construction company. This time his involvement in a drug trafficking ring got him expelled again.

The seventies made Gasqué a man of the world. He was

busted as an accessory to murder in Miami, Florida, which was pled down to three years at Raiford Penitentiary. After his release, Gasqué's career became much more suggestive. In 1974 he was spotted in Quebec in company with members of a French-Canadian crime family. Three years later his fingerprints were identified in a Parisian apartment that had hosted a summit meeting of Canadian, French, and South American underworld figures. By the early eighties, Gasqué had made Interpol's watch list as an assassin for hire. He had surfaced as a suspect in two major terminations: a bombing that had destroyed an entire squad of Spanish government agents operating in Buenos Aires; and the public execution of a French magistrate in Marseilles.

Interpol had nothing further on Gasqué for the last three years. The only report of any kind came from a Drug Enforcement Administration agent operating in Mexico who had made contact with a man closely fitting Gasqué's description. The agent had been negotiating for a large buy of "white" heroin with Gasqué as middleman. Unfortunately, the DEA agent disappeared along with his Mexican informant and the front money. They were presumed dead. The contact with Gasqué was listed as "probable but unconfirmed."

Apparently no one had ever been able to get close to Gasqué. CIA personnel in France had interviewed a prostitute he had used in 1978, who provided some information on his habits. She said that he preferred brunettes, two at a time if possible, and that he had a liking for cocaine that seemed no more than recreational. He smoked cigars, oddly shaped ones with a wrapper that was almost yellow. He also paid well for services rendered; these included every kind of submissive sexual behavior.

When Warfield finished reading the file, he was sorry he had probably done no more than break Gasqué's nose, which, from the looks of it, had been broken before. He was even sorrier that the information did not contain some kind of cross-reference to Bettina, but he had not expected it. Gasqué could have been hired by anyone with the proper contacts. Only if he were working for himself would his background be relevant. Even then his business, which seemed to be drugs when it wasn't murder, gave no real indication of his mission.

The one thing that seemed clear was that Bettina had gotten herself involved with some heavy hitters. Men like Gasqué did not come cheap. They also did not involve themselves casually in a situation that would cause them to go up against other professionals. The stakes, whatever they were, had to be worth the game.

Warfield tried to restrain the impulse to speculate, because that was no different than any other type of gambling. Until he had some idea of what was going down—and he would have that idea as soon as he met Bettina face to face—curiosity would only disturb his concentration. The essence of the kind of counterintelligence work that Warfield had practiced all his adult life was patience. It was the will to wait to act.

The problem was that Bettina had made no attempt at contact again. No messages had come into NSA or to the machine at his house. Instead, there were three calls in succession from a man who said that his name was Ned Eglon and that it was important he speak to Warfield at once.

The timing, if not the name, ruled out coincidence. When Warfield returned the call, he was told by another machine that Bettina's ex-husband had left and could be reached at his office on Sixteenth Street.

It was easy to reach Eglon, but it was slightly less easy to convince him that they should not speak over the phone. Warfield made an appointment to meet him in an hour and a half at his office. Meanwhile, he collected his car from Support Activities. It was clean. The NSA technicians had found no transmission devices or any kind of passive bugs.

Warfield was well down the parkway toward the city when he received the report on the sweep at his house. It had taken a while to complete because of the numbers that had to be dealt with. Altogether, five separate listening devices had been located, including a tap on his phone and a directional antenna strapped to the main chimney. The technology was good and current but nothing that could not have been purchased at several different outlets. The antenna had been signaling to the general coordinates of northwest Washington and any one of several thousand locations. The operation seemed very professional.

Warfield hung up the phone with its multifrequency scrambler, thinking that there was virtue in consistency. Everything so far pointed to a well-organized network. He knew that in spite of precautions he could have been followed to the Clay. At night, with radio communications and a vehicle relay, the job would not have been difficult.

But it meant that they had been waiting. They were a step ahead of him because they were no more than a step behind Bettina. Warfield left the parkway near Bladensburg and took the long circuitous way into the city, doubling back every six blocks, working his way up the spokes of the streets toward the center. As he drove, he also set up a quick meeting with Stretch Dixon on the Mall.

# Professionals

THEY met behind the Freer Gallery and began to walk up Twelfth toward Constitution. The sun had come out like a blade, slashing through the fog and heavy vapor that had drifted in from the river and the basin. Crowds of federal employees moved semipurposefully along the streets, and some early tourists milled about the open Mall like troops on bivouac.

Though he was not a commonplace man, Stretch Dixon could have fit into either group without effort. His suit and tie were off the high end of the discount rack and his brown face placed him among the dominant minority of every American city. Nothing in his manner attracted attention. He was not short or tall. He was not loose-limbed and jocular, or pumped up and Bad; but once Dixon had been a paratrooper with a beret, and only his movements, which were completely liquid, always on the verge of a stalk, might still have given him away.

"This is one mean man," he said, studying the photograph

of Roland Gasqué. "Eat your lunch and then tell you he don't like mayonnaise."

"Here's the other," said Warfield, passing across the computer-aided facsimile that he had constructed of the second man in the street. "It's the best I could do."

"Lord," said Dixon, growling. "Only Jane Goodall could love that face."

Warfield had to agree. When he was putting the parts of the Indentifax together he had been aware of the simian components—the low brow, the prognathous jaw, the nose that was virtually unbridged and as broad as the mouth. This one looked like a throwback as much as Gasqué seemed the totally modern item.

"No name?" said Dixon. "No occupation?"

"Nothing."

"They're running together, though."

"They were last night."

"At night," said Dixon. "That's scary, my friend. You have any idea who's paying the bills for that kind of talent?"

"I'd like to know," said Warfield. "They're after Bettina."

Dixon stopped and stared at the Museum of Natural History, as if he were too considerate to turn the same hard eye on Warfield. He touched the halves of his mustache with thumb and forefinger. "Bettina," he said. "What's going on here?" He peeked at Warfield. "Are you people back in business?"

"Nothing like that, Stretch."

"This is personal, then."

Warfield did not exactly lie when he said, "Very."

"I'll take your word for that, but what if I run across somebody from the departments?"

"Back off."

Dixon nodded. He was glad that Capitol Detection Inc., which consisted primarily of himself, would not have to buck any of the official legions of the government. Though no one had better lines into the District Police, or for that matter into the unofficial apparatus of politicians and pressure groups and street gangs that actually ran the city, Dixon had to be aware of the arbitrary power of the most feeble federal agency to cancel his ticket. Satisfied with the boundaries, he began to walk again in that controlled stalk, as if gravity were a force that barely affected his choices.

"So all I have to do is find a gorilla and his keeper," he said. "We're talking strictly location."

"That's right."

"I know for a fact there ain't no circuses in town," he said. "My kids keep me up on that."

"If it helps, Gasqué likes to play sandwich with dark-haired hookers. He likes a little coke on the side."

"You think that makes him stand out around here?"

"He also smokes big cigars with a yellow leaf wrapper and a very sharp taper at the end," said Warfield. "La Regionals. They're not common at all."

"That's great," said Dixon. "I'll run with that. Sixty-seven different tobacco shops in the book."

"If this was easy, I'd give it to the Bureau," said Warfield. "You might want to be alert for anything that points to northwest D.C. We have a buzz there."

"A buzz?" Dixon looked at Warfield with forbearance. "You wouldn't want to tell me what that means?"

Warfield did not want to for reasons of compartmentalization. The less Dixon knew of the details, the less he could reveal if pressed for them. In this case, however, too much security seemed the greater risk. Warfield wanted the best investigator outside of government to be motivated to his best.

"It means that there's a listening post in that area," he

said. "They were collecting from me to get at Bettina. We don't have anything like a specific location."

"Stephen, I think I can see why you want to farm this work out."

"Hire some hands, Stretch. There'll be a meaningful bonus for all due speed."

"Make sure it's a cashier's check."

Dixon touched Warfield's hand as deftly as a pickpocket and began to move away, timing the light, heading across the avenue in the direction of the Internal Revenue Service Building.

Warfield did the same in an oblique direction in case someone was on his tail. Although he hated walking the broad, dehumanized downtown streets, he liked the opportunities they provided to lose surveillance. During rush hour the streets absolutely could not be crossed except with the light, and some of the government buildings could not be accessed without ID.

Warfield entered the National Archives on Constitution and came out on Pennsylvania. One block west he passed through Justice onto Tenth, picked up his car, and drove to Sixteenth, where Ned Eglon, Bettina's ex-husband, had his offices. Warfield found a lucky parking space in the street and circled the block from both directions before approaching the building, which according to the plaque on its front was a designated historical monument. It boasted a brace of revolving doors, a lobby without one wart of modern sculpture, and an elevator in wrought iron that was little short of nostalgic.

Eglon and Ramirez were on the sixth floor. Their receptionist was a tall black woman with a Dutch accent and a Caribbean lilt in her voice. She conducted Warfield quickly and interestingly down a short corridor to an office with dark wood paneling that glistened like fur. The desk was inlaid with glove-grade leather. The paintings were post-modern. The grandfather clock that told the phases of the moon was from an older Tiffany's. The overall statement was very masculine and successful because it cost so much.

So seemed Ned Eglon. He entered the office from a connecting door looking like the incarnation of what every well-thought-out professional ought to be. He moved confidently but carefully, weight back on his heels, as if every space were a potential corridor of power. His light brown hair had a yacht bleach and tousle, even to the nape of his neck and the backs of his hands. The faultless sharkskin suit had a memory as good as most computers. Warfield wanted to muss him up until he remembered that Bettina had done that reasonably well. It must have been a constant temptation.

"I'm sorry you had to wait, Stephen."

"Look, Ned, if this is really important—"

"It is."

"Then I suggest we take a walk or find some white noise."

Eglon released his good grip on Warfield's hand and shortened his Roman forehead with a wide-eyed stare that mocked every reference to NSA paranoia that had made the rounds.

"You really think this room might be bugged?"

"I don't know," said Warfield. "Do you?"

"We handle some pretty sensitive work here, Stephen. We have the offices checked completely once a month."

"Did you have them checked this morning?"

With the thick, stubby fingers that had doomed him for the piano, Eglon tapped his leather-topped desk twice. He might have been consulting his oracle. When he had finished, he turned to the bookcase behind his chair and opened the lower cabinet, which perfectly matched the wainscotting. He flicked on a small Japanese television set to C-SPAN.

"Okay?" Eglon had spoken as if there were parallel worlds surrounding him that were equally absurd. Civilians usually assumed that attitude unless they were stupid.

"Let's start at the beginning," said Warfield, after they had both taken their seats. "You called me this morning. Early. You left a message. Three messages."

The attorney nodded. "All right," he said decisively. "I've been in touch with Bettina. She told me that she was going to meet with you last night. She also said that she'd get back to me with the results—but she hasn't. That's why I called."

Warfield was not surprised to hear that Bettina had contacted her ex-husband—there had to be a reason why he was sitting in this expensive place. But the other news was disquieting. It might mean there had been more than two men in the team and that she had not gotten clear. It might also mean that she did not trust either Warfield or Eglon after such a fiasco. In any event, Warfield judged that it would be useful for Eglon to think the worst.

"It went wrong last night," he said. "There were some people waiting. I don't know what happened to Bettina."

Eglon did not lose his composure. He touched the fretlines above his brow. "You don't *know*?"

"I was having my own problems at the time," said Warfield. "I think we have to consider the possibility that she was taken."

Although he must have been expecting something of the sort, Eglon exhibited all the symptoms of surprise. His face was rigid and his tone dull when he said, "How?"

"The 'how' would have been easy," said Warfield. "Bettina broke off our contact at the restaurant. When I went out into the street, she was gone. Two men came down on me hard.

They were professionals, but I don't think they're the kind that are going to be interested in ransom."

"You think they'd . . . hurt her."

Warfield wondered why being hurt mattered so much to the average citizen. Perhaps it was because he could not imagine anything worse happening to a woman. "They'd kill her if they thought that was best," he said. "I need to know why they want her. You've got to tell me everything that happened between you and Bettina."

"Recently, you mean."

"Yes," said Warfield. "I'm assuming that like everyone else you haven't heard from her in a while."

"That's right," he said quickly. "I hadn't heard from Bettina in almost four years. I hadn't heard anything *about* her since those drones from the Bureau questioned me when she disappeared. Do you know they followed me for three months afterward."

"Standard procedure."

"Maybe where you come from."

Warfield did not react to thc jibe. They were close together over the desk, and the scent of Eglon's cologne was suddenly sharp, as if it had been reactivated by sweat.

"When did she first contact you, Ned?"

Eglon hesitated. He ran his hand across his seamless cheeks and down to his neck, which he covered as if it were dangerously exposed. "You know we're dealing with an attorney-client relationship here," he said. "Privileged information."

"I'm used to secrets," said Warfield. "What you tell me about Bettina won't go any farther."

Eglon took the full time for his breach of confidence. He laced his hands behind his head and rolled back a notch in his leather chair. "I'm going to feel like shit if she calls five minutes after you leave. You know that."

"And if she doesn't? And you don't?"

He shook his head roughly without dislodging a hair and put his hands palms down on the desk. "I saw Bettina for the first time three days ago," he said. "Last weekend. I was down at Annapolis—I keep a boat there—and I was looking around some antique shops. Penny was with me—" Eglon used the same gesture of his hand to indicate the existence of a woman as he had used for the boat—"but she was cruising the other side of the street. She collects lap desks. I do clocks."

Warfield listened patiently—it was good that Eglon was taking the time to set the scene. The more clearly he saw things in his own mind, the better his recall would be. There was additional satisfaction in knowing that the man was dull with his money.

"Anyway, I was looking at a Second Empire mantel clock. They were selling one entire wall—paneling, mantel, firedogs, the works—and if you had a thirty-seven by twenty-three room, you were in business. There was also a lacquered Japanese screen that went with the package. I must have looked at it three times before I realized that someone was standing behind it. Spies do have a sense of the dramatic, don't they? I mean, all that anonymity must get to be a pain in the ass."

Warfield said nothing. Eglon's tone was a reminder that two men who did not really like each other were being forced to discuss the subject of their unease. It also conveyed a bit of blame, as if Warfield were responsible for Bettina's change of allegiance, her life. That was not true, of course.

"At first I wasn't sure it was her," said Eglon. "She'd changed her appearance—and her taste. She wore a pair of new hiking boots that were right out of the bargain bin. Boots, for Christ's sake. She must have gotten them at K-Mart."

"Is that the only thing you noticed that seemed out of character, Ned?"

"Everything was out of character," he said almost angrily. "She had a GI haircut. The mole on her cheek was gone. And she looked like she'd gained weight, but I couldn't be sure because she was wearing a yellow slicker. It was raining—the reason we weren't out on the water—and everyone in town had one on."

"But you were absolutely convinced it was her."

"I never really doubted it," he said. "There are things you can change—and things you can't. Bettina had more of the second kind than anyone I've ever known."

Warfield knew what that meant. Originality was bought in fractions, little things that balanced the whole, and had almost nothing to do with clothing, cosmetics, or education. It probably had most to do with an inner ear, a sense of rhythm, a way of seeing the world that was absorbed and retransmitted. Somewhere along the line Bettina had constructed a set of filters unlike any other.

It also meant that if someone were trying to pass off a double as Bettina, they had chosen a difficult subject, and they had chosen to present her to the men who knew her best. That was a daring strategy, if strategy it was.

"What did she want from you, Ned?"

"What do people usually want from lawyers?" he asked rhetorically. "Counsel. But I guess when it's for free, it's called help."

"She didn't have any money?"

The attorney leveled his stare and his voice. "The subject didn't come up."

"What did you advise her about?"

"She wanted to turn herself in," he said. "She was very nervous. She was afraid of being seen by anyone until she could have some guarantees about what would happen to her if she came in."

"Guarantees?"

"Well, let's just say she didn't want to spend a month in the country at one of those brain farms you people have."

"It could have been worse than that," said Warfield. "She could have been looking at some years in prison."

"She didn't think so."

"Why?"

Eglon hunched even closer over the desk top; Warfield could see the scalp in the part running down the middle of his head. "Bettina had something to trade," he said.

"What?"

"She mentioned someone—or something—called Kronos."

Perhaps that name, which was obviously a cover, should have meant something to Warfield, but he had never heard it before. "I don't know what she means."

"That might not have mattered," said Eglon with slight condescension. "Someone at your place would. From what I gathered, they'd want to know very much."

"Where did Bettina get this information?"

"I don't know," he said quickly. "I didn't want to know. My advice to her was to try and get in touch with you—and to keep me apprized."

Warfield would have liked to know the nuances of that conversation behind the lacquered screen. He wondered what kind of help Bettina had really begged. Apparently what had been offered was a quick shunt between ex-husband and ex-lover. Yet it would do no good to insult Eglon's integrity. What he owed Bettina was problematic.

"Did she give you any indication of where she was staying?"

"No," he said. "I assumed she was somewhere in the area, but I could have been wrong. Washington's just a few hours from almost everywhere, isn't it?"

"Did she mention any places in any context?"

"No," he said again.

"How did the reference to Kronos come up?" asked Warfield. "Try to remember exactly."

Eglon took a moment to install himself in the antique shop again. The simulation was almost certainly for Warfield's benefit. He was sure that the attorney knew more than he was letting out.

"I remember she said that she wouldn't be coming in naked." Eglon paused again. "That's what she said. *Naked.* It was a curious word to use, I suppose. Here we were buttoned up from head to foot in rain gear. I kept having visions of Bettina as some kind of flasher. But of course that's just what she said she *wouldn't* do. I think my mental state wasn't very secure at the time. It was a shock seeing her—a continuing shock."

"But her clothes were called Kronos."

"Yes," he said. "She said that she could give you Kronos."

"By that she meant NSA."

"Of course," he said. "She used the phrase Black Chamber. Isn't that what you people like to call yourself?"

No, thought Warfield. Not for a very long time. It was strange that Bettina had pulled that archaic name out of the past. Was she trying to communicate something that was not obvious?

"Are you sure she said Black Chamber?"

"Certainly," he said, all innocence. "I wouldn't have made that up. I couldn't have."

"It's a very old term, Ned. Not current at all."

He shrugged. "Well, what can I say? We were in an antique shop."

"Where the best advice you could give her was to contact me."

"Yes," he said.

"When did you hear from her next?"

"Last night," he said with no hesitation. "Bettina called me while I was having dinner at the Mayfair. I don't know how she knew I was there. But when I came to the phone she said that she was leaving to meet with you. She wanted me to know exactly what she was doing."

"Why?"

The question, and perhaps the tone, seemed to jar Eglon somewhat. He shrugged with slightly exaggerated movements. "As a precaution, I guess. She must have been worried. With good reason, as it turns out."

Warfield had conducted enough debriefings and other forms of interrogation to sense when his subject was maneuvering without purpose—or rather, when concealment was his purpose. Bettina had not needed Ned Eglon to tell her to contact Warfield. She had no need to inform the man of the meeting that he had done little to promote and nothing to guarantee. The only plausible reason for her to contact her ex-husband in the first place was to provide herself with some insurance, which would have been of a tangible kind.

"What do you have, Ned?"

He said "I beg your pardon" with so much disingenuousness that it could have been mistaken for surprise.

"Bettina would have left something with you," said Warfield. "She would have told you not to give it up to anyone. She was probably meaning to trade with us. But the situation's changed. If someone's holding her, what you have may be the only thing that can keep her alive. I don't think you can hold it back."

"I don't know what you're—"

"We shouldn't waste time," said Warfield. "The sooner I know what she has, the sooner I can move. It's best for Bettina. And best for you."

"Me?"

Warfield was determined not to leave Eglon room to breathe normally. "Ned, they had my place wired like a recording studio. It would surprise me if they haven't done the same to you. Even if they haven't, eventually they'll come to you. They'll want whatever it is. If you still have it, they'll take it."

Eglon said nothing. He might have been frightened. He should have been.

"I identified one of the men who jumped me in the street last night," said Warfield after a short pause. "In 1969 in Quang Tri province he raped a prostitute. I'm not going to ask you if you know how absolutely unnecessary it must have been to attack a Vietnamese whore. Just remember that when he was finished, he beat her until she was unconscious and then placed a hand grenade between her legs. In 1978 he destroyed several agents of GEOS, the Spanish security force, with a car bomb that killed eight innocent civilians and wounded twenty others. These are a couple of the incidents we know about. You'd have to imagine the rest."

Eglon might have done that. His eyes moved off Warfield and onto the stately cabinet of his grandfather clock, as if the old pendulum works were counting down much too fast. The shift in attention was natural and perhaps not entirely controlled. He had to make an effort to right it.

"How do I know that you people don't have Bettina?" he said. "Am I supposed to believe that *you're* harmless?"

"You can believe that I wouldn't hurt Bettina."

"I suppose I do," he said. "But I can't be sure, can I?"

"Be sure of this," said Warfield. "I can obtain a warrant to search everything that you call your own. I can have it quickly."

Eglon gave all the preliminary signs that his back was up, as every good lawyer's ought to be, but he spoke no words for a good twenty seconds. Maybe he did not quite believe in the warrant, or that it would find anything. He was, however, a man who did a lot of direct and indirect business with the government. Any trouble with one of its more powerful agencies might cause a retraction of that big swollen tit.

"Stephen, I'm willing to cooperate with this investigation as far as possible. But I can't give you what you want. You can cause me inconvenience with one of your tame magistrates. I hope it doesn't come to that."

"It already has, Ned."

Eglon stood up suddenly, scooting the heavy leather chair back against the cabinet. "Then I'm sorry."

Warfield knew that he had made a strategic mistake in threatening a lawyer with legalities, but the issue had to be forced. He left the offices on Sixteenth Street certain that Eglon held something important and that he might take steps to secure it. It would be physical evidence of some kind, and it would have been hidden, perhaps temporarily, in the hope that Bettina would relieve him of the burden.

Warfield was not counting on being led to Bettina that way, but he knew it was worth the chance. One of the maintenance workers in the building pointed out Eglon's new Jaguar in the lot across the street and, for a bounty, promised to report at once if the attorney left by the service exit. In the meantime, Warfield returned to his car. From his space in the street he commanded a view of both the front of the building and the parking lot that was nearly catty-corner.

Conducting one-man surveillance was not Warfield's idea of efficiency, but he used the time to check back with headquarters on the subject of Kronos. The watch commander, a competent but implacable sort named Amelia Worth, also known as Fort Worth, took the call with a promise to get back quickly. In less than twenty minutes, she did.

"Kronos was a Titan," she said. "The son of Uranus and Gaea, who were the original rulers of the cosmos. Kronos overthrew his father in order to be chief of the gods himself. He is usually represented as an old man carrying a scythe in his right hand, for obvious reasons. The Greeks at times offered human sacrifices at his altar. Eventually Kronos was overthrown by his son, Zeus, who established a more rational order."

"That's nice, Banner. But I was looking for something more contemporary. Something in this millennium."

"What you hear is what you get," she said.

"You're telling me there's nothing on Kronos for the last two thousand years."

"Nothing but a symbol," said Miss Worth. "What we're looking at here is a transitional figure. A bloody one. The Romans called him Saturn when they adopted him."

"Try that," said Warfield.

"What?"

"Try Saturn."

"Mariner, I can tell you right now that it's a planet. A ringed planet in our solar system. It's also the prototype of a new line of General Motors cars."

"Keep digging."

"We might do better if we had some kind of context," she said. "What is Saturn related to?"

"I don't know," said Warfield. "It may have a Latin reference."

"Mariner, it *is* Latin."

"Latin," he said. "As in south of the border."

"I see. A coincidence."

"There are such things."

"Not lately," she said. "Not where you live."

"Do your best, Banner. Don't think. Push buttons."

"There aren't many buttons," she said. "We're not strong with the amigos. That's Langley's area of expertise."

"Are you saying that you can't get to their files?"

There was a pause on the end of the line that had nothing to do with the squirt of scrambled sound. Miss Worth's voice came back guarded. "I don't think we can do it without leaving tracks."

"Take the chance," he said. "I wouldn't bother you if it wasn't vital to national security."

"Yes, you would."

"This is worth a chit for dinner," he said. "The Thai place on Connecticut."

"Done," she said immediately.

Fifteen minutes after Warfield deactivated the phone, Ned Eglon made his move. It was a clever one. The attorney walked from his building without striking any of the stiff and obvious configurations of the amateur who thinks he might be watched. Eglon looked left and right for traffic, then crossed the street with an unhesitating stride. When he reached the parking lot, the attendant took his stub and money. Some words might also have been exchanged.

Afterward, Warfield decided that they had not devised the plan on the spot but were confirming it. Their exchange was very brief. Eglon had undoubtedly called ahead to the attendant's booth, probably from a phone outside his office. He walked across the lot toward his fine car and entered it. After a five-second delay, the attendant followed him, removed one section of the wooden horse barrier that ran around the lot, and Eglon, instead of exiting onto Sixteenth Street, simply drove across the pavement, jumped the curb, and screamed out into traffic on K.

The Jaguar moved sharply, sleekly, like the cat for which it was named. By the time Warfield pulled out into traffic and left onto K, he knew that his best chance to hang close with Eglon was the cop who might stop him for speeding. Still, he managed to keep the white sedan in sight until the block before Washington Circle. When he knew that he was losing, Warfield ran the red light at Twenty-second and turned north, where he thought he saw a flash of white heading onto the Whitehurst Freeway. Warfield followed, but after that one glimpse he did not even think he saw anything else.

If he were right about the direction, Eglon would not get far away. The transmitter that had been placed inside the Jaguar's rear wheel well was functioning properly, emitting a steady signal that appeared as a sequential blip on the scope fitted beneath Warfield's dash. They had improved these things in the last few years. Both the power of the transmitter and the selectivity of the receivers had been boosted significantly. Even in large population centers, the signal carried for three-quarters of a mile with some regularity, and in more deserted areas the range was close to ten miles. The signal could of course be weakened and intermittently lost, but as long as some sort of contact was maintained, it was more or less a matter of narrowing the grid.

Unfortunately, the signal went dead for the better part of a minute. When Warfield resurrected it, the Jaguar had altered course, heading northwest along an almost parallel line.

Warfield guessed at MacArthur Boulevard and came onto it near Georgetown Reservoir, where he maintained a steady signal for the next two miles. Somewhere around Arizona Avenue the Jaguar veered directly north, then west, north again, west again, and suddenly to a stop.

The area was one of Washington's better suburban reproductions. There were Tudor mini-manors, pocket chateaux, and echoes of an earlier South. The streets broke the normal spoke-and-grid pattern of the city, doubling back and meandering in their own eccentric way. Twice Warfield thought he had zeros on the signal only to find himself one street away. He finally located the Jaguar parked in the driveway of a fine Williamsburg colonial.

Eglon could have been no more than six or eight minutes ahead. Less if he did not have a key. Warfield parked on the street where he had a partial view of the driveway and the front door. There were two other cars at the curb in front of him and another to the rear. Although there was no foot traffic and very little in vehicles, it was the kind of neighborhood where a man alone in a car for any length of time would be noticed.

Warfield was thinking that it was also the kind of place where a successful attorney might live, and when he checked with headquarters, they confirmed the brick colonial as Eglon's residence. He must have moved into the house sometime after the divorce from Bettina, because they had lived in Arlington during the years of their marriage. She had not touched that house in the settlement; in fact, she had touched Eglon for very little. The IOUs that Bettina collected never had much to do with money. Warfield could understand the kind of reckoning that had caused Eglon to agree to help her that rainy day in Annapolis, although he could not for the life of him imagine the details of debit and credit. Perhaps she had just reminded her ex-husband that once she had let him off quite cheap.

It had only taken a minute to check in with headquarters, but suddenly Warfield knew that time might be very short. The second car down at the curb on the sloping road was a grey sedan with two rear-view mirrors—one up front, one in back. It was a big, brand-new Chevrolet with a V-8 engine and a wide body and full-length seats that would allow one man to recline out of sight in comfort while holding the stem of the mirror between his knees and maintaining surveillance on the street.

Warfield knew that he must have been burned. He cursed himself for not seeing the extra mirror on his first pass along the street. Carelessness. Rust. They would have known from the message center at his apartment that Eglon had been in touch with him. They could have watched the downtown office and followed the Jaguar closely while Warfield took the scenic tour of the Palisades. Or they might have staked out the house. Those were the things that manpower could do. Whoever they were, they had plenty of it.

And it seemed that all Warfield's choices were bad. He could not assume that there was only one watcher in the street. Nor could he assume that they had not already gotten to Ned Eglon. The worst scenario put men inside the house who were in close contact with the street. They would know that they were under pressure. In that case, Warfield had no time at all.

It was amazing how often the realization that things had gone wrong coincided almost exactly with their getting worse. Warfield had decided to make his move on the man in the grey sedan—he had his door swinging open and one foot on the pavement—when the watcher suddenly dove from the back into the front as could only be done in a big car with bench seats. The engine kicked over before the movement was completed and the man lurched behind the wheel. Warfield saw none of his features except a big head of light brown hair. Standing where the Chevrolet had been, he got nothing but the license number, moving away fast.

The second sequence started like a drum roll. Warfield could not place the long ravelling sound until it bumped to a stop and he realized it was Eglon's garage door. As he ran across the street, the sound of tires barked on concrete. Warfield knew at that moment that he should have gone for his car, because it was too late. The red Audi came over the lawn in a wide arc around the Jaguar, throwing up patches of bluegrass and the whole border of pretty phlox. The tires bit back onto the driveway with a yelp and the four interlocked circles on the Audi grill pointed dead-on Warfield's belt buckle.

He feinted left and dove right. When he hit the grass at the edge of the driveway, Warfield was deep into stop-time. He could have described the three men in detail, including important facial features and the crooked eyes of the driver and the ballooning snout and forearm of the pistol-grip shotgun slicing out of the rear window on the driver's side; but when the front bumper struck the heel of his shoe, throwing him another five feet and probably saving his life, the powerful thrust of the blow emptied nearly everything in his mind and left him with this: three Latin males.

Warfield did not get the license number of the car. The shock of the collision and the absolute terror of looking full-face into the blued barrel of a shotgun that did not fire took him into a blankness that was filled completely and inanely by the sight of the large bumper sticker that said IF YOU'RE RICH, I'M SINGLE.

Warfield got to his feet without thinking and immediately fell down. He looked between his knees, expecting to see his foot at a ninety-degree angle, but he saw only bare toes. The shoe was ten feet away in a bed of yellow carnations, along with the sock.

Slowly, he rose again and put weight on the leg. It held. It would be worse later. It would probably be every dirty color of the rainbow, but it could be used for now.

With the Audi gone, an absurd stillness descended on Eglon's home. Bright bits of phlox were scattered around the front lawn like shrapnel. Slashes of bare earth shone through the thick shag of grass like wounds. It was as if he were standing in the silent aftermath of a war of flowers. He could detect no sign that the neighbors had been alerted. Except for the roll of the garage door and the screech of tires, there had been no noise, no alarm. The man with the shotgun might have cut Warfield in half but had not. That meant that the team was concerned about their cover and would not blow down bystanders unless their escape was completely cut off. The tradecraft of the man in the gray sedan had been impeccable. No doubt he had alerted the others inside the house before making his run.

Because everything about the team said that they were professionals, Warfield was not optimistic about what he would find in the house. Though the four men were disciplined and prudent, he had hurried them at their work. If Eglon had resisted, their response to the danger could have been sudden.

That made it a little harder. Warfield limped through the garage and the connecting door into the southerly sunroom that led off the kitchen before he saw the mess. In the middle of the kitchen, between islands and below a ceiling rack of shining pots and pans, stood a butcher's table. Atop the table, slumped, naked, sat Ned Eglon. His posture was very bad because his arms were jammed down at his sides by a length of synthetic rope, which had been tied around each wrist and joined through the legs of the table. His head was bowed and bloody because there was a hole in the right temple. Although he was dead, blood still dripped in the last stages of coagulation from his arm onto the maple top. It pooled around the blade of a meat cleaver that had been driven into the wood mere centimeters from his groin.

It looked like the interrogation had barely started. The team must have been waiting inside or just outside the house. They would have spent time they had not known was so precious setting up the initial shocks. They had stripped him, trussed him, and hammered the three-pound cleaver an inch deep into hard wood between his thighs. There would have been talk—quiet threats backed by hard eyes and hardware that almost certainly would have cracked Eglon wide open if they had had their leisure.

Or perhaps he had talked quickly. In either case they might have killed him for insurance, or on orders, but never for the hell of it. Whether they had gotten what they wanted or not, they wanted Eglon quiet forever.

When Warfield inspected the rest of the house, it seemed clear that the team had been waiting inside. Although he found no obvious signs of a search, there were subtle indications throughout the house that someone had carefully gone through Eglon's possessions. In the den the lock on the middle drawer of the desk had been forced, and the vertical files were so jammed that the deep side drawer would not close. By the look of the dust marks, some books on the ceiling-high shelves had been repositioned. The filing cabinets, which undoubtedly contained some sensitive material, were unlocked, and the bottoms of the thick legs of a bishop's chair in the corner had been drilled without leaving more than a trace of sawdust between the gaps of the oaken floorboards.

So they had been in the house for a while. It was even

possible that they had had no plans to confront Eglon until he appeared unexpectedly in the middle of the day. When he showed, the priorities changed, and after Warfield came into the street, any notion of precedence vanished.

At least the team had had some idea what they were looking for. Except for the name Kronos, which was an obscure reference at best, Warfield had none. He might be staring at the keys to the kingdom and never know it, but he knew that he had to look.

He spent half an hour in the den with very little result. The only information of more than passing interest was that Eglon and Ramirez, by the evidence of the files in the desk and the cabinets, conducted a lot of business south of the border. Though most of the clientele was Mexican, other Central American countries were also represented. Warfield made a list of the Nicaraguan and Salvadoran accounts, of which there were several. He also examined the contents of Eglon's master address wheel for any promising leads. One address was a keeper by the name of Penelope Worsham. "Penny" had a well-thumbed page all her own, and she had been in Annapolis on that rainy Sunday afternoon.

The three bedrooms were a blank. The disheveled one was the master, and there was no way to be sure it had been searched. The other two bedrooms had apparently never been inhabited for any length of time, though Warfield found a selection of women's clothing in one closet that could have kept Imelda Marcos for a week. If you were rich, Penny, or her surrogates, were definitely single.

Warfield felt himself resisting a search of the kitchen. He had seen dead bodies before, and he had created some, but there had always been the certainty that it was needed. Eglon had died for a reason that he perhaps did not comprehend. He had died accepting the devices of a woman who had abandoned or betrayed everyone that came close to her.

It felt that way now. Warfield was surprised that it could ever have felt any other way. And it had.

He found himself standing in the formal living room that had belonged to a man who loved antiques. No interior designer had flogged this room together. The taste was too eccentric, the space too crowded, the pieces too remarkable. The block-and-shell chest was a tribute to the cabinetmaker's art, and the butler's table was sheer cunning. A spindly canterbury and an even spindlier candle stand had defied time and common sense. The Victorian card table enfolded like a symphony of leaves and the camphor sea chest gave the room a keen medicinal smell. The chairs were Chippendale and one-of-a-kind Windsor and whatever the hell else they wanted to be.

Then there were the clocks, which he *did*. Which he had done. On the west wall was a seagoing Claggett, on the east an ornate banjo. Virtually every horizontal space held some functional or decorative piece—miniatures, watch faces, ancient travel alarms. Every time Warfield moved his eyes he came across another fragment of time. One of the last things he noticed was the clock on the mantel.

It was a beautiful instrument, white-faced and gold-plated, with the workings exposed in a rounded glass housing. The period of its construction could have been Second Empire. Eglon had been looking at such a clock the day he met Bettina in Annapolis. He had not said that he had purchased it, but he was after all a collector with instincts and avarice that might have survived the shock of seeing his ex-wife.

Warfield moved in for a closer look. The hours of the day were told by the postures of angels. The brilliant counterweighted golden balls behind the glass housing revolved slowly, very slowly. In fact their progress was too slow. The time was off by more than two hours.

The clock would be wound by a key near the lock in the

back, and when Warfield looked round at it, he felt immediately that something was wrong. The key was of the same general color of brass or gold plate as the rest of the fittings, but its surface was pitted and discolored. That was curious. A mantel clock had to be wound every so often, so it was unlikely that the key would ever be kept in a separate place. Yet it had aged differently, as if it were made from different materials or had been thrown into a damp place for years.

Nor did it wind the clock. When he tried it, Warfield heard a harsh shearing sound that ended only when the key jammed in the strike. He had more than a little difficulty extracting it. When finally it worked free, he could see that the key had probably not been designed for the clock. It looked like a clock key in outline because of the hollow pin and its obvious age, but there were several sprigs of teeth all around the radius and a single protruding bit that had certainly caused it to jam. Warfield's efforts to make it do what it could not had marred the surface of the bit so that glimmers of older, brighter brass shone through. He knew he would have to find out what the key could do where it fit.

# The Bramah Key

WARFIELD made no report back to headquarters on what he had found at Ned Eglon's house. He called the D.C. police from a pay phone once he was well away from the area, telling them that a burglary was in progress at that address. They would find the body, and that would effectively end any real investigation. It would also promote Eglon's death into the morning papers and perhaps—if there were no bombings or hurricanes—onto the television news as well. Warfield wanted that because he wanted Bettina to see it. Seeing it, the possibility existed that she might feel it. Feeling it, she might break hiding and come to Warfield again.

While he drove with some irony across the Key Bridge onto the Washington Parkway, Warfield also ran the number of the plate on the gray sedan through an old and reliable contact in the Virginia State Police. The information came back quickly and as anticipated: the Chevrolet was a rental from Dulles. Further details would have to issue from the company.

Since any professional who rented a car would have taken steps to screen his identity, Warfield put that project on vigorous hold. He exited the parkway at Washington National and wound back into Crystal City, where All-American Safe and Security had its offices. There was a time when the area had almost been abandoned to marauders, but the recent steady flow of money from the Pentagon nearby had transformed rubble into madcap high-rise splendor filled with apartment complexes, corporate headquarters buildings, and several new hotels. Only a few relics remained.

Howard Thunander operated out of half a warehouse on an unreconstructed street that led into Army and Navy Drive. Though he serviced in various ways the Defense Department machine at his back door, Howard's heart was with the intelligence agencies. He had worked for CIA and NSA for years as a consultant on very delicate matters of surreptitious entry, which was known to some as burglary. Howard was without doubt the best locksmith in the business and one of the better safe-crackers. Furthermore, he had never been in jail.

Warfield located the man at a large roll-top desk in an office with bars on the windows. Howard was partly bald and partly lame, and for as long as they had known each other he had seemed to hover on the near side of retirement. The reason might have had something to do with the bifocals, or the old vests, or the brown patches that mottled his face and hands, but more likely it was the bemused, wrinkled way that he regarded any intrusion. Howard had camped in late middle age because he liked the view.

He gave a nice greeting to Warfield but did not offer his hand. Howard never shook hands.

"You're getting old, Stephen."

"Thanks."

"Really," he said, propping a foot on the desk, tilting his

head for a fuller view. "Time was I wouldn't have heard you at all. But you tripped the infrareds on the loading dock. Just had to come in the side door, didn't you?"

"I don't want to be seen."

"Holy shit," he said, rubbing his spotted veinous hands. "We talking business again?"

"Of a kind." Warfield took the cylindrical key from his pocket and placed in on the desk atop a calendar-blotter that was still set to 1981. "Let's see if you can tell me something about this relic."

Howard swept his feet off the desk, picked up the key, and nipped the bifocals down for an intelligent perusal. He did not concentrate on the object very long. "Where'd you get this thing?"

"It came from a mantel clock," said Warfield. "But I don't think it belonged there."

"Not likely," said Howard. "Your average mantel clock would have a polygonal key, or one with two separate bits. Need some torque, those things do. This is strictly a key to a lock, my friend."

"But not your normal kind."

"Oh, no." Howard popped one of the everlasting Tums that he stored in every pocket of his many vests. He let it percolate for a moment. "This, Stephen, is a Bramah key. It could be late eighteenth century, but I'd guess early nineteenth."

"You can tell that closely?"

"It's easy," he said, sucking meditatively on his lozenge. "Almost anyone could tell you that."

Warfield did not interrupt Howard's pause because he knew the man would tell more.

"You see, Stephen, the Egyptians invented the pin-tumbler key and lock about four thousand years ago, but somewhere along the line the knowledge got lost until Linus

Yale more or less reinvented it around the middle of the last century. Meanwhile, they dicked around with poor substitutes. The Romans knew about warded keys, which is what this thing basically is. The idea wasn't advanced much until well past the Middle Ages. The history of keys is the history of portable wealth. If you don't have much in the way of personal property, you don't need to secure it. In the eighteenth century, they started to improve on the warded key with all kinds of variations. This key was of the type made by Joseph Bramah, an Englishman, and it was designed so that a wax impression couldn't be made of the ward—the bit—which was what every half-assed lock-picker in Europe was doing at the time. The Bramah key combined the sliding movement that was as old as the Egyptians with the rotary movement that was as old as the Romans. It used radial tumblers and a barrel shape. The pin on the side rotates the lock. Not unpickable, but it put the goods beyond the reach of the run-of-the-mill thief."

"You say the key is English?"

"Probably," said Howard. "Unless it was copied."

"Do you think it was?"

"No."

"Well, I found it here," said Warfield. "It must have come over with something attached to it."

"Not necessarily. Some people just collect keys, you know."

Warfield was beginning to think along the lines of collectors, where he had some meaningful associations. "I don't think so, Howard. Either someone sold the clock with a defective key, or the key was deliberately inserted in the wrong place. What I need to find is the right place."

Howard wagged the key by its bow and dropped it back onto the desk. "My advice is to look for something fairly small."

"Let's try to narrow it down," said Warfield. "Do you think it could fit a safety deposit box?"

Howard shook his head slowly but definitely. "Not any modern kind," he said. "Maybe a very old one. But it's more apt to be something like a small cabinet. Or a cedar chest. A lady's jewelry box. The more elegant, the better. These were relatively expensive keys to produce."

Warfield might never have brought the tumblers of his mind into synch if Howard had not set him thinking along the lines of small elegant boxes. He began to recall the conversation he had had with Ned Eglon in his office. He had not only said that he did clocks, but that the woman Penny collected lap desks. Warfield knew that they came in all sizes of "fairly small," and that they often had locks.

"Do you think this key could fit an antique lap desk?"

Howard swallowed the last of his Tum. He belched mildly and un-selfconsciously. "I don't see why not," he said.

Warfield left Crystal City in the snarl of early rush hour. He had spent more time with Howard Thunander than he wanted because he liked the old man and also because the master locksmith had balked at releasing his best set of picks into Warfield's care. Howard had volunteered to do any necessary entry work himself and had not taken the refusal kindly. He had accused Warfield of everything from paranoia to age discrimination before admitting that the thought of action was foremost in his mind. Howard had been missing it lately. It seemed a man was never too old to lose the craving for the wicked spike of adrenaline that came when skill and danger mixed.

Warfield had been feeling it for twenty hours now, and occasionally, as he moved with the heavy pulse of traffic in suburban Virginia, the message to sleep came in sudden waves. He hardly noticed that Penelope Worsham lived just off Lawyers Road in Vienna. Her home was a regulation split-level in an undistinguished plat on a very callow street and probably, as these things had evolved, worth a small fortune.

It was also the last house at the head of the court, or dead end. Warfield did not like the approach. He checked the street thoroughly this time, working all the way back to the intersection, and when he was satisfied, he drove off. A half mile up the way he parked at the side of a service road and walked overland toward the court, crossing a small creek and coming up over a heavily wooded rise directly behind the house. He scanned the neighborhood again with his glasses.

Nothing. The street was totally inactive. It could have been the middle-class annex of a ghost town. There were no cars in the street and only one in a sunken driveway near the intersection. Warfield had come out of the copse of birch trees onto the verge of a small herb garden when he saw the police car enter the block. The brown-and-white sailed up the street into Penelope Worsham's drive and stopped.

A uniformed officer and a woman emerged from the squad car. He led her by the arm to the breezeway, took her keys, and opened the door. The black-haired woman had to be Penelope Worsham, laid low by the news of Eglon's death. Even from a distance Warfield could see that she was wobbly and the cop solicitous, if only because the big bulky man seemed so constrained in his movements. He held the door, her arm, and her purse as if everything were contagious.

The cop remained in the house for almost half an hour. He was probably not one of the investigating officers but more of a chauffeur. He stayed long enough to settle her down, put on the coffee, have her call a friend. When the friend arrived in a powder-blue Camaro, the cop rolled immediately, leaving the two women alone in the house.

Warfield gave them twenty minutes together, knowing that he had paid a price for his caution and thinking that he could not lose more by it. He checked the street again with his glasses, and seeing nothing but a station wagon returning from a day-care run, moved to the front door. The Schlage lock, he noted, would not have been difficult to pick.

The tall brown-haired woman who answered the door was understandably annoyed. Her brow knit in big cable-stitches and her tone was brusque as she said, "Yes."

Warfield flipped the phony ID that he carried as a matter of routine. "I'd like to speak to Miss Worsham," he said. "I realize this is a bad time."

"It's a goddamned evil time," she said, with her hand still on the door. "Give her a break."

"I wouldn't bother Miss Worsham if it wasn't extremely important," he said. "Could you please tell her that someone is here to find out who killed Ned Eglon."

The woman shook her head as if she had her teeth in something. "Look, she's already spoken to the police."

"I'm not with the local police." Warfield held up the ID in the nice plastic case again. "I'm a special investigator with the U.S. Attorney's office. I'd appreciate it if you'd tell Miss Worsham exactly what I said."

The brown-haired woman was about to tell Warfield just what he could do with his bogus shield when from the hallway behind her Penelope Worsham hove into view. She had unfashionably long black hair parted in the middle, like Eglon's; it half-hid her face. In a general though more subdued way she resembled Bettina—the dark hair, the blue eyes with heavy lids, the very fine sweep of her limbs and body. But the eyelids, Warfield realized, had been swollen to heaviness by recent tears, and the hair was actually a shade of dark brown. Penelope Worsham was less a copy of Bettina than an echo. Even in her sorrow she would never be taken for more than an attractive woman.

"It's all right, Marcy," she said. "I'm all right."

"You're not all right, Pen. You're not even all here."

"I've never been more here," said Penelope Worsham. "More anywhere." She turned to Warfield very slowly. "I heard what you said: that you would find out who killed Ned."

"Yes."

"No one else said that, Mr. . . ?"

"Stevens. Warren Stevens."

That was how Warfield got in the door: with a promise that he believed was the truth. Penelope Worsham believed it too. Although she was disoriented by her grief, the same force had moved her instincts well out in front of any civilized defenses. Without being asked, she sent Marcy into the kitchen on the ground floor. She sat in a stubby overstuffed chair in the living room while Warfield occupied a third of the couch. That was still not close enough—she edged up in the chair until her arms on her knees almost touched Warfield. She looked at him with hallucinatory directness, as if into the depths of a dream. People silently petitioned their executioners that way, and their priests and lovers.

"I did talk to the police," she said with a precision that was remarkable and no doubt misleading. "I mean, you see these things on television, and you read the books, and you know it's all a lot of stupid hype, but the thing you don't know, the thing you can't even begin to realize unless it happens to you and you talk to them and you look them right in the eye and you ask them what's going to happen and suddenly you know it's . . . nothing. Absolutely nothing. They look like cops, but they're just goddamn bookkeepers."

Warfield never contradicted anyone who arrived at a correct conclusion in the very hardest way. He said nothing, which he knew would serve best.

"But you're not a bookkeeper, Mr. Stevens, are you? You're something else."

"Yes."

"I don't think you're with the U.S. Attorney's office either. And your name's probably not Warren Stevens."

"It could be."

She seemed to accept that ambiguity; she seemed to like it. "Just tell me one thing," she said, holding his eyes with her own universe of intensity. "When you catch them, will you kill them?"

"I promise you they'll suffer."

She closed her eyes deliberately, almost peacefully, and did not open them until she spoke. "That's good enough."

Warfield had the cylindrical Bramah key in his front pocket. At the end of the couch to his left was a lap desk that had been placed on a custom-built stand to serve as an end table or perhaps a conversation piece. At the other end of the couch was another lap desk on a similar stand. They were not mates, but they were both old. Neither looked as though it would accept a Bramah key.

"I'm going to ask you a couple cop questions first," he said. "Do you own a red Audi?"

"Yes," she said, balling her fist against her cheek. "They stole it, I know, but as far as I'm concerned they can keep it. I left the car at Ned's because when I took it to the garage on Monday, they wouldn't do anything with it. The accelerator sticks sometimes. It's a very dangerous thing to drive, believe me. I've had it in for repair four different times, but I've gotten no satisfaction from the dealer."

That might have explained the crazy way the car had careened out of the garage and down the driveway, as if it were out of control. It did not explain the bumper sticker as bold as a tupenny whore. Warfield did not see that kind of woman before him.

"How long have you and Ned been going together?"

"Six months on and off," she said. "Mostly on for the last three. We liked to believe we had an open relationship—and it started out that way—but we let it get very serious."

"Then you'd be able to tell me if you noticed anything extraordinary—erratic—in Ned's behavior recently. Say in the last week or so."

"The police asked me that too," she said, expressing her contempt for their methods. "And I told them, yes, he'd been acting strangely. He didn't sleep at all last night. He got up several times to use the phone."

"Do you know who he called?"

"No," she said. "He used the extension in the den. It was late. I suppose he didn't want to disturb me."

Although the calls that Eglon had made were probably to Warfield, there was no sense in passing up the chance to elicit a willing response from Penelope.

"Did Ned give you any indication of what might be bothering him last night?"

"I really don't know," she said with a hopelessness that could only be true. "We were reasonably confiding people, Mr. Stevens. But we both have jobs. We have—we had—our own concerns. If they were business-related, we tried very hard not to lay them off on each other. We tried to have quality time together."

She tipped her head back suddenly, as if she might control her tears by the angle of egress. Warfield thought that the reference to "quality time" had caused the reaction. Romance died a hard death within that phrase. Penelope knew it and mourned it. She wanted time back now, all of it, the good things and the dross.

"Can you tell me when you first noticed this change in Ned?"

The question brought her back. "Actually, he was irritable for the last couple weeks, but I didn't pay much attention to that. He worked long hours, and very hard. Sometimes it got to him in little ways. I deliberately didn't notice because if he wanted to talk, I knew he would. But I couldn't ignore what happened Sunday night. We were driving back into the city, and we were on Millwood near his house. Ned was a very good driver, and he'd traveled that street a thousand times, but last Sunday night he zigged when he should have zagged. All of a sudden the road curved and we didn't. The car jumped the curb onto the right-of-way before he stopped. Even after we stopped Ned didn't seem normal. For a minute, he lost it. Everything."

"Where had you been that day?"

"At Annapolis," she said. "We were supposed to go out in the boat, but it started to rain and the winds got real crazy."

"Did anything special happen that day?"

"No," she said. "We had lunch. We did some shopping."

"Were you together all the time?"

"Most of the time," she said, clutching the open throat of her blouse as if trying to hold the memory. "I wasn't with Ned when he found his clock, but we met right afterward."

"You say he bought a clock?"

"It's right there on his mantel in the living room," she said. "He made quite a thing about it, I remember. We were almost to the car when he turned right around and went back to the shop. He said he'd forgotten it when he ran into one of his clients."

"Did you see this client?"

"No," she said. "I was across the street in another shop. I'd found something that I liked too. A lap desk."

When Warfield turned to look pointedly at the fairly small

wooden box on the stand between them, Penelope shook her head. "That's not the one," she said. "This was a real beauty. I haven't had it mounted yet."

"Is it here?"

She nodded.

"Do you think I could take a look at it?"

Although she seemed surprised by the request, Penelope said, "Of course." She rose unsteadily to her feet. "It's in my room."

She must have meant the bedroom, because she walked to the stairs that led to the top level and disappeared in the first door on the right. Almost immediately she came back out, carrying what must have been the finest piece in her collection. It was not much bigger than a breadbox, but very elegant. Made of dark satin-smooth wood, the lap desk was strapped at the corners with brass. In the center of the lid was a brass plate embossed with the initials of the original owner. She placed it in front of Warfield on the coffee table before the couch. He could see at once that the lock, which was also clad in brass, demanded a radial key.

"It's English," she said. "Early nineteenth century. A gentleman's possession. In those days no person of real substance would ever go anywhere without something like this. It was his line of communication. I'm sorry that I can't open it, because the inside is very interesting. I've misplaced the key."

"I think I may be able to open it," said Warfield. "I'd like to try, with your permission."

Though she clearly did not understand the reason, Penelope nodded her consent.

Warfield was glad of that, and very glad that he had found Penelope at home and cooperative, because the radial lock would have taken Howard Thunander, or any good locksmith, half an hour to pick. How long it would have taken

Warfield was debatable. If the Bramah key did not work, it was possible that he would find out.

"Does this look like the key that you misplaced?"

She stared at Joseph Bramah's cunning invention for a moment, then took it from Warfield's hand. "This looks like it," she said. "It's a distinctive one, isn't it?"

"Yes," said Warfield. "I found it inserted into the back of Ned's mantel clock. It didn't quite fit there."

He hoped she wouldn't ask any questions, such as why she hadn't seen him at the house with the police, and she did not. Penelope worked the Bramah key easily into the lock. The lap desk clicked open. She lifted the lid to display a row of wooden inserts covered in green velvet. These would have kept the inks, the powders, the quill pens and wax. Touching a small metal catch on the inside of the lock, Penelope swung the row of inserts forward to reveal the compartment below, which would have contained the writing paper. Instead, there was a manila envelope, twelve by fourteen.

"Is that what you're looking for, Mr. Stevens?"

"I don't know."

"Neither do I," she said. "This compartment was empty when I bought the desk."

"Did Ned have access to it?"

"I suppose so." She smiled for the first time, wanly. "Of course he would have."

"When did you notice the key was missing?"

"Yesterday. I tried to open it because I was thinking of having it relined." She touched the envelope with her fingertips, then withdrew her hand hurriedly. "You don't want me to look at this, do you?"

Warfield thought that she might accept a simple no, but he felt that he owed her a bit more. "I think it would be better if you didn't," he said. "Ned ran into someone at Annapolis—maybe a client—and I think that person gave him something to keep. I think it's in that envelope—and it may be the reason why he was killed."

Looking at the plain manila envelope, Penelope finally began to lose it. Everything. The emotion that she had been holding escaped in soft rhythmic whoops, terrible and fierce. When Warfield moved to comfort her, Penelope stood suddenly, wrestling herself away. She took two steps into the center of the room, stopping before the cold hearth of the fireplace. She wrapped her arms around her body, compressing it, trying to manage it.

In that she was successful. Her face when she turned back to him was so rigid that it seemed waxed. "My name's Penelope," she said. "Not Pandora. Just please don't have me wait ten years. Take the envelope, Mr. Stevens. Get them—whoever they are."

What Ned Eglon had apparently died for was a negative, and a black-and-white print of the same that showed two men walking side by side on a beach. They did not seem to have posed for the photograph, which had been taken with a telephoto lens that obscured the background somewhat. In the upper left-hand corner was the thick straight trunk of a tree. It was probably a palm.

The man nearest the tree was younger and taller. He wore form-fitting trousers and an open-necked *guayabera*. He was perhaps in his early thirties with a dense head of hair that rose as if it had been styled and moussed. Except for the color of the hair, which was light, he would have passed for the typical young and monied Latino.

There was the jewelry—the cookie-sized wristwatch and the chains around the neck that probably secured Krugerands or Chinese Pandas. There was also the hauteur—the macho sense of pride and swagger that had never gone out of fashion south of Disney World. The young man's walk was cocky, loose-limbed, and the way he held his body suggested that he was listening closely to the words of the fellow on his left. He might have been listening, or it might just have seemed that way because his posture and configuration were so similar to that of the man next to him. The effect was that they seemed closer together than they really were. Warfield liked the second interpretation best, because the more he looked at the young man, the less likely it seemed that he would listen to anyone for very long.

The second figure was quite old. His dress was more businesslike—wing-tipped shoes, pleated pants, and a white shirt with the cuffs rolled back and the top buttons undone. Although like the other he seemed to inhabit the tropics, Warfield would have guessed his origins as middle European. His head was three-quarters bald and three-quarters square. His face had not shrunk with age; it still retained a strong foundation of flesh and bone, especially across the broad forehead. His mouth was a thin slash. The sharp nose was also thin, supporting a pair of spinsterish glasses. Perhaps due to the correction in the lens, the old man's eyes appeared larger than life, bulbous and robotic, as if they had seen everything but change.

Warfield did not recognize either of the men, though he felt a worrisome suspicion that he should. There was something public about them, as if they might be businessmen or politicians who had come to a meeting and decided on a walk together in a secluded spot where their aides could not interfere.

The spot had a name. On the back of the photograph was written "San Juan del Sur."

The handwriting appeared to be Bettina's. Warfield wondered, though not for so long, how she had managed to acquire a picture taken in a resort town on the southern coast of Nicaragua. But then he reminded himself that although we were waging war against that country, it was the most peculiar kind of war—undeclared, unacknowledged, apparently unfunded. The two countries still maintained diplomatic relations. There was still a tourist trade of sorts. Anyone could visit San Juan del Sur with proper papers and the will.

Warfield felt himself smiling inadvertantly at the photograph. He had no idea why it was important, but he knew that it would be. The identity of the two men might provide the answer. It could probably not be otherwise if the photograph had caused a man's death.

Warfield was also beginning to have an understanding, which was little more than a feeling, of why Bettina had run so fast and so long. And why she was still running hard.

# Kronos

WARFIELD was late for dinner. He had spent some time securing the negative and snaking across midtown traffic, and it was well after eight when he entered the restaurant on Connecticut. The place was indeed Thai. He stood for a long moment in the lobby, sampling the familiar smells. He loved the odor of soy and ginger and sesame and satay, the garlic and curries and lemon grass. To Warfield these were the memories of peace within war; they were epitomes.

The atmosphere must have been equally pleasing to Amelia Worth, who had enjoyed a posting to Bangkok in the early part of her intelligence career with CIA. Given a choice, she probably would have remained there for the rest of her professional life, but her name was one of those that had appeared in the Covert Action Information Bulletin, the tattler that broadcast the identities of American operatives in foreign lands for the benefit of the free press and the KGB. Being blown like that had lent Amelia a certain notoriety that complemented her naturally feisty nature. She was five feet two inches tall, thirty-six years old, single, low-breasted, as pretty and brittle as a Liberty Bond poster. In high school and college she had probably been a cheerleader, and popular, until the boys found out how very smart she was.

"I ordered the crispy whole fish," she said by way of greeting. "And the shrimp in pepper-garlic sauce. You drink vodka straight, don't you?"

"Stolichnaya."

"I won't have it at my table," she said without the ripple of a smile. "The man assures me that there's a perfectly good Swedish substitute."

"You're going too far, Amelia."

"It surprises me that they carry that Russian dreck at all," she said. "I made them promise not to reorder. As for you, Stephen, you'll be just fine."

She said that because she could see the waiter coming with the drinks. He was an occidental male, and from a distance of ten feet, he seemed patently gay. Closer up, Warfield wasn't so sure. It was possible that Amelia had badgered him into that thoroughly neutered state. He seemed awfully glad to get away from their corner booth, which was enclosed on three sides and a good distance from the windows.

"A toast to your health," said Amelia. "By the looks of you, one's in order."

Warfield raised his glass and took a hit of the vodka. It was not bad, or memorable.

"I've had a long day, Amelia."

"Really," she said, without much malice. "The last time we talked you were hobnobbing with lawyers. Is that strenuous?"

"More than you know," said Warfield. "Ned Eglon was killed early this afternoon. A team of four men took him right out from under me. I have three of them as Latins but nothing more."

Though she was certainly surprised, Amelia did not digress unnecessarily. She came right back with procedure. "You didn't report that, Stephen."

"I'm doing it now," he said. "I want you to know that I notified the civilians. The details should be all the way through the pipeline by now."

"We could have kept a tight lid on this," she said, rimming the edge of her green cocktail with her fingers. "But that's not what you wanted, is it, Stephen?"

"Bettina had to know about this, and I don't have any other way to tell her."

"You're assuming that she cares," said Amelia. "Or that she didn't order the execution herself."

"I don't believe that," said Warfield. "And neither do you. Bettina gave Eglon something to keep. The team was looking for it. If Bettina had wanted it back, all she'd have had to do was ask."

"Perhaps," she said, quickly and sharply. "But what if he understood its value and didn't want to return it?"

"Bettina's not a killer," said Warfield. "Even if she's everything short of that."

Amelia said nothing as the waiter reappeared with a mound of seared ribs and hacked chicken. She studied Warfield with disconcerting curiosity until the man had gone, leaving the food, with its extravagantly subtle smell, between them. Amelia began to pluck at once from the pile with her chopsticks.

"You think that Bettina's not dangerous, Stephen, but that's only because you don't have a reasonable assessment of the potential of a female agent. You assume that she's less capable than a man—less ruthless—when in fact it's often the opposite. A woman with Bettina's training and intelligence is *more* capable than a man. She's automatically accorded the one thing that you or someone like you works years—hell, forever—to gain. And that's trust. A man trusts a woman *before* he sleeps with her, and afterward his ego won't allow any suspicions beyond the obvious one—jealousy. You trust Bettina now, Stephen, at this instant."

"No."

"Good," she said. "I'll take your word. Now tell me what convinced you away."

"The hole in Eglon's head," said Warfield truthfully. "Bettina had him loaded with some very heavy weight and didn't give him a clue about what could happen to the bearer."

Amelia nodded as if her thesis were proved. "Do we have any idea what this material is?"

"I do," he said. "You don't yet."

"What does that mean exactly?"

"It means that I want to hear what you've got on Mr. or Mrs. Kronos. Now."

Amelia was unaccustomed to that kind of talk from erstwhile subordinates. Although she was watch commander on this mission, she was also one of Jack Brindisi's personal assistants, his main trouble-shooter entrusted with internal security. Her reports would go directly to the DAD. Warfield did not discount the possibility that she was sitting in this booth wired. His suspicions were heightened when she smiled broadly, dispelling every trace of her professional mask.

"I deserved that," she said, dandling chicken with her chopsticks. "But now that we're even, I can tell you that you're not going to like what I've found. Not unless you're a history buff."

"I'm getting to be."

"As long as you're appreciative," she said. "Believe me, I

had a hell of a time locating any reference to Kronos. There is no information under that heading in any computerized data bank serviced by the United States government. But you said to check *all* the files, and finally something surfaced. I have a friend at the Bureau who has very good access. He came up with the cross reference."

"You didn't alert them, did you?"

"In this case, no," said Amelia with a faint puzzling smile. "We're talking about *hoary* things, Stephen. The information is so old even an antique dealer wouldn't be interested. And if there is some mindless antiquarian left over there, he lost interest years ago. They're into undercover stings now. A sexy new image."

"Don't be too sure, Amelia."

"Let's pretend that I am," she said. "You see, you were right about the Latin American connection. The information on Kronos was found in the Bureau's old Amigo file. Remember, they had authority over all intelligence collection for that area before World War II. Hoover kept it right through the war, in spite of the objections from OSS and everyone else. But afterward the Civilian Intelligence Group was formed. In the middle of 1946 General Vandenburg took over as director of CIG. He was the nephew of Senator Arthur Vandenburg. Using his political clout, he pulled together all the old elements of the OSS that he could find. He also went after Hoover's Latin American section and took it."

"But not everything."

"Never everything, Stephen. You know that. Collectors don't give up their choice items."

"Is it choice?"

"At the time it was very choice," said Amelia. "If Hoover had managed to convert that three-by-five card into a living body, they might have given him back Latin America for Christmas."

Warfield was feeling such a nice buzz from the vodka, the appetizers, and Amelia's pregnant tease that he did not mind that the waiter came at just that moment with the main course. The fish was a gorgeous golden brown topped with a fragrant sauce and brilliant vegetables. The shrimp were stir-fried, swimming in a thick lather of spices and savories. Both dishes were under assault before Amelia began to speak again. She did not miss a beat as she gnawed voraciously on the fish head that Warfield had coveted for his own.

"So, Stephen, have you ever heard of a man named Heinrich Müller?"

Warfield had, perhaps, but his memory was roving another continent at the moment. "A Nazi official," he said.

"That's like saying Ghengis Khan was a nomadic chieftan, my dear. In point of fact Heinrich Müller was head of Section IV of the Reich Security Headquarters, better known as the Gestapo. He held that position from 1939 until 1945, through all the greatest horrors, and he was the effective head of the organization for much longer. Müller was an odd duck among the Nazi hierarchy because he was very competent, the complete professional. He served in the First World War as a flight leader on the eastern front, and afterward he became a member of the Bavarian police specializing in the surveillance of Communist Party functionaries."

"A lot of people have made their careers that way," said Warfield. "Not only Germans."

Amelia shrugged with her eyebrows. "That was one of the reasons that Hoover was interested in him, and also one of the reasons why Heydrich hand-picked him to head the Gestapo. Müller had an extensive knowledge of Soviet police methods, which he acquired in Russia itself. He spent time with the NKVD in Moscow, studying their organization. Some people think he never allowed his contacts to lapse. During the war it was known that Müller often slipped false intelligence to the Russians through their agents in Germany, but it would have been easy to maintain real communication by the same means. In any case, he was never blown because of it. Müller was last seen in the Führerbunker on April 28, 1945, two days before Hitler committed suicide. His burial was recorded on May 17, 1945."

Amelia left off at that point, though she had not reached a stopping place. Throwing down the clean bones of the fish head, she pursed her lips and said, "But guess what?"

"The body wasn't Müller's."

"Close," she said. "The body could not be identified as Müller's. Or anyone else's."

"That doesn't prove he escaped Berlin."

"Not in itself," said Amelia. "But there were persistent rumors that he had defected to the East through his Soviet contacts. I back-checked this through existing records. There was a report by a German communist writer named Ludwig Renn who claimed that Müller had been seen behind the Iron Curtain after the war. Renn was a leading figure in the wartime Free Germany movement among anti-Nazi writers in Latin America. He later returned to East Germany. His idea was that Müller had made a deal with the Russians that enabled him to lie low in the East until he could perfect a cover. That would be consistent with Müller's history. He saw himself as a policeman, regardless of party affiliations. In fact he wasn't admitted as a member of the Nazi party until 1939 because some influential party members considered his early work with the Munich state police to be anti-Nazi. But he shifted with the prevailing winds, or at least he seemed to."

"So you're convinced that Müller was a double agent."

"It's a strong possibility," she said. "Admiral Canaris, the German chief of military intelligence, thought so. One of his counterespionage agents traced radio transmissions from the

Nazi party chancellery in Berlin to Moscow. At first they suspected Martin Bormann, Hitler's secretary, until they learned that Müller had a basement shelter built secretly near the chancellery complex. If Canaris hadn't been executed by the Gestapo after the attempt on Hitler's life in 'forty-four, he might have uncovered Müller."

"But he didn't," said Warfield. "And Müller went over to the Russians even though they were killing everything in Berlin."

"If anyone would have had the means to contact the Russians safely, it would have been Müller," said Amelia. "Even if he wasn't their agent, the Soviets would have listened to a man with his credentials. They listened to men with a whole lot less. In fact they sought out any competent German official, even if he were SS, to help in restructuring Germany to their specifications. In Müller's case, the advantages were clear. The Russians could deal comfortably with a man who held dossiers on every important individual in Germany—and the rest of the continent. Think of the possibilities."

Warfield did not have to think very long. The Russians would have dealt for the records of every *dead* individual of importance in Europe, and who was to say the files stopped there? By the end of the war the Gestapo had taken over the records of all Nazi intelligence, including those of Canaris's Abwehr. The chances for blackmail and extortion were nothing short of global, and Müller, if he were as cunning as he seemed, would have held back some particularly fine items against that rainy day.

"So we can say, for purposes of discussion, that Müller went over to the Soviets."

"Yes," said Amelia. "It seems almost certain. He was supposed to have been seen in East Germany by Renn, and in Albania and the motherland by others."

"All right, Amelia. I'll go along with the script. Now tell me what Heinrich Müller has to do with Kronos?"

Amelia gave every indication that she was not overly confident about the next step. She dipped both hands in the finger bowl filled with lime water and commenced a long rinse before taking her small steaming towel. It was as if things might have gotten too messy for her taste at last.

"According to Mr. Hoover—God rest his soul—Heinrich Müller *was* Kronos. He entered Argentina in the late spring of 1946 on a Vatican passport. Hoover's man in BA was a member in good standing of the German community who knew Müller on sight. His report said that Müller had undergone some cosmetic surgery and had done his best with disguise, but that no one could hide a head that square or change those eyes. And not too many people with Bavarian accents deposited fifteen million dollars in their personal bank account. Hoover's man was a financier, which was how he came to hear about Herr Kronos."

"Müller used that name?"

She nodded. "Mr. Hoover could not have thought it up."

"Where did Müller get fifteen million dollars?"

"That's the interesting part," said Amelia. "The way the story goes, about five mill was put out in bribes. The rest of the money was invested in Argentinian government bonds with long maturities. That's like buying a bankruptcy and giving all the executives golden parachutes. It was a flat-out guarantee. Hoover's man maintained that no one would do that unless he was diddling with only *part* of his fortune. The money was paid in dollars from Credit Swisse, which was the favored banking institution of Nazi officials. Although he couldn't get detailed information, Hoover's man received the impression that Herr Kronos's credit had not been tapped out. You have to remember that Müller was the head of the most corrupt organization for plunder ever known to man. All questionable transactions were done in diamonds with steep discounts to karat value. No one questioned the head of the Gestapo. Not Kaltenbrunner, not Goebbels, not even Himmler."

"So Kronos put a down payment on Argentina. Then what?"

"He disappeared, of course," said Amelia. "The Argentine station lost Kronos in mid-1946, shortly after the first contact. There have been numerous unconfirmed reports of Müller all over Latin America in the years since, but they're like UFO sightings. Bolivia, Paraguay, Brazil—to name a few. But not even the Israelis still think he's alive."

"They thought that about Mengele too."

She said, "Yes."

There were a hundred questions of substance and speculation in Warfield's mind, but the first was the most important. "Do you have a photograph of Müller?"

Amelia reached into her purse, which was half as big as she was. A file folder emerged from it as if she had hardly plumbed the first layer of substrata. "This is the works on Müller," she said. "Career highlights. Two glossies. You can keep the file. It's unclassified."

Warfield did not waste time with the biography but went straight to the pictures. What he saw was a very interesting possibility. The man named Heinrich Müller, head of Amt IV, RSHA, the Gestapo, had thinning hair and a wide forehead. The first photograph had been taken in 1928, when Müller, a member of the Bavarian Political Police, was in his twenties. The second photograph, dated 1942, showed Müller in his gray uniform jacket, black riding breeches, and jackboots, standing next to his mentors, Himmler and Hitler. Of the three, Müller seemed the most German and the most convincing. Beside Hitler, who looked like a cheap comedian, and Himmler, the eternal clerk, Müller's solid presence was a virtual anchor. Here was no philosophical mystic. Here was a very hard cop with a shell casing for a head and eyes like a desert bird.

There was also a progression in the hairline and waistline from the first photograph to the second, an intriguing one that Warfield tried to press forward another forty years. The basic parameters were there. A man in his eighties might very well have lost his hair. His body could easily, inevitably, have thickened. The mouth was a good match—thin, almost lipless, very unusual. Of course the nose was wrong, but that would have been the thing that bore change best. It was remarkable how much character a nose imparted to a face, and how much surgery could alter the basic disposition. Unless Warfield looked closely into Heinrich Müller's eyes, he might not have taken him for the man on the beach.

But Warfield did look. Those eyes had condemned millions—*millions*—and they had recorded the fact like a camera. Nothing showed. While Hitler dabbled with astrology, Himmler with herbal remedies and hypnotism, Heinrich Müller read his files. They were all numbers to him—the Jews, the Gypsies, the Slavs, the politicals. That gaze was as messianic as a plough. Warfield recognized it because sometimes he saw it in his mirror—in his own eyes. It meant that a man had succeeded in disconnecting the things he saw from the things he felt. He had eradicated soul. Both the man on the beach and the head of Amt IV had done that very well. The worst part was that after a man had done it, he often came to like it because of what it gave back: the feeling of invulnerability.

No man with Heinrich Müller's eyes would have joined the orgy of self-extinction in the Führerbunker. If anyone in Nazi Germany had worked out a foolproof escape route, it would have been the head of the Gestapo. He would have no illusions, like Goering had, that the Americans might shelter him. He would understand that no country pretending to morality or justice and still in possession of its own soul could deal with him. Therefore, he would go to the Russians with his goods. He would exploit the contacts he had never allowed to lapse. Forty years later, those events would place him in conference on a socialist beach.

Maybe.

Warfield realized that he was allowing the memory of Ned Eglon's death to validate the photograph when in fact a dead body could as easily validate a lie. He supposed that it all depended, as Amelia had said, on whether he still had some trust in Bettina. The answer was not easy but it was simple: Warfield did not trust her motives or emotions or moves; he did trust her resources. If anyone could have put that killer cop on a beach for an afternoon stroll, Bettina would have been the one.

"I think you'd better put this file back in the safe, Amelia. Stamp it 'Special Compartmentalized.'"

She took the announcement very calmly. "You're being coy, Stephen. What do we have here that makes 'Top Secret' just not good enough?"

"We very well may have Kronos."

"You mean Müller."

"I mean Kronos. Now you tell me—how much are we interested in him?"

Amelia stared at the bones and congealing juices in the plates, and without altering her eyes looked at Warfield. "I would say definitely yes. But I don't know how urgent the yes would be. You have to understand that Kronos-Müller would now be more than eighty years old. Catching a buck Nazi is one thing, but a toothless old bull . . . It's hard to say."

Warfield found it suddenly difficult to keep the anger from

his voice. He also found it useful not to have to. "You mean that the White House doesn't put a high priority on capturing soul brothers, is that what you're trying to tell me?"

"Watch it, Stephen."

"I'm being objective," he said. "There's nothing political in this."

"I think there's something else in this, and her name's Bettina, but I'll pretend I'm stupid."

"You don't have to change character, Amelia. Just kick this back up to Jack. Tell him I've got a line on the biggest Nazi left in the world, a man that raped half of Europe, who also appears to have gone over to the Russians after the war. Stress that last point. Say Russian *communists*. Say *reds*. Tell him that I have some indications that Kronos is linked to the current government in Managua."

Amelia Worth's mouth had not fallen open since she tied her first tooth to the knob on that swinging door but it did on this warm summer night as she was confronted with a statement that fulfilled almost every primal wish in darkest Washington. Daniel Ortega's bowels on a stick would have been better, just barely.

"Are you sure of this, Stephen?"

Warfield felt a chill blast of air conditioning eddy through the tall booth. It was the ghost of Lenin no less, bearing maxims from beyond the grave. They all had to do with deception and desire.

"Just pass what I said on to Jack. Tell him I want a response from the highest levels right away. I want a deal: Bettina's guaranteed safety in exchange for Kronos."

Except for the vestiges of surprise, all harmony vanished from the face of Amelia Worth. The light, the sweet chiding, the care with which she had kept her best profile turned toward him throughout the long meal—it all went away. She stared at Warfield as if he were numbers.

"Bettina set us up once before, Stephen. She'll do it again. This time she'll take you—and God knows how many others—along with her."

Warfield did not know how much he cared about Bettina anymore. He would have been lying if he said he did not, but it would have been a much worse lie if he said he did not care about this mission. Warfield wanted to see it through more than anything he could remember. Linking it to Bettina's safe passage seemed to be the one sure way to guarantee that end.

"I want the deal," he said.

"Or what?"

"Or you lose your ticket to this show."

Amelia did not like that either. She took it with a quick grimace. "You know, they're going to have you fluttered."

"No lie detectors, Amelia. I've told you fifteen low-down dirty fibs already."

"You've told me almost nothing," she said icily. "But I'll pass along your request. I'm sure Jack will be interested. He'll also want to know what kind of assurances we have that you'll deliver."

"You can tell Jack that he'll have Kronos—or my head—whichever comes through the door first."

"I won't say it like that, Stephen. It's melodramatic as hell. And he would hold you to it."

# PART TWO

# TARGET ACQUISITION

# The Stud

WARFIELD awoke the next morning with some very good after-tones from his dreams and some very bad second thoughts about the things he had said the night before. Mission fatigue had caused the excess, but he knew that he should not have pressed Amelia Worth so hard and that he would never have done it if Bettina had not been involved. That was the same as saying his emotions were involved, which was very nearly the same as saying he was untrustworthy. At one time or another, Warfield had flagged the files of dozens of others—agents and ordinary citizens in sensitive positions—for exactly the same sin of the heart. The thought that someone might be doing it to his file was disquieting.

Love and its lesser forms were the staple of espionage. No intelligence service would exist but for the man who needed money to support his mistress or had been caught in a compromising position with someone else's. NSA's greatest security breach had occurred in the early sixties when two men in key positions within the Puzzle Palace had defected directly to the Soviet Union. They had taken good booty and declared good political reasons for their action. No one at the time had known that they were lovers.

Which was more than could be said of Bettina and Warfield. Everyone had known of their affair, including the DAD. It had begun in Prague, in a one-room apartment in the Old City that was supposed to be a safe place. It seemed that way until the moment when someone thumped at the door with what sounded like a thirty-pound sledge. Until that time, they had never touched each other with the intent to love or experiment, because they were not the kind of people for either, but as she walked him to the closet-sized john with his broken foot she was stripping off her clothes and dousing her hair and putting on her robe—all within easy reach of a cripple.

They had touched, inadvertantly, and that, given the chemistry of the situation, had been enough. When she returned to fetch him after discovering at the door a drunken student ranting about love and a woman named Helena—when she was sure that he was a student and that something called love was loose in the hallway—Bettina acknowledged the change that had occurred in those moments of panic and proximity. She shrugged off the robe, and on the ledge of the claw-footed tub, with Warfield agog at her nakedness and helpless in the mechanics, they began the thing that would endure beyond sense or regulations.

They were told to break it off, of course. Each in turn refused. Each was threatened with termination, and when that had no effect, they were told that they would never work together again. Warfield could not help feeling that the prohibition—and the love that had caused it—led in the end to disaster in Central America. If they had still been working together, Bettina might never have gone to El Salvador and her disgrace.

So there was guilt at ten o'clock in the morning, and a wee bit of anger. By now the details of their relationship would have passed across some imposing desks. Men whose business was the bottom line would have weighed the dangers against the payoff promised. Warfield's trump was that he knew how badly they needed a score. The conflict in El Salvador was grinding on aimlessly. The Contra offenses in Nicaragua—if they could be called that—had been blunted by home-grown defense forces and the refusal of Congress to grant more than humanitarian aid to those lovely "Freedom Fighters." Warfield was banking on all the bad signs to counteract the suspicion that he was simply pussy-whipped.

He checked out of the motel on 95 South where he had spent the night and into a pancake house across the way that featured real butter and fake syrup. The phone call to his encoded lock number produced two messages.

The first was the unmistakable voice of Jack Brindisi speaking one terse word. He said: "Yes."

Warfield was thinking that World War III might start in exactly the same way—same voice, same chain of command—but the word was very welcome because it was his go-ahead. The conditions had been accepted by the DAD and his superiors, of which there were few.

The second call on the recorder said that Capitol Cleaning had his suit ready. The voice wasn't Stretch Dixon's, but the procedure was. It meant that he had some information of substance to relay. Fifteen cents and five minutes later, when Warfield was already back to the city limits, Dixon's return call came through.

"I've got a line on your Canadian."

"Good work, Stretch."

"A classic piece of detection," he said. "The man just can't break his old habits. It seems like he's always got to have two hands in the bush."

"Where are you?"

"Foggy Bottom," he said, as if it were Mars. "Stephen, I think you might like to stop by and talk to this lady. She knows more than she's telling, but she's like everybody in this town—patriotic. I think she's looking for a congressional commendation—or maybe just some insurance."

"This is the sandwich?"

"No, sir," said Dixon. "This is the sandwich-maker. We're talking about the finest deli in D.C. She's got take-out service all over the tristate area. Thirty-eight flavors. MasterCard, Visa. Wouldn't surprise me if she graduated from the Wharton School of Finance."

"I'm on my way."

The address that Dixon gave led Warfield to a sedate block off Twenty-second Street. The building was a very well kept brownstone with polished brightwork and painted grillwork and a waterfall of ivy down the bricks. Warfield rang the bell for the Parkins Foundation as he had been told to do.

Stretch Dixon answered the door with a comatose smile that would have suited the butler. "You always wanted to see how the upper half's lower half lives. This way, sir."

Warfield followed him down the hall, which was equipped with motion sensors, and through a door with a magnetic alarm system. Next they passed through a nondescript anteroom with one heavily curtained window before entering a double living room that was a shocking blast of Moderne. The furniture was sleek, aerodynamic. What was not blonde was white, and what was not transparent was shimmering and tubular. The rug on the floor was a pale arctic green. The neon palm tree on the wall flashed a cool blue. The natural order of the planet was represented by an ancient bronze cash register and a baroque telephone that stood on either side of a massive jet-black desk like household gods.

Between them sat a woman of great beauty. Her form was

covered in an iridescent white morning garment. Her auburn hair was plaited in one long thick pigtail that snaked around her right shoulder onto the exposed upper halves of her breasts. The cleavage was deep, like a fissure in the earth. Her eyes were like earth. The bones, the complexion, the limbs all had combined in an idolatry that obscured her age. This woman was not too young or too old for anything. Warfield was not completely sure that she was real until she moved her tinted lips.

"He's cute, Stretch."

Dixon gave a low groan of disapproval. "I suppose that plain vanilla has its charms."

"I'm Shiloh Parkins."

She stood up, flooding the area with white folds, and offered Warfield her hand across the desk. The grip was firm and fashionably cool. The faint accent, which was no more than the way she sloughed her vowels, might have been Virginia, or even Arkansas, by way of the Wharton School of Business.

"Warren Stevens."

Dixon laughed. "You're going to confuse this lady," he said. "I already told her your name and what you approximately do. She said she never met an *American* spy before."

"We don't use that word," said Warfield to Shiloh Parkins, her hand still in his. "We're intelligence officers, and we collect data. Mostly, we sit at desks."

"You don't look it," she said, removing her hand slowly from his. "I have a great deal of experience with bureaucrats. They might be concerned with power, they might be consumed by it, but they're rarely powerful men."

"She's good," said Dixon. "I told you she was very good."

Warfield said nothing because that was clear. Shiloh Parkins spoke with the accrued authority that success brought to intelligent people. Her beauty made that judgment seem infallible. Her politeness and low sensuous voice as she asked him to sit and if he would like something to drink bore the kind of solicitude that undermined strong nations. Warfield accepted the velour chair but declined the drink. He wanted to keep some sort of control after Stretch Dixon left the room.

"I understand that you may have some information on a man I'm interested in," he said. "His real name is Roland Gasqué. Stretch must have shown you a picture."

She had seated herself opposite him in another soft chair with the white garment hitched to display a long leg that was as sleek and well-turned as the lines of the room. "I couldn't identify the photograph," she said. "I'd never seen the man myself. But you know, sexual preferences are almost as good as fingerprints in some cases. Not very many men will request two women of exactly the same type at the same time."

"Brunettes."

"Yes," she said, stroking the silken end of her pigtail. "Dark haired and large breasted. Middle aged. I think we're looking at a mother fixation here. That sort of insistence usually indicates an unresolved inner conflict. I should have been more aware."

"Was there trouble?"

"A bit," she said. "There might have been a good deal more except for Leona—one of my best. She's done a lot of fantasy work with clients. It takes a very intuitive type to handle that kind of situation."

"What kind?"

Shiloh Parkins pursed her lips until they were bee-stung. "Most women—even most sexual therapists—do not like being urinated upon. Something like that has only one object. Degradation. It's the next thing to violence. What I mean is, violence can be the next step."

The CIA report on Gasqué had not included that detail or that insight, but they had obviously not interviewed a woman with the analytical skills of Shiloh Parkins. She could have been crunching numbers for the Pentagon.

"When did this happen?"

"Last night," she said.

"Do you think it would be possible for me to talk to these girls?"

Choosing the most economical gesture, she swished the pigtail twice. "I'm afraid I couldn't allow that," she said. "I have to protect the identity of my employees. I'm sure a man in your line of work can understand that."

"These are moonlighting housewives, I suppose."

Shiloh Parkins shrugged a bunch. "We could be talking about any occupation," she said. "You'd be surprised at the number of my therapists who began their work in college. Call it tuition augmentation. Afterwards, it might be a new car, a grand tour. It might be any number of excuses, but basically they like the hours, the work, the financial rewards. They're not . . . whores, you understand. Approximately sixty percent of their dates do not insist on sexual consummation. What that means is that men like to talk to women. They like to talk to attractive women whose main concern is their company. And the talk is sometimes very interesting. I screen my clientele as carefully as possible. Mistakes like Mr. Gasqué are mercifully infrequent."

Warfield did not think that she was lying, but there had to be a reason for her obvious concern with security. The police would hardly be part of that concern. The process of client selection would be her weak point, though it might be very strong indeed.

"How do you do your screening, Miss Parkins?"

"Shiloh," she said.

He spoke her name. There was absolutely no discord in it.

"We operate strictly on an out-call basis, Stephen. I accept only the best referrals from people I know—some very important people by the way. My therapists go directly to them, usually to their homes or to some neutral ground."

"In other words, you could tell me where the two women went to meet Gasqué," he said.

"Yes, I could."

Her smile was like a wink of summer lightning. It was an invitation to dicker.

"What can I do for you, Shiloh?"

"I need a man," she said, as if she really needed a coat. "He would have to be physically capable, but even more he would have to be intelligent and discreet. A man who knows his way around this city. His job would be to deal with . . . delicate situations. He would have to be firm sometimes, and always careful. I think you know the type of man I need, Stephen. He would be someone like yourself." She smiled again, more broadly and for longer. "Less dangerous, perhaps."

Sometime soon, Warfield thought, he would have to work on his eyes in that mirror. If Shiloh Parkins, who wanted a first-rate troubleshooter, wanted something less than what she saw, then the hunter in Warfield was far too obvious. It would not be very difficult to find someone less "dangerous" because there were lots of those around, but it probably meant that the incident with Gasqué had been more than a routine hosing. The freak must have frightened her girls and herself considerably. Either that, or, in spite of beauty, brains, and money, Shiloh Parkins found that she was lonely at the top. Possibly, it was both.

"I may be able to help you, Shiloh. Give me a day or so. I'll try to find at least two candidates." Warfield smiled, hoping to extinguish the look of the predator. "I think it's important that you have a choice."

She waited a moment, as if searching for sarcasm in his

tone. Finding none, Shiloh gave a short businesslike nod and a long lingering smile, one that had surely launched myths if not ships. She dipped into her pleated bosom and pulled out a small piece of note paper. Reaching across the space between them, spilling the folds of the white garment and baring her breasts all the way to her rich roseate nipples, she handed the paper to Warfield.

"This is the address where they went."

He took the paper but did not unfold it. "I'd like the sponsor's name too," he said. "The man who introduced Gasqué."

"I can't do that," she said quickly.

"This is important to me, Shiloh. I have to get to this man."

"There are some people who can't be gotten to, Stephen."

"Not this time."

"Every time," she said. "It surprises me you don't know that."

"I don't," said Warfield. "And it's unfortunate that you do. What people know is sometimes the only thing that keeps them from being what they might be."

She pulled back into her chair, the pleated white garment cupping itself to her breasts like hands. "I'm happy with what I am, Stephen."

"Then I apologize."

With a brisk movement, she whipped the thick pigtail around to her back. "Do I lose my man now?"

"No," he said. "I'll find you someone. That's a promise."

Warfield sent Stretch Dixon ahead to check out the address that Shiloh Parkins had supplied. It was in northwest Washington, close enough by dead reckoning to qualify as the receiving station for the directional antenna that had been broadcasting the minutes of Warfield's private life.

They must have been bored by the experience. Visiting the Parkins Foundation had reminded Warfield of how much people were willing to pay for human companionship—even if it was only companionship—and how much he was not. The women that he had escorted and attended in the last three years had not been satisfactory or satisfied. There had been one very staunch lady who had given Warfield so much good company over a six-month period that they had both nearly mistaken it for love, but in the end she had been unable manage the absences, physical and emotional, that were a part of what was left of his life. She had been a good lover too, but she did not bring to the act the feeling that every time was the last. Only one woman had ever done that.

And Bettina was still missing. There were no outside messages waiting for Warfield at NSA's downtown offices. He could have said that he was surprised that she had not reacted to the news of Eglon's death, but of course that might have been exactly what she had done. Bettina's response could have been to remove herself from danger completely, especially if she thought that her proof had been lost to the wrong people. That's why the link to Gasqué was important. He could know everything about where she had been and something about where she was going.

The equipment that Warfield had requested from Amelia was waiting in the parking lot off Fourteenth Street. It was primarily a surveillance van with several refinements, such as the cryptosecure mobile line and the set of laser-enhanced parabolic receivers. There were also the "special needs": one Italian front-opening eight-and-a-half-inch knife with a large faceted grip; one SIG 210-2 9 mm automatic pistol, as accurate as the Swiss could make it and one of the few still available with single action; one HK 93 assault rifle with the new and very good scope-mounting system; one infrared and one starlite scope; a 7 mm Mauser; a silenced .22; some Kevlar body armor; some scaling tools; and a supply of surgical gloves.

Before leaving the area, Warfield also put in a pouch a copy of the photograph that had been taken on the Nicaraguan beach. He did not mind keeping headquarters current as long as they were one lead behind. It would be interesting to see if the specialists could verify Heinrich Müller's reappearance from the slim evidence of the photograph. They could also have a crack at the identity of the second man, that young *español.* Not knowing where the picture had been taken, headquarters might have a difficult time sorting him out, but the omission could also result in an unprejudiced search. Because of Bettina's handwritten notation, Warfield assumed the man to be from Nicaragua, when in fact he could have come from anywhere.

It would keep them busy and off his back in any case. He did not think he would be shadowed by anyone out of Meade, though they might have rigged the van to transmit. If they had done that, Warfield knew he would not find the device short of tearing the truck down to its frame, and perhaps not then. Besides, there was always some advantage in having folks think they knew exactly where you were.

Which was northwest D.C., off Utah, almost midway between Rock Creek Park and the Chevy Chase Country Club. Warfield arrived at the address shortly after noon. The condominium development was called Arcadia Farms, and what it reaped were tax advantages. The landscaping looked very sweet with flowering shrubs and lush swale gardening. The tall oaks were the oldest inhabitants; the buildings had obviously been built around them. The condos were single-story, each joined to one other in a cluster.

Sixteen thirty-two G lay on the right side of the road, abutting the tall property-line fence and adjacent to a large blue dumpster. It was the left one in its group and had the finest view of the communal garbage. If any of the units were rented out often, that would be the one.

Warfield had parked at the entrance to the road, out of sight of the target except through powerful glasses, but Stretch Dixon found the van inside three minutes. He appeared beside the driver's side window dressed in coveralls that said: Maintenance. Although Warfield had been scanning the area constantly, he had neither seen nor heard Dixon until the last second, when the side mirror suddenly filled with his impassive brown face.

"Two bedrooms along the outer wall," he said. "A kitchen and a big living room for the rest. There's a sliding glass door that goes out onto the back patio, but the curtains behind it are shut. Also," he said with a pause, "one oversized skylight."

"Anybody home?"

"One for sure," said Dixon. "The stud."

"You saw Gasqué?"

"He moved the garbage out to the garage about ten minutes ago," said Dixon. "I don't know why he doesn't take ten more steps to the dumpster, but I guess that's what makes him a cool-hand professional. Instead of showing himself, he shows himself and his car."

"A dark green sedan?"

"That's a Charles."

It sounded like the vehicle into which Warfield had been invited two days ago. Knowing that Gasqué had held on to the car when he should have traded it for another made the situation seem better. A man who was sloppy in one respect might be in others. He had been careless with his sexual therapists too, though no doubt he had paid well for what he hoped was silence.

"Thanks a lot, Stretch. You can go home now."

"I think I'll hang around," he said. "This man can't be as dumb as he seems."

"You must be desperate for the money."

"Or something."

Warfield did not want an argument that he might regret winning. Dixon was as good a backup as anyone was likely to get. "All right," he said. "There's a ninety-three in the back. Take it and work your way up to that skylight. Shoot anything that moves too fast."

Dixon smiled like the memory of a smile and moved around to the side of the van, where he swung open the sliding door and jumped in without causing the slightest movement in the suspension.

"That's what I like," he said. "License to kill."

"In the green bag you'll find a set of suction clamps with a harnass and power pack," said Warfield. "I'm told it works almost every time."

"It's one story, Stephen. I can *think* myself that high."

"Do it."

When Dixon left the van, he carried the automatic rifle in its plastic case in his left hand, as if he were a doctor of maintenance on his usual rounds. He made no attempt to diminish his presence. If anyone stopped him, it would be to complain about the service they were not getting nearly enough of.

Warfield strapped on the Kevlar body armor, knowing that if he did not shut down this operation in less than fifteen minutes he would be broiled alive in the noonday heat. He chose the 9 mm automatic and the silenced .22 revolver, confident that these and Howard Thunander's heirloom picks were sufficient for the work.

There was no need to worry about external security—if Dixon had not found any countermeasures no one would. The heavy plantings of ornamental bushes and tall sea grass around the fringes of the unit gave easy access to an intruder. In less than five minutes Warfield was standing on the patio at the rear of the condominum. The large hydrangea that screened the space from the neighbors also threw a nice dappling of light and shadow across the sliding glass door and the curtains beyond. The breeze, light and erratic, changed the pattern from moment to moment in a very helpful way.

Warfield found that he did not even have to use a pick on the door lock because it was less a lock than a heavy clasp that operated with a finger button on the inside handle. Using the leverage of his bent knees against the top runner, Warfield managed to lift the sliding door the quarter inch or so that was necessary to edge the clasp apart. Slowly, he slid the door open a foot, trying to block any sudden draft that would cause the curtains to billow. Then he was in, standing behind the drapes, and the door was closed again.

One quick look told him there was no one in the area. There were several pieces of furniture scattered about the large living room, rental modern and unlovely. There was a fireplace that ran all the way to the top of the cathedral ceiling, some fifteen feet from the skylight and Stretch Dixon's long shadow. When Warfield was certain he saw no movement in the living room or through the pass-through window into the kitchen, he moved into the center of the room and gave a hand signal for Dixon to come down from the roof.

Without waiting for his backup to appear, Warfield stepped across the carpeted living room to the bedroom immediately off it. That room too was empty except for the furniture—two chairs, a cot, and a makeshift console running the length of one wall. At a glance there appeared to be at least three receiving units, which were hooked up to the same number of recorders on the folding tables.

A set of wires ran from the console into a large walk-in closet. Although a party could have been thrown in the space, it was empty but for several cardboard boxes. The wires ran directly through a man-sized hole cut in the low ceiling. No doubt a fairly sensitive antenna lay up in the rafters.

By the time that Warfield had checked out the closet, Dixon was down from the roof, standing at the entrance to the radio room with the HK 93. Warfield indicated "Nothing" and motioned for Dixon to cover both entrances. Dixon nodded, stepping aside as Warfield passed. He took up a position just inside the radio room with his back to the equipment. Dixon was invisible two steps from the doorway, and he was not stupid enough to enlarge his profile with the muzzle of an automatic weapon.

Warfield quick-looked the kitchen and started down the short hallway that led to the second bedroom. It was tricky going because of the clear plastic runner laid as wide as the hall. It could not be rolled up without making a sharp crackling noise or possibly being seen by someone inside the bedroom, so he used a slow heel-and-toe sidestep to move down the hall. On the left was a utility closet, wide open, with a washer and dryer that from the smell of the place had not been used very often. The bathroom stood directly ahead, unoccupied. But the same was not true of the bedroom on the right.

Roland Gasqué lay under a sheet and pink spread. Though his lips were partly open in sleep, softening his face slightly, he still looked like he had been fashioned by an ancient iron-monger. Those were hard interlocking plates in that face, the bones so prominent they seemed to have been hammered out. The eyebrows looked like they had been sewn to the skull.

Warfield did not know why the sight of Gasqué made him angry; it might have been because he thought something like that should not be allowed to dream peacefully. Something like that should be made to tell the truth for once in his life. There was only one way it was ever going to happen.

Gasqué's form was well defined beneath the pink spread as he lay on his side. His legs were drawn up in the fetal position. Warfield aimed for the left knee just below the patella. The .22 cartridge made its entry noiselessly. Roland Gasqué awoke screaming.

He would have aroused the neighborhood if Warfield had not moved immediately and stuck the barrel of the revolver as far into Gasqué's mouth as he could. Still, it took a moment for control to arrive. Gasqué bit down on the barrel of the revolver with big misshapen teeth before he knew what was happening. His hands groped wildly at the covers for the thing that gave him such pain. Then his eyes locked on Warfield.

"That's right, Roland. This is called Shit Creek."

Warfield threw Gasqué's pillow aside and found the short .45 he had seen in the street the other night. He tore the covers aside to reveal a 9 mm Spectre auto-loading pistol with a fifty-round magazine, thumb saver, and three boxes of ammunition. No wonder Gasqué had slept peacefully.

Warfield put the .45 into his waistband beneath the body armor. He secured the fifty-shot pistol, and chambering the first cartridge with one of the ambidextrous cocking handles, brought the weapon to bear on Gasqué's chest.

There was quite a bit of blood coming from the knee, seeping through his hairy hands into the sheets. The blood was the same color as his bikini underpants. Huge hot tears filled his eyes, boiling down his cheeks. The sight could have caused an ordinary citizen to confuse Gasqué with the rest of the human race. Warfield did not. The silenced .22 stayed in Gasqué's mouth until he had put his hands behind his back to be cuffed. Warfield did not relax until both hands were completely immobilized. Then he decocked the automatic and laid it on the rug beside the bed.

Gasqué was whining now. He screamed again when Warfield sat him on the edge of the bed with the damaged knee straight-legged in front of him. When the barrel of the .22 wagged close to his face, he stopped.

"We have to talk, Roland. You remember me, don't you?"

Gasqué nodded once.

"You know what happens when I get a wrong answer?"

In case he did not understand, Warfield tapped the other knee with the silencer. Gasqué nodded twice.

"From the beginning now," said Warfield. "How did you find me the other night?"

"Followed you," said Gasqué in a high voice that belonged as much to the pain as to him. He was breathing heavily because he was at the top of the mountain and still climbing. "Had you wired."

"Who did the electrical work?"

"Deuce," said Gasqué.

"That's the ape?"

Gasqué said yes.

"What's his real name?"

"Clarence," said Gasqué. "Clarence Dupard."

No one would make up a name like that for a fellow human being. Warfield was convinced that nothing so far had been invented, but now they had reached the tricky part.

"Where is Clarence?"

"Out," said Gasqué.

"You mean he's looking for the girl?"

"What girl?"

"Don't say that, Roland. She's the reason you hurt so bad. You tell me where she is and I'll take away the pain." Warfield placed the cold blued silencer directly against the flesh of Gasqué's one good knee. "Until then I enjoy it."

"I can't tell you," he said quickly, sucking air deeply. "If I knew I wouldn't be here now."

"Tell me what you do know," said Warfield. "Who wants her?"

Gasqué screwed his face up like foil. "What can I tell you about a million bucks? I can offer you a share. You interested?"

Warfield was not but he tried to keep his tone noncommittal. "Roland, no one pays a million dollars to have somebody killed. You could snuff half the Congress for less."

Gasqué knew that if anyone did. He would never have mentioned numbers if he was not hiding something; the mention of such a large number all but proved that he was.

"It's the total package," he said, sniffing deeply again, trying for a purchase on the pain. "It's the girl and the kid. They want the kid back alive."

There was a point in almost every interrogation when a wild unexpected element inserted itself, and these were the things that the interrogator lived for. Warfield was sure that he had not shown surprise on his face. He tried very hard to incorporate the new assumption without showing amazement in his tone.

"Where did she get the kid?"

Gasqué laughed as if the worst part of him had been touched with a wand. "I don't know how they do these things," he said harshly. "They lay down on their backs. They spread their legs. It starts."

"This is *her* child?"

"That's what I was told."

"Who told you?" said Warfield. "I want you to be very specific now, Roland."

"The contact," said Gasqué. He shook his head suddenly,

as if aware that the answer was not good enough. "A man named Esteben Cruz."

"Mexican?"

"Nicaraguan," said Gasqué. "In Mexico."

"Description?"

"Tall for a Nica," he said. "Lots of hair, lots of jewelry, good body."

The description sounded promising—it fit in a general way the young man on the beach in the photograph.

"Light hair?"

Gasqué nodded, grimacing with a spasm that forced his ugly teeth together.

"Intelligence?"

"How the hell would I know?"

"You'd know, Roland." Warfield put the silencer against the good knee again. "I want you to concentrate."

Gasqué primed himself with three deep breaths that came from way down. "Look, I've dealt drugs and I've dealt with intelligence types. You get beyond a certain level, they're the same kind of people. Hell, sometimes they *are* the same people."

There was more than a grain of truth in what Gasqué said. The people with the greatest need for security were the big drug dealers. The people who could provide it best were those with intelligence training. Sometimes they did provide it.

"You're telling me that he was a professional."

"You were a greaseball, he'd be you."

"But Roland Gasqué didn't ask for guarantees," said Warfield. "You took his personal check for seven figures."

Gasqué ground his teeth so hard that Warfield could hear the snap of something as it broke. He spit three times before he spoke. "I got three and a third wired to Paris."

"Whose three and a third?"

"Don't ask me who's paying the bills," he said, gulping the words. "You know how these things work. Point to point you're better off chasing piss down the river. I don't know where the money came from. The bank knows but they don't want to know. Somebody puts up that kind of money, half's for the job, half's so there's no return address."

Warfield refused to believe Gasqué if for no other reason than the increase in the number of his words. Pain made for short answers, and panic was probably the only thing that could lengthen them. Something stood between the truth and the fact that he would never walk well again. It was something powerful. Slowly, Warfield cocked the hammer of the revolver.

"Take a deep breath, Roland."

"You can't do this!" he said, snorting, almost screaming. "You can't just shoot holes in me! You better kill me! You don't and I'll fucking kill you! I'll find you and I'll . . ."

Gasqué never completed his oath or Warfield his promise because at that moment both men heard the sounds.

First came a bump, as if someone had stumbled on the stairs or a door had reached its stop, and Warfield knew by the look of hope in Gasqué's eyes that it was the front door, that it had opened, and that although the sound was not much for volume, it was ten times what Stretch Dixon would have produced in a headlong flight.

The sound meant that someone was coming—someone was here—because the next thing in sequence was Dixon's voice screaming an incoherent spool of sound that almost certainly was Warfield's name. Overlapping the sound, swallowing it and shattering it, came the bark and whistle of automatic gunfire.

There was no time for anything but cover. Warfield grabbed the autopistol off the floor and vaulted across the bed. He rolled onto his back, cradling the weapon, then swung back with the block sights resting on the plane of the bed, framing the doorway exactly.

For a second there was a lull in the firing. Suddenly, Warfield heard the sounds—*whisk, whisk, whisk*—that meant someone was coming down the plastic runner in the hall.

Warfield had no idea who or what it was, but he knew that if it had gotten past Dixon it was as fast as it was deadly. He was sure that the Spectre could take down anything, including a full-sized bull, but when Warfield had decocked it he had unknowingly put the trigger on a very long pull. He fired as the figure of Clarence Dupard, also known as Deuce, flashed across the doorway low in a dead roll toward the adjoining bathroom, and the heavy kick of the auto pistol was just a fraction of a second late. The black man might have been hit but he was not all the way down.

And then it all blew up. Warfield hated automatic weapons and the freaks who used them, which was almost every freak in the world these days, because they made time and skill the enemy. They made everything irrelevant except who could point fastest and how many rounds could be gotten off. Dupard could snake that stubby MAC-10 around the doorjamb and send round after round shrieking into the room and the bed and ricocheting off the slab beneath the carpeting and crashing through the venetian blinds over the dresser and shredding the dresser to chips. He could and did have Warfield hugging the green wall-to-wall, firing blindly over the bed from his back, hoping, praying it would stop.

But it did not stop—suddenly it got louder. There was another automatic weapon in play, the 93, Stretch Dixon, and for a moment the rounds stopped helling into the bedroom. Warfield rolled clear of the bed and fired full-face into the figure of Clarence Dupard not fifteen feet away in the bathroom. He was being hit from two directions, he was being torn apart and his flesh splashing all over the white tile, he was being mulched, but until his head was nearly cut off his shoulders the rounds kept coming from the MAC-10, swinging wildly into the bedroom again and down the hall again. Finally there was quiet.

Warfield knew that he had been attempting to fire an empty magazine for the last two pulls. He knew that he had been hit somewhere on the left wrist and that he had taken two solid blows of .45 calibre high up on the body armor and that his right shoulder was numb. He knew that Clarence Dupard was as dead as King Kong. But not until Stretch Dixon came into the room did Warfield look toward the figure of Roland Gasqué on the bed. What he saw was a man who had had his throat torn out and his skull completely shattered.

# Humint

THE restaurant was attached to a motel not far off the beltway in a region of dense commercial clutter. It was no more than a mile and a half from Arcadia Farms, but it might have appeared at any interstate exit in fifty states. The decor, for some reason, was Western, wagon wheels here and there, bull-horn pulls for the draft beer, electrified oil lamps at the leatherette booths. The steak and fries were as lean and mean as a free range.

"I don't see how you can eat," said Dixon. "I don't even see how you can chew."

"Habit."

"I should have done what you said, Stephen. I should have gone home. I let that son-of-a-bitch surprise me. Gasqué started to scream, and then all of a sudden this damned animal comes through the door like Doctor Death. We're in the suburbs—the *suburbs*—and he thinks he's in the jungle. Some damned banana republic. I'm telling you, there ain't no sense of *proportion* here."

"There's a lot of money involved, Stretch."

"We talking Ivan Boesky now? Carl Icahn? How much money does it take to make a man think he can't die?"

"Not very much really," said Warfield. "If Gasqué wasn't lying about the money, and if he got his final payment, and after he deducted his expenses, I don't see how he could have cleared more than a couple hundred thousand. He splits that with Clarence, he's got even less. Then there's always the chance that Clarence mistakes him for watermelon pie."

"Typical ethnocentric remark," said Dixon. "I don't suppose you noticed young Dupard's earring."

"Earring?" said Warfield. "I didn't even notice his ears."

"He had two," said Dixon. "One was in the bathtub. Attached to it was an earring with the motif of Baron Samedi. The Tonton Macoute used to wear those little items of dress."

"You think he's Haitian?"

"I think we're going to have one hell of a time asking him about that," said Dixon. "He's going to need more than voodoo to be walking among us again. But it makes sense. The organization went all to hell when Baby Doc split for Paris. You say the Canadian likes France almost as much as he seems to like Old Mexico. It's got the potential to play either way."

Warfield found himself nodding in agreement, which increased the more he recalled of Gasqué's file. "I think it plays best with French pastry," he said. "Gasqué speaks the language and he has a connection to organized crime in France. He's worked in Argentina and Mexico, but he could just as easily be working under contract from Paris or Marseilles."

"If I remember, he was doing a deal for white heroin there in Mexico," said Dixon.

"Right."

"A man with Mexican connections for the dope would be doing brown or black tar," said Dixon with considerable expertise. "White heroin is an import item. It generally comes in through the Middle East and gets expedited through France. You know—the old French connection." Dixon raised his eyebrows and a second later his index finger. "But look, here's the man who can tell you all about it."

Warfield did not know how Dixon had spotted the car for what it was because the late-model ragtop in no way resembled an ordinary government vehicle, and it had pulled into a parking space at the far end of the lot, barely visible from the window booth where they sat. Nor did he think that Dixon had seen John Slaughter for more than a passing moment once or twice in his life. Yet when the car door opened, the large figure that uncoiled from the front seat, looming high over the roof, was unmistakably that of Warfield's former colleague.

"I still can't believe you're going to work the DEA on this."

"He owes me a favor," said Warfield. "Now he owes me two."

"They wanted Gasqué bad, did they?"

"These drug-enforcement types are peculiar," said Warfield. "They resent people who kill their agents. They even resent them dead. Slaughter's got just enough grease to be able to control the investigation."

"And get your ass out of the grinder."

That was the plan. If it did not play, Warfield could always plead diminished capacity. That defense had worked for John Hinkley.

"You'd better get going, Stretch. I'll be needing you again."

"I didn't hear that, Stephen."

A moment later, Warfield did not see or hear Stretch Dixon. Even his car, a Mazda, seemed to operate silently. It was not, however, invisible, and Warfield could only hope that no one in the vicinity of Arcadia Farms had noted the plate. The knowledge that a civilian was involved in this business could rattle the cage all the way to the top.

But Slaughter had not seen Dixon, and even if he had, Warfield was convinced that the DEA agent did not have anything resembling total recall. Slaughter, as he passed through the front door, stopped, and looked, seemed to have changed little. He had the milky blue eyes and the thick drift of bright white hair that spoke of polar nights and winter kills.

Slaughter had worked for NSA, and Section Turnkey, for seven years. He had given his wife to divorce and his only son to drugs because of his absolute dedication to his work. When the section had been dissolved, Slaughter transferred to DEA and the one thing left in life that interested him: stopping the traffic. In lieu of that, he usually had to settle for stopping the men who moved the goods. Warfield was counting on that.

He rose and came to greet Slaughter halfway across the room from the window-booth. They shook hands. Slaughter's was thicker and meatier than Warfield's steak had been.

"It's good to see you again, Stephen."

"I happened to be in the area."

Slaughter gave him a thin crusty smile. "I'd like to know what's going on," he said. "You want to fill me in?"

Warfield gestured toward another booth on the opposite side of the barbecue flame pit that rose in a series of steplike hearths up the center of the restaurant. They ordered black coffee from a very attentive waitress dressed in tight buckskins.

"I really can't tell you much, John. A little over an hour ago I received information that Roland Gasqué and a man named Clarence Dupard could be found at sixteen thirty two G." Warfield paused. "Did it check out?"

Slaughter blinked slowly. His eyes, which had seemed clouded, tightened their focus like agates. "It was kind of hard to tell," he said. "They didn't slip on the soap, those two. In fact they were all over the lot. Literally."

"My information was vague as to disposition."

"If I knew what that meant, Stephen, I'd probably be pissed off."

"Look, John, I'm working on something collateral here. I had an interest in those two."

"Is that what you call it?"

"This is a sensitive matter."

"I know what that means, Stephen. I remember."

"You know I've given you good value," said Warfield. "You've been looking for Gasqué for a year on that Mexican thing."

Slaughter accepted the comment with gratitude that seemed curiously like anger. He stared at Warfield's arm as it rested against the window sill. With the cuff raised two inches, the bandage on his wrist was visible. It had been a very lucky wound, almost bloodless, more like a long rip that had creased between the artery and the tendon, touching neither.

"Cut yourself shaving?"

"He's off the street, John."

"All right," said Slaughter. "I'll admit that I'm happy."

"Good," said Warfield. "If I turn anything else that belongs to you, I promise you'll have it right away."

"I appreciate that, Stephen. If you need any help, let me know. I've got plenty of manpower."

Warfield knew that was true. Being in drug enforcement in the eighties was like being in oil in the Middle East in the seventies. The country's major growth industry had its own growth bureaucracy.

"We're very compartmentalized on this right now, John. But I could use some information."

Slaughter gave a sardonic roll of his big broad hand. "My computer is your computer."

"I'd like to see your file on Gasqué," said Warfield. "On Dupard too, if you have anything."

"I'll send it over."

"Also a man named Esteben Cruz," said Warfield. "A Nicaraguan, possibly living in Mexico. He may or may not have a connection with drugs, but if he does, I'd like to know."

"Okay."

"And I'd like to see the tapes."

Slaughter seemed honestly surprised. "The tapes?"

"The ones that Gasqué and Dupard were taking off the wire," said Warfield. "They were in the back bedroom."

Slaughter did not speak for several moments. He seemed to grow frostier. "Stephen, you're sitting here telling me that you whacked those two. You call me in to cover your tracks. Now you want to siphon off evidence in an MPD investigation. What's the matter, you didn't have time to cop?"

"Something like that."

"You know the police have a fairly decent description of two men who were seen leaving the unit. A salt-and-pepper team. You could pass for the salt."

"But we all tend to look alike."

"Stones," he said. "You always had them, Stephen."

"Listen, if you can't get me the originals, I'll take copies. But I have to have them ASAP."

Slaughter shook his head slowly, ponderously. He was one of the few men on the face of the earth who could use that gesture to express agreement and be understood. "We're going to be all even after this," he said. "No more 'Remember Kabkan.'"

Warfield smiled. Kabkan was a village in a remote part of Iran near the Russian border where Slaughter had spent the worst sixteen hours of his life. "I never mentioned it, John."

"I noticed that," he said.

It took sixteen stiches—several more than he had expected—to close the cut on Warfield's wrist. No one at the Fort Meade infirmary would believe that the wound resulted from a suicide attempt, which meant that the watch and eventually Jack Brindisi would learn of it. Warfield wondered how long he had before they called him down. Deciding it would not be very long, he put in an appearance at the room in the basement of the Operations Building labeled HUMINT.

He supposed it was an inside joke. SIGINT stood for Signals Intelligence, NSA's primary mission, including everyone's current favorite, satellite photography and relay. Human Intelligence, however, had taken a back seat at NSA, a reminder of what could go wrong with a source that could not simply be unplugged.

But there was nothing like a flesh-and-blood operation to generate excellent morale. Warfield received everything but salutes from the folks on duty in the watch room. One was a young computer specialist named Mike Koricke. Like so many who communed with the binary gods, he was tall, thin, and visited by the kind of nervous humor that comes from standing too close to the surge of logic. Ralph Greenspan, who was short and thick, was an older man whom Warfield had known for years, one of the few in the entire organization who knew how to use the full resources of

NSA's extraordinary library.

The surprise was that Amelia Worth had been replaced as watch commander by Ellen Pena. She was a language specialist, the earth mother of Sector V, Latin America. Ellen had raised four children and gone through three husbands while rising steadily through the ranks at NSA. Part of her legend held that she was never fluttered because her emotional response to all questions registered such utter calm that the lie detectors could not be geared down to her metabolism. The other part of her legend was true: Ellen had been a member of the team that for months had lifted the private conversations of every Moscow-based Soviet official who used his mobile phone to discuss affairs of state, and lesser, more important, affairs. The operation, one of NSA's great successes, had reached deep into the Politburo.

Warfield was glad to deal with Ellen because in passing information up the chain of command a lot depended on the tone it was presented in. Ellen understood operational necessities as well as internal politics. She did not react with outrage or panic when Warfield informed her of the fire fight in northwest Washington. He even got a small chain-smoker's smile as she received the news that DEA had agreed to cooperate with both silence and intelligence.

"Jack will shit an actual red brick," she said, sailing forward in her spring-loaded chair and putting both arms flat on the desk. "But that was good work, Stephen."

"Slaughter's a good man."

"Yes," she said. "And if I'm not mistaken, he owes you big voucher."

"Not any more," said Warfield. "He'll relay what I requested. After that, we'll have to stroke him with feathers for the time of day."

Ellen's shrug rippled through her soft unbelted dress. She

had a strong ropy body that had not thickened in middle-age and a complexion that had not been dulled by tobacco. Word had it that she lifted weights and gave a good massage. Warfield was not aware that gym work could result in feminine product like that. If Slaughter required further stroking, Ellen could always be put to the job.

"Let's hope we don't need to," she said. "Gasqué's jacket will give the police an excuse to turn the matter over to DEA. And they will get good statistics out of it." She paused, squinting through a gray haze of smoke. "What did we get?"

"Not a hell of a lot," said Warfield. "Gasqué was being paid very well for running the operation—a million green, he claimed. His contact was a Nicaraguan named Esteben Cruz. A cutout, possibly."

Ellen agreed with a flourish of a fresh cigarette. "Seeing as how the Nicas don't have a pot to piss in, that makes sense."

"They have Soviet helicopters."

"And a starving people," she said. "Besides, there are all shades of Nicaraguans."

Warfield had not thought of it in quite that way before. There were indeed Nicaraguans of the left and right, plus a large percentage, as always, smack in thc middle.

"You know, Ellen, the description I got from Gasqué might be a match for the young man in the photograph."

"We'll research that," she said. "But so far we've got nothing on him here. We're checking all other photo banks, including the Bettman Archives in New York." She paused for a quick puff. "What about those four men who took out Eglon? Could he have been with them?"

"It's possible," said Warfield. "I didn't get a good enough look, and I didn't have time to pull it out of Gasqué. That damned zombie Dupard brought the house down fast. I had some doubts about the cool million until he came charging through the door."

"That's *prima facie* evidence all right," she said. "We'll run a check on him too."

"Have you heard back on the photographic comparison with Heinrich Müller?"

"I just got the report," she said, passing the folder across the desk to Warfield. "It's five pages long. At least half of it is gibberish about bone structure and basic head shapes. Apparently there is still such a thing as phrenology. The upshot is that there's an eighty percent chance that the subject in the photograph is really Müller. The man's age and something called the corneal index are very close in alignment. They could be more certain if it weren't for the nose."

"According to Hoover's man in Argentina, Müller had had cosmetic surgery."

Ellen agreed. "It looks good," she said. "Possible."

"You mean she looks good. Bettina."

Ellen had of course been waiting for that name to come up. She lit a second cigarette with the butt of the first. "What did you find out about her?"

Until Ellen asked that question, Warfield had not realized how smart Jack Brindisi's personnel move had been. If Amelia Worth had asked the same thing, she would not have gotten an answer worth reporting. But Ellen had known Bettina well. They had been friends. They had been better friends than most women because neither as a rule cultivated her own sex. Warfield realized that he trusted Ellen too much as a result, but his intuition also told him that he needed a second opinion.

"What I learned doesn't make much sense," he said. "Gasqué told me that he had no idea where she was. Bettina wasn't even his primary target. Apparently he was only trailing her to get at her child."

"*Her* child?"

"That's what I said."

Ellen reacted by stubbing out her cigarette with stern finality. She did not reach for another. "I don't know why I'm surprised," she said. "I know she always wanted children."

"*Bettina?*"

"Yes," she said. "Is it a boy or a girl?"

"I didn't think to ask."

"Men," she said without hope.

"Does it matter?"

"Not really," said Ellen. "But the equation's been changed. If there's a reason why she came back, that would be it."

"I don't understand."

"She must be running from the father of the child," said Ellen. "Who else would want her dead and the child alive?"

Warfield did not see how it could be that simple, but the explanation certainly provided a motivation that had previously been lacking. It could also explain why she wanted to return to where she was known and could be protected, and why she had shied completely when the first contact went bad.

"What are you thinking, Stephen?"

"That if she had a child, she wouldn't give it up."

"No, she wouldn't."

"And that we'd better find Dad in a hurry."

"Yes."

# Beta Shift

But nothing happened quickly. Warfield spent the next two hours in the watch room being mildly frustrated. He read the anthropometric report on the comparison of the two Müllers, which added very little to Ellen Pena's précis. The only addition that seemed worth noting was that the hand size and shape appeared to be virtually identical. The author of the report considered that significant. And if the look in Müller's eyes were added to the eighty percent probability, Warfield figured that the new number fell in the area of ninety-five. That was very high. That was as near to a sure thing as an agent in the field usually got.

Warfield was hoping that some item would correlate with Müller out of the parade of new research, but nothing seemed to fit. Mike Koricke ran Clarence Dupard's name through every computerized data base in the free world, and in some places not so free, and came up with a blank every time. The lone reference that tallied concerned Deuce, Clarence Dupard's nom de guerre. Someone using that name had been connected with the kidnapping of a British military attaché in Paraguay. A call to MI-6 supplied no additional information. The attaché, who had been ransomed and released, thought he had overheard one of his captors referred to as Deuce. No elaboration as to sex, age, or color was available. But Dupard had possibly been involved in a kidnapping, and in essence that had been his mission with Roland Gasqué. Warfield liked the symmetry, if nothing else.

The name Esteben Cruz generated even less text. Someone by that name had served as minister of defense in a Colombian cabinet back in the late forties, but he was far too old to be the man on the beach, or Gasqué's contact, even if he had been of the correct nationality. Ralph Greenspan volunteered to research the minister's family ties for sons, grandsons, or other male descendants who might have come to own the same name. No one, including Ralph, was optimistic about the chances.

Just about the time that all immediate leads petered out, Warfield took a call from John Slaughter. He seemed to be in fine spirits, as if reporting nothing of substance pleased him very much.

"I have zero on this Clarence Dupard," he said. "He appears to be one of the few killers on this planet who was not involved with the traffic in illicit substances."

"Too bad."

"It gets worse," he said. "You want to listen to the spiel on Roland Gasqué?"

Warfield told Slaughter to go ahead, but he might have saved himself the trouble. Slaughter's history of Gasqué was the same one Warfield had called up two days ago. Only when he began to probe along the outline indicated by Stretch Dixon did the facts begin to grow into something more.

"Where was Gasqué getting his heroin?"

"It was white," said Slaughter, as if color were as important to him as to a painter. "We think it came in through the French in Argentina. Maybe they shipped it direct to Mexico, but that really doesn't matter. Once the stuff hits Latin America it's as good as delivered anywhere below the border. You've got Air Coke, Air Smack, Air Weed. These people do not give a shit—in government or out—as long as they get their fair share. There isn't a head of state in the region who makes more than an enterprising custom's agent—unless he really wants to."

"So you think that Gasqué was working for a syndicate in Argentina."

"It was a big piece," said Slaughter. "Forty kilos. Too much for someone like Roland to handle on his own. There had to be another level of support. You'll notice he's done work for the organization from time to time in the past."

"In Buenos Aires."

"And Marseilles," said Slaughter. "These are the same people we're talking about. The Corsicans run most of the traffic in Marseilles. Their cousins are in B.A. If it sounds like the Mafia, that's because it is like the Mafia. Sicily. Corsica. Island people run very tight conspiracies. You don't infiltrate agents or informants very easily. When you do, sometimes you don't get them back."

"Gasqué wasn't Corsican."

"Neither are all these folks," said Slaughter. "But there are enough to keep it a tight operation."

"How long has this connection been going through Argentina?"

"A long time." Slaughter yawned wearily into the receiver. "At least since the end of War Two. Our dope peddlers had to up and leave Marseilles because a lot of them were in very bad odor at the time."

"What smells worse than a drug dealer, John?"

"I'm going to tell you," he said. "A collaborator."

Warfield's antennae immediately went into a mode of full prejudice. "Collaborators," he repeated. "I suppose this is Frenchmen helping out the Germans during the war."

"What it is, Stephen, was French gangsters hunting members of the Resistance at the direction of their friends in the Gestapo."

Warfield liked the way that sounded because it sounded perfect. "So they moved to Argentina when things grew uncomfortable in France."

"The ones that had to," said Slaughter. "The others stayed at home and worked the same old stand. Except now the business was bigger. Latin America never had much in the way of an *efficient* drug trade before the Marseilles connection was established. The Europeans were entrepreneurs in a fertile and disorganized market. You want to know why we have the problems we have today, you have to look to those pioneers in Argentina. They showed everybody what kind of profits could be made by people who were completely ruthless and well organized."

Warfield did not think Slaughter was exaggerating in any way; he might even have been leaving something out. "Have you ever heard of anyone in the German community in Argentina being involved with the French?"

"Not to my knowledge." Slaughter paused because he was trying to trace the parameters of Warfield's operation while seeming only to give information. "The Germans might have invented heroin, but they were never big traffickers. And the Marseillais didn't need anybody to show them how to cook or how to network."

Warfield believed that too, and he knew that if Heinrich Müller's name had ever surfaced in a narcotics investigation, the fact would have been noted with great interest.

"Thanks a lot for the background, John. It's been a great help." Warfield did not allow time for an acknowledgment. "Now what about my tapes?"

"You don't let up, do you, Stephen?"

"Priority, John."

"Well, let me tell you I've got two men transcribing the tapes now. Two full-grown men, government issue. You might have the stuff later tonight, but I can tell you you're not going to like it. I listened to some of the talk, because you piqued my interest. Believe me, I never heard such drivel."

"Let me be the judge."

"Absolutely," he said. "And by the way, forget this bastard Cruz."

"Why?"

"He broke my machine," said Slaughter. "You ask your people if they ever heard of a Beta Shift."

"You better back up, John."

"All right," he said. "I fed the name into Bemis—that's our 3034. We got nothing. No recognition at all. But I started thinking how Latins are with their surnames. What if Cruz was the mother's maiden name, like they use sometimes. That would make it Esteben Something Cruz. Esteben Jones Cruz, for instance. The middle name would actually be the father's name. Say, Esteben Jones. So I ran it that way through the interagency machine and came up with a possibility. The man's name is Esteben Molenaur Cruz. Or Esteben Molenaur, as we have it."

"I underestimated you, John. That's brilliant."

"I thought so too," he said without humor or humility. "Until we tried to call up the file."

"What happened?"

"I honestly don't know," he said. "The display came up and said 'Beta Shift. N/A.'"

"In other words, there's information on this character somewhere, but access is blocked."

"That's it, Stephen. I talked to my nerds about this, and they don't know what to think either. I told them not to fool with it. I figured it's got to be CIA or you people."

"That could be."

"You going to tell me?"

"When I find out, John."

Warfield was glad that Ellen Pena was out of the room when Slaughter called. He hated to think that his own people were sandbagging him, and if they were, he wanted to find out. Casually, without insinuating that the matter was important, he asked Mike Koricke to retrieve all available information on Esteben Molenaur.

Although Warfield was careful not to look directly over Mike's hanger-thin shoulder at the terminal, he could tell from a distance of fifteen feet that something had not gone quite right with the search. Mike entered his command, waited, and waited some more. His pale blue eyes took on a wintry glaze as he repeated the process at greater length, perhaps using a different command and entry. Finally, he gave up with a shrug and turned to Warfield.

"There's nothing from Vulcan on this," he said. "But the interagency data base knows the name."

"What does it say?"

"That's the problem, sir. I'm getting a response I've never seen before."

Warfield moved in for a closer look. The tight yellow letters on the dark screen read BETA SHIFT N/A.

"Why wouldn't it just say 'Access Denied'?"

"I don't know," said Mike. "It's almost as if someone's trying to confuse the origin."

"A bandit?"

He shook his head. "A hacker would just get in and raise hell. He'd destroy the file before he could make any kind of substitutions."

"So this was done by someone with good access."

"Very good," he said.

"Any ideas as to whom?"

"Not the man who updates the data base," he said. "Not a secretary. This would probably be a high-level administrator—or one of his assistants."

That narrowed the field down to several hundred people in government, which was actually quite an accomplishment. "Is there a way around the block, Mike?"

He knifed his legs together, clasped his hands, and stared at the screen. "It would be easy if you knew the password of someone who does have access," he said. "But you'd have to know who that is. Like I said, I've never seen these instructions before. I wouldn't know who to impersonate."

"Is there another way in?"

"I could try to change my security profile," he said, as if he would rather change his blood. "But I'd probably trip alarms. Violations are logged, you know." He held up his hands, which were as skeletal as prostheses. "If you want, I'll go for it."

"Let's hold off on that," said Warfield. "Do we have any other alternatives?"

"A hundred," he said, without hint of exaggeration. "The only problem is that they all take time."

"How much?"

"Days," he said. "Maybe weeks." Mike held up a finger like a five-penny nail. "Unless you got lucky with the backup tapes."

"Where are they kept?"

"No idea," he said. "But I think I could find out. For a

machine like this, they'd have backup on-site and off. They might even have double backups."

"How many people would you need to get this done?"

"A few," he said. "And a lot of luck."

"We'll see if we can't get Jack to spring for both."

Warfield was not surprised to see Ellen Pena as he stepped from the elevator on his way to the deputy assistant director's office. Although she had not told him where she was going, Warfield had assumed that the watch commander had left to make her report to the DAD. It would have been verbal. Everything about this operation was off the books.

With Ellen's report out of the way, Warfield thought he would not have to wait long on the DAD. He was right. Like all upper-echelon intelligence officers, Jack Brindisi worked long hours as a matter of routine. There were always a hundred ongoing projects to tend, as well as special operations, and the appointees who were his superiors could rarely be trained to grasp more than a fraction of that number or choose among shades of importance. If intelligence work were a cult requiring great devotion and personal sacrifice, then men like Jack Brindisi were its spiritual leaders.

His office did not distinguish between day and night. The dense blackout curtains were always drawn across the windows and the internal shields that protected against voice and radio emissions further dampened every sound. The rug was thick and dark. The furniture was spare, dark, and unpretentious. The ornaments on the walls were mostly certificates framed in cheap dark metal. This was not a run-of-the-mill executive power place but a functional and secluded black chamber where a modern alchemist plotted his transformation equations.

Jack's sole weaknesses were his pipes. He had hundreds, a

good dozen on the top of his desk, and in his mouth was a sea-coral brier that must have cost a small fortune. He usually spent as much time shredding the tight navy flake tobacco into the bowl as he did smoking, but the purpose of the two rituals was the same because it allowed him to build a world of concentration within the many worlds of NSA. When he put the pipe aside without emptying the bowl, his subordinates grew wary. That meant his thought was finished, and perhaps their project too.

"We're already outside our guidelines on this," he said, putting the pale brier aside. "I don't like widening investigations that aren't sure of their purpose."

"We're sure of that," said Warfield. "We just don't know where it's going to stop."

"We know where Bettina's last mission went."

"Nazis are safe, Jack. If something goes wrong, we can pull back at any time."

"That's exactly what I'm saying here, Stephen. And while you're at it, define 'wrong.' Try to keep in mind that most citizens are alarmed by automatic gunfire in their bedrooms."

"We're covered on that," said Warfield. "And 'wrong' in this business is being uncovered. That hasn't happened."

"DEA knows," he said.

"DEA in this case is John Slaughter. I'd trust him with my life."

"You're already trusting him with your career," said the DAD quietly. "Believe me."

That was plain enough. If it were any plainer, Warfield would be shipping out his résumé to private security firms. "I want a decision," he said. "Either I get a free hand on this, or you can activate my resignation."

The DAD gravitated slowly toward a new pipe from the rack on his desk. That was a good sign. The one he chose was a meerschaum with an enormous, intricately carved bowl that could have passed for the figurehead of an old wind-ship. He began to pack it with tobacco.

"It's my feeling that if I accepted your resignation, Stephen, you'd pursue the matter on your own."

"A man should listen to his feelings."

The DAD finished crumbling, shredding, and packing his good burley. He looked up at Warfield with renewed interest. "I know you're holding some things back, Stephen. You're making it very difficult for me to evaluate the potential of this mission."

"Jack, if I told you all I know, you'd replace me with a CAD-CAM system."

"There's always that risk," he said.

Warfield knew that it was time to take it on. "All right," he said. "The photograph of Müller was taken on the beach at San Juan del Sur. In Nicaragua."

The DAD applied to his wooden matches. He lit one off a striking plate on the pipe rack and put it to the meerschaum bowl, which resembled the head of Leon Trotsky. When the room was thoroughly suffused with smoke, he began to speak.

"That's quite a lovely spot," he said with something that resembled affection. "The resort that Cornelius Vanderbilt built."

"I didn't know that."

"Most people don't," he said. "Before the Panama canal was constructed, the only way to move customers to the California gold fields safely and efficiently was across Central America. Vanderbilt's ships followed the old pirate route up the San Juan River from the Caribbean and across Lake Nicaragua to La Virgen. From there he built the only macadam road in Central America down to the Pacific coast at San Juan del Sur. He transported his passengers in sky-blue carriages right to his hotels and his docks. Made a fortune. Another fortune."

"You seem to know a lot about the place."

"I've been there," he said wistfully. "When I was young."

"You were never young, Jack."

The DAD clenched the bit of the pipe in his teeth, as if he were about to blow more smoke. Then he pulled it out of his face abruptly and smiled. "But I was," he said with the sympathy of reminiscence. "All men grow through stages. All countries too. USA was a very young thing at one time. And it might have been that we lost a bit of our moral authority down there in Nicaragua. Vanderbilt, you know, sponsored the American adventurers who took over the Nicaraguan government in the 1850s. They were thrown out eventually, but their legacy was the dream of a united Central America for Central Americans and a policy of forceful intervention by the American government. When the dictator Zelaya took steps to realize his dream, we moved in with the Marine Corps for the next twenty years so we could run their country for them. After the marines left, Somoza took over with a National Guard that had been trained by us. The Guard was a very good engine of repression for quite some time. That's one reason the Sandinistas hate us the way they do. They know that the Contras—the Freedom Fighters—are composed of a lot of old Guardsmen. They know that the Contras are the only thing that stand between them and the realization of their dream."

Though Warfield knew most of the story, he was surprised to hear it from the DAD. "Understanding both sides of the problem will make you a liberal, Jack."

"Is that what a knowledge of history means?"

"I'm afraid so."

"Don't be afraid," he said, dousing the spark of revelation as he set aside the second pipe. "Just bear in mind that there's a congressional vote coming up to restore direct military aid to the Contras. Anything we can dig up that tends to strengthen the administration's hand will be most welcome. I want you to understand that."

Warfield understood completely. It meant that certain kinds of evidence were acceptable, desirable; other kinds were not.

"I can't promise anything, Jack. All I can do is lay it out."

"As long as we understand our positions."

"We do."

"Then you can have whatever you need," said the DAD. "I'll give you forty-eight hours to wrap this up."

# Sister George

NE hour later, when the transcription of the tapes came into NSA's downtown office, Warfield gave instructions to hold them there. He needed to be moving. He did not have one lead that could be acted upon, and would not have one, it seemed, until Mike Koricke and his newly formed team turned up something on Molenaur-Cruz.

Warfield had not protested when the DAD mandated a deadline because he knew he had pushed too hard already. Jack Brindisi had put more than a little of himself on the line over this operation. As long as only one man was exposed, NSA had deniability in hand. If anything went wrong with Koricke's mission, no number of resignations could stop the flak. The team was going to have to enter a secured government installation, retrieve the material from among a thousand possibilities, and leave the premises unremarked.

It could be done. It could even be kept within the family if discovered. But that event would have repercussions, the kind that might ruin careers.

The pressure was on Warfield to be quick and very careful.

That was the kind of pressure Bettina had been subjected to when she cracked. He was glad to hear, on the way into town, that the six o'clock news carried the DEA version of the violence in northwest Washington. Two men, known drug traffickers, dead. Metropolitan Police investigation proceeding. Both exaggerations were within the limits of tolerance.

Warfield was satisfied with the broadcast, though he did wonder what the cops would think when the medical examiner dug that .22 slug out of Gasqué's knee. Possibly, they would realize nothing from it unless they did a close ballistic comparison, because the HK 93 that Dixon had used was pretty much the same caliber. The rifle had been left at the scene in the interests of a tidy wrap. There had been no time to do anything but relieve Gasqué's body of its handcuffs.

Warfield's main regret about that bloody mess was that he had not been able to find out anything about the men who killed Ned Eglon. He had promised Penelope Worsham that he would bring them to grief, if not justice. Grief seemed better. He was convinced that pain was the thing that would finally bring him to Bettina.

Curiously, when he arrived at the downtown office, Warfield was able to listen to her voice again. The transcriptions that DEA had made were contained in three bound notebooks, but there was also a single cassette on top of the stack. The note from John Slaughter said, "Mariner, I thought you might want this for your private listening pleasure. It can be kept or deep-sixed. We are now into a period that begins with the words: Remember Arcadia Farms."

Warfield might have laughed. He had no illusions that the cassette was the original. Slaughter would never destroy evidence in a police investigation, and his files were as deep as anyone's. One day there would be a knock at Warfield's door. Fate would be standing on the threshhold, white-haired, ham-handed, smiling.

In the meantime Warfield was free to listen to the sound of his own voice captured on a thin strand of magnetic tape.

His mother's call. She knew who he worked for and something about what he did, but she always insisted that government jobs were good because of the early pension. His broker, because everyone was into the stock market these days. A solicitation for charity. A solicitation for discount shopping. A call from Karen, who worked at Commerce, and occasionally on Warfield's mind. A call back to Karen, setting up a date that he had completely forgotten. Two messages from NSA. His return call. And late that night, Bettina.

Warfield listened to that very short conversation at least ten times. Some of the repetition was pure indulgence, an aural drug that exhumed the past and distilled it through his blood. He realized that an extremely vulnerable man had answered the phone. The shock in his voice was naked. The surrender was quick. He recalled that when he had hung up the phone, his hand had been shaking.

With the headset over his ears and the world shut out, Warfield eventually came to think that he heard something beyond the words and their nuances. Bettina had asked him not to hang up. He had not. There was a pause of two or three seconds before she begged his help, and in the pause Warfield heard a background noise. Using the suppressor and the treble enhancer, he was able to flesh out the sound until it was right at the verge of coherence. In fact it was a high wheeling shriek muted by distance from the mouthpiece.

A baby's cry, he thought. A child's cry.

Warfield knew that he could be misreading the sound, but if he were not it meant that Bettina and the child had been together two days ago. Since no more than an hour had elapsed between the time of her call and her appearance in the street outside the Clay, Bettina could not have been more than forty-five minutes away. That ruled out a quick plane flight from any distance. That ruled out nearly everything but a fast car within a thirty-five-mile radius. It also meant that someone must have been looking after her . . . what? The cry gave no indication of the sex. The cry disappeared, overridden, as soon as their conversation resumed.

He wondered if Bettina had told Ned Eglon about the child. Thinking that he might find out, Warfield attacked the pages of transcription in the bound notebooks. The texts of the conversations were all Eglon, home and office. Much of the time it was impossible to tell who he was talking to, and usually that did not matter because John Slaughter was right: the results were drivel. The conversations were much the same as Warfield's had been—stolen minutes of little substance yielding little reward. A fast scan revealed no exchanges with Bettina.

But Warfield forced himself to examine every conversation. He could have delegated the work to the office staff, which had been increased for the duration of the mission, but he did not want to chance their unfamiliarity with the operation or widen knowledge of its details in any way. Less than half an hour later, Warfield was sorry for his discipline. It took another forty minutes for him to begin to be glad.

At about three o'clock on Monday afternoon, Eglon had received a call from a client that his secretary had announced as "the Maryland Interfaith Coalition." Warfield read the transcription with minimal interest because religious matters always put him into a trance. Not until the two parties began to exchange information about a robbery that had taken place did Warfield really become alert.

Apparently Interfaith's offices had been broken into. Eglon seemed to have a working knowledge of the incident, but he seemed concerned, perhaps surprised, when he was told that some things had been stolen.

EGLON: What's missing?
INTERFAITH: Our mailing list for one thing.
EGLON: Is that basically it?
INTERFAITH: It's difficult to be sure. We think they may have taken some of our correspondence. And we haven't been able to locate the copies of the depositions that were given about the raid on the UPE farm.
EGLON: I want you to make a complete list. Everything.
INTERFAITH: Is there really something you can do, Ned?
EGLON: Not with the local authoritites. Not right now. But if a pattern can be established—
INTERFAITH: Pattern? They've hit the Rights Commitee, the Exchange, the Task Force—
EGLON: I know. But these are a string of low-grade burglaries right now. We certainly can't prove conspiracy.
INTERFAITH: I didn't know we had to prove anything.
EGLON: Wrong. I need reports of every violation before I can go to Justice.
INTERFAITH: Is there a chance they'll listen?
EGLON: Some. I still have contacts there. Anyway, we've got to touch all the bases.
INTERFAITH: Sports metaphors.
EGLON: It's how we communicate.
INTERFAITH: No, actually, we communicate through the media, but they're all *barbosa.*
EGLON: What?
INTERFAITH: It means slugs. It also means idiots.

Warfield found himself nodding in agreement, though from the other side of the fence. He had never heard of the Maryland Interfaith Coalition, but had understood almost immediately that it was a United States–based Central American support group. UPE were Nicaraguan state farms—prime targets for the Contras. Apparently one had been hit hard enough to rate special notice. And apparently someone cared enough about it to try and suppress it. What was surprising was that Eglon seemed to care. Warfield wished he had the tapes so that he could hear the tone of the man's voice.

EGLON: Look, sooner or later the press will have to investigate this. They can't stay blind.

INTERFAITH: The press is manipulated. You make a mistake if you think they're liberal or conservative or anything else. They're attracted to power regardless of the source.

EGLON: That's a good argument. We'll have it some time.

INTERFAITH: I think I'm being intentionally walked.

EGLON: Nothing like that. Just remember the practical damage is manageable. You can recompile the mailing lists. And there must be other copies of the depositions.

INTERFAITH: There are. Witness for Peace has them in D.C. and New York. We made sure they were scattered.

EGLON: Good. I'll be in touch, Alicia.

INTERFAITH: Go with God.

And so he had gone two days later, victimized by another burglary while holding a different piece of evidence from Central America. The four goons who had taken him down had conducted a thorough search of his house. The coincidence was too much for Warfield's taste. Coincidence and murder were mutually exclusive.

He called back to headquarters for priority research on Eglon's client, on the other Central American support groups, and on whether there had really been a series of burglaries. He also requested a check on the offices of Witness for Peace to see if they had been hit, and any available reports on Contra activity against UPE farms.

Some of the answers came back quickly. All the support groups, which were uniformly sympathetic to the Sandinista revolution and the rebels in El Salvador, had made the FBI's watch list some time ago. None were thought to be engaged in espionage, but the Bureau had no doubt that their resources were assisting the forces of liberation throughout the hemisphere.

All that went double for Interfaith. The organization was composed of Protestant and Catholic religionists dedicated to a hands-off policy for Latin America. Beneath the letterhead, however, the group was run and policy determined by a nucleus of Catholic laymen and clergy, many of whom had experienced the harsher realities of life in that region. Their sympathies made them sworn enemies of the various bands that comprised the Contra command. The "Freedom Fighters," although not an effective army, were a potent force for anarchy. They had raised hell with the Nicaraguan rural economy, raiding crops, destroying animals and machinery, killing everywhere. Unfortunately, no records of an attack on any UPE farm existed because no records of that kind were kept by the Contras. Usually no records existed from the other side because no witnesses could be found. The Interfaith depositions must have been the exception.

Lack of statistics was one thing that did not plague any police agency in America. The pattern that Eglon had discerned was quite clear in the information that began to arrive via landline and computer. A series of burglaries had occurred over the past two weeks, all connected directly with the support groups. The bag jobs clustered about New York and Washington, but there were also reports out of San Francisco and Los Angeles.

So it was a bicoastal operation, if not a big one. None of

the work had been done on the same day, which meant that one unit could have been responsible for all the break-ins. The fact that the two West Coast entries had occurred on successive days tended to reinforce that idea. And, yes, Witness for Peace had been hit in New York.

Warfield found himself thinking about the four-man team that had raided Eglon's house—and the promise he had made to a distraught woman. If he was to keep it, Warfield would need all the information he could get.

Penelope Worsham answered her phone on the seventh ring in a voice that seemed filled with sleep. She said, "Hello." Actually, she said, "Hell."

"This is Warren Stevens. I'm sorry if I woke you."

The pause that followed was nearly seven rings long. "Oh, yes. You didn't wake me, Mr. Stevens. I haven't slept at all. It's the dope."

"I can call back."

"No, please," she said, as if she were surprised by her own voice. "Go ahead."

"I wanted to ask a question about Ned's work," said Warfield. "I'm interested in one of his clients—the Maryland Interfaith Coalition—and I wondered if you might know anything about the case."

"Does this have something to do with—"

"Yes, I think so."

Another pause: three rings' worth. "I know a little," she said, almost drawling with drugs. "Ned gave help to political causes—more like political pariahs. I guess he thought he'd made enough money and could afford to donate some time. Only he didn't do ACLU work, he did things he thought were more progressive. Central American groups were high on the list. The Interfaith Coalition, the Mothers for Solidarity. You actually needed a program for the players, and I'd be surprised if they weren't all communist fronts. But Ned didn't care. He took on the legal work for free."

Warfield could not say that he was surprised by Eglon's political leanings, but he was shocked by Penelope's last statement. Eglon must have been truly committed to do *pro bono* work for any cause.

"How long had this been going on?"

"Quite a while," she said. "Mostly the work was nothing of consequence. The thing with Interfaith was a little more. Ned was convinced that some sort of conspiracy was directed against them and some others. Harassmeent. Break-ins. It was like a Watergate dirty-tricks type thing, with the government possibly involved."

"Is that why you didn't mention it to me?"

"One of the reasons," she said quietly. "Also because I guess I didn't want to think of him angry."

"Was he?"

"Yes," she said with soft regret. "We had a kind of fight about it. I mean, I can listen to political arguments. I can even agree with them. The Contras probably are a bunch of thugs—butchers—and the president is probably a very limited man. But Ned went overboard. He complained to me and everybody who would listen, but I don't think he got much attention. Another paranoiac. Who really gives a damn, right?"

No one that Warfield knew. The agitation against the administration's Central American policies was very much in a minor key. Even the college students, who were not threatened by the draft or an imminent war, seemed to care less.

"Tell me, did Ned ever talk to you about his ex-wife?"

"No," she said. "Almost never. I knew him for two months before I was aware that he'd once been married."

Warfield could believe that. He had also heard it qualified. "Could you tell me what you mean by 'almost never'?"

"He told me about what she'd done—the embarrassment she'd caused," said Penelope, as if she might be the one to be embarrassed. "And he complained because once he had to send her money."

"Money," said Warfield. "Was that recent?"

"A couple of weeks ago," she said. "Maybe less. As a matter of fact, I think it was sent through one of the groups we were talking about. I remember Ned saying that he didn't mind working for nothing, but that he resented it when his clients cost him money. I think one of those fallen nuns hit him up. That little bit of a woman, what's her name?"

"Alicia?"

"Yes," she said. "Alicia Fenster. She used to be famous."

So Eglon's contact with Bettina in Annapolis had not been the first. Warfield had suspected as much. Though he still could not prove that Eglon and his ex-wife were coconspirators, there was every reason to suspect that Bettina, if she had known of Eglon's sympathies, would have exploited them. Warfield wondered why Eglon had resisted disclosing the evidence he was holding in the face of threats that he must have known were real.

"Penny, whose idea was it to go to Annapolis last weekend?"

"Ned's," she said. "The weather forecast was bad—couldn't have been worse—but he insisted on going."

So the meeting had almost certainly been arranged beforehand. The smell of conspiracy within conspiracy rose in Warfield's nose like the kick of smelling salts.

"Well, thank you, Penny. You've been a great help."

"I don't mind at all, Mr. Stevens. If it means something to you."

"Yes, it does."

Information on Alicia Grogan, AKA Alicia Fenster, AKA Sister George, was easy to obtain. Her file was thicker than Heinrich Müller's, perhaps because she was considered more of a present danger. The material made it clear that she was something like the spirit of an era—one that had gone a little rank.

Born and raised in a suburb of Chicago, Alicia Grogan had become a St. Agnes nun at the age of nineteen. After completing her training and education, she had gone out as Sister George to teach in the more savage parts of inner-city Philadelphia. The year was 1967, and one of the young nun's first missionary works consisted of leading her social sciences class on a midnight raid of the Federal Building in Newark, New Jersey, where goat's blood was poured liberally over the records of the local draft board.

For the next year or so, Sister George was one of the most famous clerics in America, vying for antiwar headlines with more established religious celebrities. Unlike others, however, she accepted the edict of her order when told that she was to be transferred to a less visible post in Central America. Her superiors—and *Sixty Minutes*—probably thought they had seen the last of Sister George.

For a while that seemed to be true. She taught English and etiquette to the sons of the El Salvadoran upper class, and later, when she was transferred to Nicaragua, worked among the *costeños* of the Caribbean, the *campas* of the highlands, and the university students of Leon. When she was brought to Managua in 1977, Sister George had paid her dues with several serious illnesses and a clear sense of resignation to the will of mother superior and Anastasio Somoza.

Of course the Sandinistas were active by that time, and since so many of them were college students whom she had known in Leon, it was natural that Sister George would put liberation theology to its ultimate test in practice. She supported the FSLN as much as they would let her, supplying intelligence, reliable contacts in areas where they had few, safe houses where they had none. In late 1978 she was taken and beaten by the Guard, taken and tortured by the Guard, but revealed nothing. Many who knew her were taken, tortured and murdered while apparently revealing very little.

When the Triumph, as it was known, came to pass on July 19, 1979, taking everyone, including the FSLN, by surprise, Sister George hit the media again. Appointed by the revolutionary government as a spokeswoman, she toured the United States, speaking to audiences everywhere, lobbying for U.S. government aid to the Sandinista regime. She testified before Congress as to their benign intent, aligning herself with moderates in the State Department and against hard-liners at CIA who argued that Nicaragua had been "lost."

Although that small battle was won, the war had already been decided at the polls in 1980. The newly elected administration gave CIA carte blanche to "find" Nicaragua again through every covert means. The president divorced liberation theology by adopting the Document of Santa Fe, and Cardinal Obando y Bravo of Managua began to expel every radical Catholic in the country. When he put the boot to Sister George, she responded by leaving the church, marrying a Capuchin priest, and carrying on the work by every overt means.

For the last six years, Alicia Fenster had worked intermittently for the Ministry of Education in Nicaragua while maintaining American citizenship. She divided her time between countries, bearing two children in the process, including one on a flight into Washington. In mid-1982 she founded the Interfaith Coalition when the economic recession forced all foreign policy issues into the kind of retirement that every American administration yearns for.

Interfaith's avowed purpose was to stop the funding of the "secret" Contra war against Nicaragua. Their success to date had been middling. For five years vast amounts of money had been put into the counterrevolutionary effort by the U.S. government. Sister George had had a victory of sorts when in 1984 Congress had restricted Contra aid to "humanitarian" purposes. But in 1986 it was widely expected that full military assistance would be restored.

For that reason Alicia Fenster had come up on the hemispheric shuttle again. She had been in town for the last three months, living in a house near the western shore of Maryland that her husband and children occupied year-round. Though she was not under routine surveillance and her phone was not wired, several government agencies kept loose tabs on her whereabouts.

Warfield had no trouble finding the small town or the house where they lived. The area was a little too far out for easy commuting to the District, and a little too seedy to have been discovered. Not more than a mile from the house was a gigantic landfill dump that could have serviced half the state, and perhaps did. The trucks and bulldozers worked even at night, under brilliant arc lamps, with thousands of sea gulls wheeling through the quadrants of darkness and light like bats. That intrigued Warfield. He would have thought the gulls rested at night, and that the human beings and their equipment did too.

The house, an L-shaped ranch, stood on a bit of a hill overlooking a small pond. The front yard and the pond were lit by a battery of spotlights. The interior lights were on too. As Warfield knocked on the screen door, he could hear the television tuned to an all-news station and the voices of children engaged in water play. From a distance, the two commotions seemed very similar. He had to knock twice before an adult could be summoned.

The woman who came to the door was in her forties, old for child-bearing but vivacious in most other ways. She had a tropical tan and tropical crow's-feet at the corners of her large brown eyes, but she also had that startled gamin look that had poked out of so many newspapers in the sixties. The T-shirt she wore over her slim chest said PUNO EL ALTO.

It meant "Fist in the Air," which, if Warfield remembered correctly, was the name of a Sandinista radio broadcast.

"Yes?" She said it like a teacher who had acquired the authority of administration; she spoke like herself.

"My name's Warren Stevens," he said, displaying that ID one more time. "I'm an investigator with the U.S. Attorney's office."

"That's possible," she said. "You don't look like FBI."

She had not opened the screen door or given her name. Knowing the drill in every detail, she would volunteer nothing to any sort of cop.

"Mrs. Fenster, I don't want this to be an adversary proceeding," he said. "I'm investigating the death of Ned Eglon. My interest is in finding out who killed him. Anything else is irrelevant."

She said, "That's what you think."

"A couple of questions? A few minutes of your time?"

She sighed and her hand flitted to the small crucifix that hung from her neck, resting above the slogan. Shaking her head at last, Sister George (he could think of her by no other name) pushed open the screen door and led Warfield into the first room off the vestibule. It was the family room. The television burned like a forgotten genie in the midst of chaos. Books and papers, including the *Congressional Record,* stood knee-high around two filing cabinets supporting a slab of wood that served as a desk. The remaining furniture, which looked like it came from Goodwill, was obscured by newspapers, plates, glasses, ashtrays, two cats, and every imaginable children's toy. Children's shrieks and splashes could be heard from an invisible bathroom down the hall.

"Sit," she said, using a slightly less insistent voice of command.

Warfield sat on the long, corrugated couch. He was immediately aware that he had sat on crackers.

Sister George turned the television down but not off, as if

telling Warfield his place exactly. She put herself down at the other end of the couch, crossing one blue-jeaned leg over the other in a display of hostile body language.

"The president of the United States killed Ned Eglon," she said in that same aggressive tone. "You have to understand that—or you understand nothing."

"We didn't find his prints at the scene," said Warfield.

"You didn't look hard enough," she responded quickly. "His bloody hand is over everything."

Warfield did not care what they talked about as long as he was in the door and seated. "Possibly," he said. "Not everyone agrees with the administration's Central American policies."

"Are you allowed to have an opinion?"

"If I don't act on it."

"A true contemplative," she said, smiling with a great deal of force. "It's clear you're not a stupid one. More's the pity."

Warfield took that small admission for his entrée. "I understand that Ned Eglon was handling a legal matter for you," he said. "Something to do with a break-in at the Interfaith Coalition's office."

Plainly, Sister George did not want to get down to cases, but she nodded slowly. "The break-in was one in a series of harassments against the movement in this country. Ned promised to bring it to the attention of the proper authorities. I think you'd be safe in operating on the assumption that his interest in our affairs had something to do with his death."

"Are you referring to the documents that were stolen?"

"Yes."

"As I understand it, they were depositions taken about an incident at a UPE farm in Nicaragua."

Sister George did not seem surprised that he knew details. Political dissidents always saw government as a monolith, and worse, as an efficient monolith. They were perhaps the only ones who saw it so. The ex-nun looked down her short thin nose as if down a rifle sight.

"You seem to know quite a lot, Mr. Stevens."

"I'd like to know more."

"Are you sure?"

"Completely."

"All right," she said, pinching in her cheeks like a very prim lady. "The slaughter at Totogalpa was one of many such *incidents* in Nicaragua today, but it was also one of the worst. The people at the farm were virtually unarmed. All the men were mutilated and killed. Their heads were cut off after their eyes had been torn out. The women were made to touch the dead bodies of the men. Then they were raped. Their throats were cut unless they were pregnant, in which case their bellies were opened with bayonets. The letter C was carved into the foreheads of everyone, including the children."

"C?" said Warfield.

"They were one of Cruz's bands," she said. "He is what is euphemistically referred to as a Contra leader."

Although the evidence had already headed in a direction that Jack Brindisi and his superiors would not like, Warfield felt that he had to pursue it. "Would this be Esteben Cruz?"

Sister George looked at Warfield as if he were an item she was buying for someone else. "This would be Erich Cruz," she said. "Esteben, the fellow you know, is his brother. They're the very worst of a very bad lot. They're what your tax dollars have bought."

"Nicaraguan?"

"Only in name," she said, diverting the question. "They're men without a country. Mercenaries. They were heavily involved in the drug trade throughout Latin America until someone made them a better offer. It is really more fun to kill with sanction, isn't it? It really is much better to think that your atrocities might cause an entire country, rather than mere money, to fall into your hands. It's all that and secular absolution to boot."

She was quietly angered by her own words now; so was Warfield, in his way. "Mrs. Fenster, if you don't mention Totogalpa, I won't mention the Moskito Indians."

"Oh, yes," she said with thick sarcasm that seemed at odds with her slight frame. "The massacre of the Moskitos. I don't suppose it would interest you to know that there have been no massacres. The Indians along the Rio Coco were resettled because of Contra attacks. They were given the choice of crossing over into Honduras or evacuating to new settlements in Tasba Pri. No one died except in Jean Kirkpatrick's mind. She said—on nationwide television—that two hundred and fifty thousand Moskitos had been put into concentration camps. Mister Stevens, there are no more than seventy thousand Moskitos in all of Nicaragua. Believe me, I know. I've lived in that area."

"Reasonable people can differ," said Warfield. "It's sometimes called the art of diplomacy."

"That's the kind of cynicism that excuses everything," she said with anger. "That sort of attitude allows a B actor who happens to be the consumer's president to stand up in front of the National Association of Evangelicals and say that two hundred pastors in Nicaragua are in jail. I could tell you that there are *no* priests or ministers in jail in Nicaragua. Not five, not three, but *none.* I would be absolutely correct because I know the *truth.* That's why those documents were important. They bore witness to the *truth.*"

"You didn't keep copies?"

"We did," she said. "Those were stolen too. The Witness for Peace office in New York was raided yesterday."

Warfield noticed that she did not mention the organization's other office in Washington. There was probably a reason.

"You have no way now of presenting the evidence?"

"We may," she said. "But you will never know."

Warfield did not challenge her because he was satisfied with the information that had come out. It seemed obvious that Gasqué's operation had been feeding the break-ins. There was also the strong suggestion that while the letter C was being carved in flesh in Nicaragua, someone was going to great trouble to delete in the United States.

"Mrs. Fenster, I can promise you that if I turn up any of your documents, I'll see that you get them."

"In the interest of truth?"

"Yes," said Warfield.

"And the truth shall make you free," she said mockingly. "That's the motto of the CIA, isn't it? But what it means is that the truth is only available to a very select few. An elite."

"I'm not with CIA, Mrs. Fenster."

"And what about the man who's been watching this house?" she asked. "I suppose he's with the U.S. Attorney's office too."

"What man?"

"C'mon, Stevens," she said. "The *Somozista.*"

Before Warfield could respond, Sister George got to her feet, walked to her makeshift desk, and began rummaging seriously among the papers. "Here's his picture," she said, returning to the couch. She handed him a color print.

When Warfield looked at the man in the photograph he was sure at first glance that he was staring at one of the team who had killed Ned Eglon. The Latin male with the eyes that seemed slightly mismatched might have been the driver of Penelope Worsham's car. The longer he looked, the more sure he was of the identification. Those had been crooked eyes that ballooned from behind the wheel of the runaway Audi.

"Can I keep this?"

She smiled less than angelically. "I've got more," she said. "Take it and run it through your contact files. I'm sure you'll find he's one of your deniables."

Warfield thought of asking her how she had first spotted a professional watcher and then obtained such a clear shot of him, but remembering her history through the repression in Nicaragua during the late seventies made the question redundant. Sister George would be familiar with all the tricks of spies.

"When was this man watching you?"

"The last time I saw him was two days ago," she said. "You'll have to check your logs for precise times."

There was no sense arguing with her because clerics were always right even when they were out of uniform. Just how far out was proved when the room suddenly filled with the damp bodies of two children and a large adult male. The latter, though not introduced, had to be Serge Fenster, the defrocked Capuchin who was Sister George's husband. He seemed too big for a priest. Six foot three, two-fifty-five, a little loose in the gut but formidable. The oldest child, a boy of about four years, resembled his father in the hair and in the belly. The youngest, a girl of three, looked like her mother, or the image of her mother that had shadowed the country like a bad conscience fifteen years past.

"They want *Billy Goat's Gruff,*" said Serge plaintively. He ignored Warfield and the children who batted about his legs. "I can't handle that again, Al."

"I'll read them their story," said Sister George. "The CIA is just leaving."

Serge seemed immensely relieved and not at all surprised to see a purported intelligence agent in his family room. He bent down to kiss and tousle each child. After he had peeled them from his limbs and Sister George shooed them down the hall toward the bedrooms, Serge extended his hand toward the door.

Warfield got up to leave without complaint. He had taken a step and a half when the picture window at his back all but exploded into the room. There was a loud dull thud against the glass and a flash of something airborne. Warfield crouched and whirled, his hand on the grip of the SIG 9 mm in his hip holster. From the corner of his eye he saw the object that had struck the glass fall outside the thick panes. It was spheroid and white.

"Easy," said Serge. "It's just the gulls."

Warfield did not understand for a moment. Sister George and her flock had not bothered to turn around or alter course. Serge was smiling with his huge carnivorous teeth as he took three steps that placed him by the screen door. He opened it and pointed.

"We're on the flight path between the dump and the shore," he said. "The gulls are confused by the picture window. They think they can fly through it."

Warfield had moved to the front door to stand beside Serge. He saw the gull on the ground, stunned but already attempting to totter onto its feet. There were other gulls nearby in the air, circling, as if aware of the troubles of their brother.

"It happens twice a week," said Serge. "I think they eat too much garbage. They fly too low. They fly into the spotlights and just keep going."

The gull was on his feet now. The other gulls circled and stalled, screaming the weird rasping cry of their species. The clamor was intense, ejaculative, almost human. Clearly they were encouraging the gull who had collided headlong into the window. With a hop and two flaps of his wings, the stunned gull finally rose off the ground. He pumped several times and swooped into a rising glide that brought him swiftly to the level of the others. He began to scream with delight. Flying away, they all began to scream.

Warfield almost let out his own cry of relief. He was

thinking back to the tape of his conversation with Bettina. There had been a rasping cry in the background between words that he had taken for that of a child. It could have been a child, but the sound was more likely the controlled shriek of a gull. Of gulls. Warfield was suddenly sure of that. He also knew that the distance from this house to Annapolis was a short twenty-five miles. Downtown Washington could be reached in an hour or less. At night, less.

"I have something to tell you, Serge. I hope you'll listen."

The big man smiled like a linebacker. "You can't be worse than the troll," he said. "By God, I hate that troll."

"My name's Stephen Warfield. I know that Bettina called me from this house two days ago."

Serge did not reply. He was reading the quarterback's eyes, waiting for the snap from center and certain mayhem. Warfield thought that he had guessed correctly.

"The meeting with Bettina didn't come off because I was followed," he said. "They had me under audio surveillance until they picked me up at the Clay."

"Your phone was tapped," he said helpfully.

"So was Ned Eglon's," said Warfield. "The same men who were listening to him were listening to me. Now he's dead. Two of them are dead. Four are still around. One of them was watching this house the other day. They're all killers."

Serge did not blink or react visibly, but he spoke to the problem. "I know that," he said. "What do *you* want?"

Warfield wanted to tell Serge that he was nearly as outraged as Sister George had been; that he could not bear to think that the *Somozista* in the photograph was being paid with his tax dollars. Whatever those billions were appropriated for, their disposition did not include the murder of American citizens in their homes.

"If you have a safe method of contacting Bettina, I'd like you to tell her to get in touch with me right away. I can protect her."

Serge did not respond. His stolid calm made Warfield wonder if the *Guardias* had ever paid their visits to Capuchin priests. The look in his eye was either the confidence of a very big man—or prison patience.

"I'll make you the same offer," said Warfield. "I can protect your family if you can bring them in."

Serge shook his head. He put his hands in the pockets of his pants, which had been cut down to shorts. "She'd never agree to that," he said. "Never."

"You can't talk to her?"

"Not about this," he said. "No one can."

Warfield did not ask the ex-priest what he meant by "this." He could have said "that" and been more noncommittal. The choice of pronouns seemed to include the whole range of their conversation—the misguided birds, Bettina, the threat to his own. It was a kind of admission.

"You know, Serge, I can't find innocence on either side of this," he said. "The FSLN tracked down Somoza in Paraguay. They fired a rocket propelled grenade in his face."

Warfield knew at once that he had said the wrong thing to the wrong man. Serge folded his hands but not in prayer. He put them behind his head. Reclining against the screen door, a spotlight illuminating his crown like a fierce halo, he said, "Amen."

# Kind of Blue

WARFIELD decided to give the Fensters an hour or two in case they tried to contact Bettina. He parked at the side of the road beyond a rise three hundred yards away, but still within range of the high-powered night-vision scope capped in the roof vent of the van. They would probably not use the phone—not with all the talk of audio surveillance—but just to be sure Warfield called into NSA's circuit-intercept unit and alerted them for traffic. He also called Stretch Dixon in case he needed relief.

Warfield did not have great hopes that either Alicia or Serge Fenster would break security at his convenience. Alicia had had on-the-job espionage training, and possibly Serge too. But the surveillance was double-pronged because of the chance that the man in the photograph might reappear. The strategy was like playing two long shots in the same race. Luckily, Warfield could do most of the research that had to be done without leaving his post.

The van he had requisitioned from Fort Meade was a younger, more sophisticated brother of the one he had driven in the afternoon. It had all the surveillance equipment that technology could supply, plus some new and innovative hardware. The computer terminal could tap directly into Vulcan and its sister networks, and the AUDRE system worked on the same direct feed. AUDRE stood for Automatic Digitizing and Recognition. The scanning unit was basically a large camera that used sensors rather than film. Any photograph fed into the unit automatically recompiled the image into the computer. A search of the knowledge base could be completed in less than three minutes. Hours—even days—of ID work might be saved.

Were saved. The machine's sweet hum filled Warfield's ears as he slipped the photograph of Sister George's nearly anonymous Latin male into its maw. A positive identification of the man with the crooked eyes came up on the flat screen in something less than two minutes.

His name was Tulio Villazon. He had been born in Cardenas, Cuba, in 1949, and had fled the country with his parents a little more than ten years later to escape Castro's government. Tulio's father, Carlos, had returned to Cuba as a member of the CIA-sponsored Bay of Pigs invasion. Trained in Guatemala, launched from Nicaragua, captured on the beachhead, Carlos did not return to his family for almost five years.

Those teenage years without a strong father had apparently led Tulio to trouble. In 1967 he was arrested for shoplifting and given a suspended sentence. In 1969 he was arrested for armed robbery but the charges were dropped. In 1972 he had been charged and convicted of possession of marijuana with intent to distribute in the town of Hollywood, Florida. Tulio Villazon spent the next eighteen months in Raiford Penitentiary.

Warfield knew two things about Raiford: it was a hard place, a killing place, and it was also the place that Roland

Gasqué had abided at the same time. Their sentences overlapped. One piece of the puzzle fit.

The rest of the information on Villazon came from the old Centac files. The man had never been convicted of any crime after his stay at Raiford, but Centac, which had been an elite and effective drug intelligence unit within DEA, had followed Villazon's career at a distance. In 1976 he had been identified as an interpreter and liaison man between the Colombian drug family of Hector Aleria and various American distribution networks.

Villazon made many trips between Latin America and the States in the succeeding years. People sometimes died when he came to town, but nothing could be proved. In time he prospered by his association with Aleria, acquiring a Panamanian wife and a comfortable house in Colon. He was said to be on familiar terms with the head of the Panamanian security police. In other words, he was one of Hector Aleria's paymasters. Villazon was no longer a cheap thug; he was an expensive one.

At that point the file on Villazon ran out, perhaps because Centac had been disbanded by the current administration on a recommendation from CIA. Not surprisingly, Centac operations were taken over in unequal parts by CIA and FBI. The result was an uncoordinated snarl that spelled bureaucratic gridlock and dead silence.

What Warfield had left was a man who could have known Gasqué and who certainly knew the drug world well. On balance the fit was very good. The only drawback seemed to be that Villazon was bound hand and gun to Hector Aleria. Would his master have put him on lend-lease for this special job?

Thinking that he might make the fit tighter, Warfield put in a call to John Slaughter at his home. The DEA man seemed to have been expecting some intrusion into his life.

He sounded affable and relaxed, yawning into the receiver at regular intervals.

"Do you know a man named Tulio Villazon?"

"A bad *hombre,*" said Slaughter. "We never caught him."

"He's in town, John."

Slaughter's tone became more invigorated. "Where?"

"No idea," said Warfield. "I called to see if you could tell me something about him lately. And where he might hole if his primary command post went down."

"Are we referring to sixteen thirty-two G?"

"I believe so."

Slaughter might have died in his recliner by the silence that took over the line. He spoke at last, as if from a tomb. "You know he worked for Hector Aleria. Maybe still does."

Warfield saw no reason to contradict Slaughter. "Right," he said. "The drug runner."

"Drug runner," said Slaughter, scoffing at the characterization. "We are talking here about a man whose cash flow equals twenty percent of Latin America's GNP. You don't ask how many air*planes* he's got, you ask how many air*lines*. You don't ask about his *pets,* you ask about the *zoo* in his theme park. Are you beginning to understand?"

"He must be a pillar of the community."

"You still don't understand," said Slaughter. "He *is* the community. One of his cousins is a general in the Colombian army. Aleria doesn't bribe the military to look the other way, he uses them to guard his airstrips. They *load* his planes with dope. He doesn't have banks wash his money, he *owns* the banks. One in Panama, one in El Salvador, one in Miami. That's at last count."

"I don't suppose he'd have any trouble putting up a million dollars for a job."

"Pocket change," said Slaughter.

Warfield believed that if the DEA said so. "You've never been able to put pressure on him?"

"You'd have to bring down most of the governments south of the Rio Grande to do that," he said seriously. "And then you'd have to replace them with martyrs. Aleria kills anyone who threatens him. Politicians, judges, members of his own organization. We've nailed perps stone cold, twenty-to-life five counts, but no one ever rolled over on him. That's a death sentence, pure and simple. And he doesn't stop with you. He takes out everyone you hold dear on this earth. Wife, kids, your damned parakeet. After the dust settles, it's like you never *were*."

"He's just a man, John. He can die too."

"I like the way you said that, Stephen."

Warfield hoped so. In fact he did not see anything—anything—wrong with the elimination of individuals who were a menace to the lives of millions. On the contrary, he saw enormous wrong in allowing the menace to exist unchecked.

"First I need Villazon," he said.

"What do you know besides the fact that he's in the area?"

"He's running with three other Latins," said Warfield. "I'm almost sure they were operating on instructions from sixteen thirty-two G. I think they've been in town at least a week."

Summarily, Slaughter said, "All right."

"What does that mean, John?"

"It means that I'll get back to you when I have something."

Warfield had no doubt that he would. While he waited for what might be a long time, Warfield checked on the status of Mike Koricke's mission.

Some progress had been made. The team had located the

backup tapes in a secured warehouse complex on Bolling Air Force Base. Though the area was restricted, no trouble had been encountered in gaining access to the building. NSA, which was within the Department of Defense, could pass without question among its many divisions. If the team found what they were looking for fairly soon, the penetration would not provoke comment at any level. That was the theory.

Headquarters Intercept also reported a sequence of phone calls to and from Sister George's number in the last fifteen minutes. The first had been placed to a D.C. number—the rectory of St. Thomas the Apostle Catholic Church. The phone had rung three times without being answered. The originator had then hung up. It was the intercept analyst's opinion that a signal had been given.

Within ten minutes a call—probably the return call—had come in to Sister George. It originated from a pay phone within a mile of the church. The exchange had been brief. The voice had been a man's. He had arranged a meeting for twelve-fifteen on the following day at the Woodley Park Zoo, saying that "the bison and camels were back." Again, the analyst's opinion was that a signal had been given. The agreed meeting might go forward, but the actual meeting, or drop, would almost certainly take place elsewhere, probably at a designated time plus or minus the hour.

Warfield agreed. Since there was no way of knowing when the contact would occur, he decided to continue surveillance of the house until something broke in another direction or the Fensters made their move. He was glad to see Stretch Dixon arrive in his rotary-engine special. After acquainting Dixon with the surveillance equipment and the situation, Warfield lay back in the reclining front seat of the van for some much-needed rest.

He was asleep within five minutes. The meditation techniques that he had been taught by his old Taiwanese master rarely failed to clear his mind. Once clear, his mind became a *tabula rasa* that transmitted and received in all directions. If the slate were properly erased and the head inclined always to the left, Warfield enjoyed deep dream-filled sleep and the certainty that he would awake, or be awakened, instantly in the presence of danger. Neither the method—nor the alarm—had ever failed him in his life.

Warfield had also learned long ago to participate in his dreams to the extent that he had some control over his presence in them; but he had no say in the content. What blossomed on his mind-screen now was intensely pornographic. Bettina appeared after the introduction. He had not dreamed of her in months, perhaps years.

But she came on like a succubus now, her body latticed in bizarre black straps and strings. She moved slowly, lasciviously, to the background music, lush Wagnerian rock. Her face had the haunted look of a Lil Dagover, frail, other worldly, but her body from the tips of her rouged nipples to the shaved and quivering pudenda were pure Ilse Koch. She had a whip. She wore big boots, new and shining with oils. She danced for him, exposing every curve and declivity, and when he was erect, wondering how he had managed to generate something that big, Bettina mounted him in the chair to which he was tied. Enveloping him sweetly, surrounding him with the smell of musk and leather, she spoke his name: "Stephen."

But the voice was Stretch Dixon's. He said, "Stephen, we're on the move."

He had slept twenty minutes. Awake, alert, and completely regenerated, Warfield took the wheel of the van and backed it into the turnabout at the side of the road out of sight. Seconds later, the Fenster's car, a less than new

Toyota station wagon, passed in the road. Serge, the big priest, was at the wheel.

Dropping Dixon at his car near the service station, Warfield followed the Toyota onto the state road that led past the dump. He ran lights-on and lights-off for another mile and a half until Dixon caught up and took the point. Thinking that the station wagon was headed in the direction of Annapolis, Warfield lay well back. He was surprised when less than five minutes up the road it swung onto a steep paved driveway and disappeared from view.

For a moment Warfield did not realize that the Toyota had entered a drive-in movie theater, the Vanity. The Marquee lights were unlit because of the lateness of the hour. Even the access lights were dimmed. The second feature must have been well underway with no further customers expected. In these days of cable and VCR, it was surprising that the theater was open at all.

Dixon had parked at the bottom of the drive. He jumped into the van when Warfield pulled alongside.

"He went in," said Dixon, making his face a parody of disbelief. "You absolutely sure this guy is a priest."

"Former priest."

"Well, he's fallen hard," said Dixon. "These flicks are kind of blue."

They were indeed. Warfield could see the big screen filled with dangling parts and gaping orifices while they were still at the ticket booth. There was a lot of skin, a lot of lace and leather. Apparently that was how an anachronism survived the onslaught of newer technology.

The drive-in lot was uncrowded, no more than five scattered rows deep around the cinder-block snack bar and projection building. They spotted the Toyota three rows toward the back, hull-to-hull in the densest row. Serge was still behind the wheel, filling the wagon to its roof. Warfield parked the van several rows beyond the last, not wanting to be obvious or to become obvious by blocking anyone's view.

"You want the speaker inside?"

"I don't think we need dialogue, Stretch."

Dixon hummed, amused and beguiled. "You think this is *Wet Rainbow* or *There She Blows*?"

*"There She Blows."*

"How do you know?"

"The tattoo. It's a harpoon."

"Jesus," said Dixon. "I didn't know other people had dicks that big."

Neither did Warfield. The man was strapped to a large shipboard mess table, and he was being eaten. The female partner was anatomically correct but outlandish. She had a chest that would have disqualified her as a chimney-sweep, prominent genitalia, and big black boots. The mouth and its capacity were awesome.

"What time is it, Stretch?"

"Twelve twenty-five," he said. "It's ten minutes late unless we're doing plus or minus."

"I say it's plus fifteen. He makes his move any minute."

"ESP?"

"A feeling."

"Well, there's plenty of that around."

There was indeed. The female had redirected her concentration, climbing atop the mess table, her shining new boots treading dangerously close to the precious parts of the fettered male. She danced above him, then went down on her knees, mounting him. The impalement was swift and stunning.

"You win," said Dixon. "There he goes."

"I'll take him."

Warfield allowed Serge Fenster to walk half the distance to the snack bar before leaving the van. He found it only mildly disturbing that Serge wore a baseball cap and had changed his cut-off jeans for long pants. The man's size was right and reassuring—tall, big shoulders, big gait. When he disappeared into the doorway that led to the restrooms, Warfield picked up the pace.

Serge had seemed unconcerned, very casual, as he walked. He had not looked back, hurried, dawdled, or acted the prey in any noticeable fashion. He had not glanced at the titanic bout of humping that filled the huge screen. Warfield was not more than twenty feet behind Serge when the door swung shut, but when he entered the men's room less than ten seconds later, no one was visible.

There was no way out of the place except for a casement window that was too small for a big man's girth. He had to be in one of the stalls, and sure enough, the third one down, half-hidden by a urinal, contained a pair of shoes. But no pants were heaped on top of them. And the shoes were not the ones that Serge had worn earlier.

Warfield made the decision that took him into the second stall and atop the toilet seat looking over the divider. What he saw was the slogan on the bill of the man's cap. It said NICARAGUA LIBRE. Next he saw an uptilted cherubic face that was not Serge Fenster's.

"Sorry," said the big man with the big grin. "This one's taken."

Knowing that he had been too, Warfield wanted to bring the whole stall down around this second outsized priest. There were probably not more than two of them of the same bulk on the entire East Coast. They had probably been on the same defense at Boston College.

"If I had the time, Father, you'd be eating that damned cap."

But Warfield had no time now. He ran back out the door and through the terraced rows of cars surrounded by shrieking bolts of climax from a hundred different speakers. Clever bastards. They had chosen the biggest public distraction in five counties for their switch. They had chosen the proper moment to unfocus.

Stretch Dixon knew that something was wrong immediately. He had the van started and in gear by the time Warfield exploded onto the front seat.

"That wasn't Serge," said Warfield. "Did anyone leave this place while I was gone?"

"One car pulled out from next to the wagon," said Dixon. "Red late model GM."

*"GM?"*

"Buick, Pontiac, Olds," said Dixon. "They all look alike, you know."

But just to be sure they checked the Toyota. Nothing was inside but a copy of the *Barricada International,* a Nicaraguan weekly. The wagon did not even have trunk space to hide in.

"They could have made the change while we were at the ticket booth," said Dixon. "Hell, they could have done it before they left the house."

In either case there was no hope. They could strike out blind on the highway and expect that the man who had lost two professionals would hold to a main road in clear view of his pursuers. They could return to Sister George and put a gun to her head, but that had been done before to no result by men with less compunction.

Warfield found himself staring at the big screen with anger. Superimposed over a pair of boots on a mess table, the credits were rolling. Four people had written the dialogue. A whole crew for the special effects. Then there was nothing but the boots, and a rather cute FINIS.

"Boots," said Warfield. *"Boots."*

"What about them?"

Warfield did not know, but his mind could not retain any other image or thought. He went back and forth with it several times until he remembered that he had heard about boots in connection with Bettina. Eglon had said that she was wearing a pair of bargain bin specials that day in Annapolis. Of course, he might have been inventing details, or he might have unintentionally provided a lead.

Warfield got headquarters on the mobile line and Ellen Pena out of her nap. He told her to clear her head for duty, and within five seconds she said, "I'm awake."

"Now I want your first response," said Warfield. "Why would a woman wear new hiking boots for an excursion into town?"

"I can't think of a reason," said Ellen, drawing out her thought in spite of directions. "Unless she were trying to break them in. They'll give you real problems if you do any serious hiking when they're brand new. I know that."

So did Warfield. There was nothing quite like the feeling of blisters, broken blisters, and finally blood in your boots. That was something to be avoided even if the risk was to be noticeably unfashionable.

"I want you to get into the Bureau's files on every member of the Interfaith Coalition," he said. "No, make that every member of every pro-Nicaraguan group on the watch list. Find me someone who lives in the mountains—or owns land there."

"'Lives' is probably feasible," she said. "'Owns land' is too rich for any computer."

"Give me what you can get."

"Copied," she said. "Stand by, Mariner."

The waiting took the best part of half an hour. Warfield had Dixon head for Route 50. He reached it and put the van on a steady eighty-five miles per hour without once saying what he really thought: that Warfield was flailing, desperate, crazy. He did not say it because that was too obvious. They were inside the beltway, the van's supercharged engine roaring with the speed and heavy load, when Ellen's answer came back.

"There's one piece of luck," she said. "We have only two possibilities."

"Rank them."

"The first is not too promising," she said as if it might be even less. "It's an address outside Cumberland, Maryland. But geological survey has the area as marginally rural, almost a suburb."

"We'll hang fire on that onc."

"The second is in the Blue Ridge Mountains," she said. "RFD 4 Flint Hill. That's south of Front Royal, on the eastern side of the range. I may be able to pinpoint the location by satellite."

"Is that the complete address?"

"I have a no number," she said. "On something called Camelback Road."

The bison and camels are back, said the wise-ass priest. Warfield did not need the expertise of NSA's code breakers to tell him that Camelback Road was almost certainly the place he was looking for. Stumble around for a while and he might come up with a bison too.

"Do we have life forms at this address, Banner?"

"Her name is Peggy Toth," said Ellen. "She's with the Maryland Interfaith Coalition."

Warfield was beginning to feel lucky again. "We're headed for Flint Hill. Thank you, Banner."

But Ellen Pena did not sign off. She kept an open mike for several seconds before speaking again. "I have one more item, Mariner."

"Go ahead."

"It may be nothing."

It usually wasn't when they said it like that, but Warfield told her that he was listening.

"I was off watch when the information came in on this man Cruz," she said. "When you found out his name was really Molenaur. I suppose that's why I didn't see the connection right away. Actually, I didn't see it until I woke up from your call."

"What connection?"

Ellen still seemed reluctant to put her mouth where her intuition was, but she finally broke silence with a bang. "The name Molenaur is Dutch. One of my languages. Molenaur in English is Miller. And Miller in German is—"

"Müller."

# Canned Goods

WARFIELD tried not to force conclusions from what might be simple coincidence. Müller and its equivalents were one of the most common surnames on earth. German immigration to Latin America had been significant long before World War II. A man of Heinrich Müller's cunning would not have chosen an identity that correlated so well with his past. Warfield could think of no reason but naked pride that would cause Müller to use such light camouflagc for himself—or his family.

Because the name Molenaur was not linked to Müller except through two much younger men named Erich and Esteben. Both, according to Sister George, had been drug traffickers, and Erich, according to the same gospel source, was the leader of a group of Contra insurgents. Esteben had been the man who set up Gasqué's mission. Possibly, he was also the man who had been strolling on the beach with Müller.

What was tantalizing was that so much effort had been expended in trying to eradicate all traces of the Müller-

Molenaurs. The four-man team had killed Ned Eglon in an attempt to retrieve one photograph. Break-ins had occurred all around the country in an attempt to suppress documents that identified Erich Molenaur as something more than a Contra leader. And brother Esteben had simply disappeared from the memory of some of the most secure and comprehensive computer systems in the world.

The stench of conspiracy was enough to wake the dead, and in the middle of it stood Bettina. Her call had begun the investigation, her evidence had fed it, and only her presence, it seemed, could end it. What Warfield could not believe was that his sole hope of finding her rested on the cry of a sea gull and the devices of a pack of radical out-of-date clergy. But since she would not come out herself, perhaps because of the child, no other way of locating Bettina was left.

While Dixon drove through the dark Virginia countryside, Warfield called up Heinrich Müller's file on the computer. He had requested that the information be augmented from every available source, and the amount of additional data was significant. If he had been asked about what he was looking for, Warfield would have said it was the explanation of why Müller would risk exposing himself, his name, or both in Central America in his eighty-fifth year.

The problem of every renegade Nazi was this: he could run, he could hide, but he could never be a man of visible influence in the world again. Even if he had amassed a fortune great enough to buy an entire country in Latin America, he could not exercise his power without fear of reprisal. Such a man as Klaus Barbie, the Gestapo "Butcher of Lyon," had been secure in Bolivia until he surfaced publicly, offering his memoirs to the highest bidder.

There was an exception to the rule of course, and that was the Nazi who preserved his health and influence through the intelligence services. Barbie had done it, working as a V man for West German intelligence under ex-SS General Reinhard Gehlen. Many others had too. The Gehlen Org had been a haven for any Gestapo or SS man who could prove that he hated communists more than he had loved Hitler. Likewise, the Russians and East Germans plumbed the same human cesspool in their search for experienced personnel. It was doubtful that they would have rejected the services of Heinrich Müller if he had been assisting their efforts before Germany's collapse.

But if Müller had not been a Russian agent before the end of the war, it was questionable that he had become one afterward. His persecution of communists during the thirties had been thorough, brutal, and monumental. His detection of Russian spies during the war had been spectacular. Müller had undone not only the famous *Rote Kapelle,* or Red Orchestra, but his Gestapo had eliminated almost every other communist network. The Russians that Warfield knew were not that forgiving. Unless Müller had come over carrying his files and bonafides, he would have been destroyed—suddenly or slowly, but in any case, painfully.

It was not easy to accept Amelia Worth's conclusion that Müller had been a Soviet mole. There was no proof of it. Müller had received training in Russia, but with Nazi party approval. He had organized and trained the Gestapo like the Russian Security Police because there was no finer model for repression. His accusers, such as Admiral Canaris and SS General Schellenberg, were also his rivals in the business of Nazi intelligence. And although Müller made his bones through his prewar knowledge of the communist party apparatus in Germany, there was another explanation of why he had been elevated within the Nazi establishment.

The report originated with a story in a Socialist newspaper in Munich, had been fleshed out by various conspiracy theorists, and had to do, again, with love. Because the love was that of the most wretched man on earth, the story was wretched. Adolph Hitler loved Geli Raubel. That she was his niece did not matter. In late 1931, during the Octoberfest in Munich, a time when almost any sin is permissible, Geli shot herself with Hitler's pistol in Hitler's apartment on Prinzegentplaz. She had also beaten herself and broken her nose before committing suicide.

The Munich police did not think this altogether strange, because Hitler was at the time already an important political figure in Germany. The Nazi party had won twenty percent of the vote in the 1930 election, and the Nazi storm troopers, some 250,000 strong, were winning the battle in the streets against the communists. The investigating detective from the Munich police, a man named Heinrich Müller, realized these things immediately. He caused any incriminating evidence to disappear. Then he sat back and waited for the rewards he hoped would come.

That was the alternative theory of Müller's rise to prominence. Warfield liked it better because it solved some inconsistencies. Müller had not been well liked by certain members of the Nazi hierarchy, yet he had risen to become virtual head of the Gestapo by 1935. By the time he was finally admitted to the Nazi party in 1939, he was already the official head of Amt IV and a general in the SS. It seemed that he had skipped several necessary steps in his climb to power. In Warfield's experience, mere competence was not enough to accomplish that feat.

But Müller was always good at his job. He was the man who ran the operation that ignited World War II. To begin the shooting war, it was necessary that a pretext be established. The Nazis planned to stage a border incident with Poland, a false incursion into German territory. The Poles would be charged with violating the sanctity of the motherland, and they would be attacked in overwhelming force.

To prove the authenticity of the incident at Gleiwitz, Müller ordered up freshly killed corpses from the concentration camps, which he then salted all over the area. These men were called "Canned Goods." The operation, a famous one in the history of secret warfare, came to be known by the same name.

Warfield had no doubt that Müller was an extremely clever man, the most resourceful of all Hitler's intelligence officers. His grave in West Berlin had been properly registered. For eighteen years someone had placed flowers on the site every Sunday. The existence of the grave, and the attention to it, had certainly inhibited any search for Müller. When the body was finally disinterred in 1963, the investigators found a skeleton composed of the bones of three different men. None of them belonged to Heinrich Müller.

That basic piece of misdirection had served him well. The several reports that had been filed on Müller in the intervening years were apparently disregarded. Probably not even FBI had believed in Kronos. But there was one quite detailed report that claimed to have traced Müller's escape route. Warfield read it with interest.

The CIG report asserted that Müller had left Berlin in May, 1945, after secreting himself in a private bunker until the shooting stopped. With very good paper, he passed north and westward into the Allied-occupied zone, slipping through several checkpoints, until he arrived at his destination—the Danish Royal Castle at Gråsten. The castle had been an SS hospital, crowded to be sure. Müller, after plastic surgery, looked so much the inmate that he stayed at Gråsten several weeks.

When he finally left Denmark, Müller traveled with his new face and an even better set of papers to Munich. A few days later he arrived in Austria. From there Müller went by way of a series of safe houses through the Brenner Pass into northern Italy. His escape route was one of the first webs spun by Die Spinne, the Spider, the organization that throughout the postwar years would secure freedom for many high-ranking Nazis on the run.

Shortly afterward, Müller arrived in Rome for the second and most important stop on the underground route—the Vatican. There a group of pro-Nazi clerics, led by the infamous Bishop Alois Hudal, provided quarters for Müller until near the end of 1945 and gave him credible documentation as well. He lived comfortably at several different locations, including a sojourn at the Teutonicum, a monastery within the walls of Vatican City.

In his six-month stay, Müller left the protection of the Vatican only once, and for a very pressing reason. He journeyed to Switzerland, where he visited with a woman named Countess Gisela von Westrop, the mistress of Ernst Kaltenbrunner, the former head of Reich Security, and Müller's direct superior. Countess von Westrop had delivered, both during and after the war, massive amounts of money to Swiss banks, along with equally large quantities of gold and jewelry, most of which came from the bodies of concentration camp victims. With Kaltenbrunner in Allied hands, von Westrop signed over to Müller a portion of the funds on hand.

Müller remained in Switzerland only long enough to establish friendly relations with his bankers. With his letter of credit in hand, he returned to Rome briefly, then shipped out to the island of Corsica, where he stayed at a nearly inaccessible villa close by Mount Cinto. He waited there approximately three months before taking a berth on a vessel bound for Argentina.

At that point the report ended, but Warfield would have stopped reading anyway because the bells were ringing so loud that he could hardly keep his concentration. Corsica to

Argentina. If that route had gone by way of Marseilles, it would have *been* the French connection. During the war the Marseilles underworld had worked as ferrets for the Gestapo. When they were looking for a friendly place to relocate after the war, the man who could show them where and how was the man they would protect. Laden with venture capital, he was the man they would honor and obey.

And the timing was nearly perfect for the sighting of Kronos-Müller in Buenos Aires. Mid-1946, or slightly earlier. When correlations like that appeared, there were only two possible explanations. Either someone had concocted one with knowledge of the other—or the report was accurate.

The someone who had submitted the report was code-named Mother Hubbard. The information had been received at HQ CIG, the organization that had been the successor to OSS and the predecessor of CIA. It was logged by a CIG administrator who gave only his personal sign: BR.

Warfield went to work at once hunting down the name of the source and the sign of the person who had receipted the report. It took some time, backtracking through the computer, shunting between headquarters and six different machines plus some older microfilmed records that had never been transcribed; but when Warfield arrived at the two conversions, he knew how Bettina had managed to resurrect the cold spoor of Heinrich Müller.

Mother Hubbard was the code name for the Countess Gisela von Westrop, the mistress of Ernst Kaltenbrunner. Although she had been a committed fascist and a member of the Nazi escape committee, Kaltenbrunner's arrest in 1945 had shaken her confidence. His death by hanging in October, 1946, had distorted her contemplation of the thousand-year Reich. She had come over to CIG shortly afterward, bearing information that was thought to be valuable. Her usefulness ended when she was shown to be an unreliable source, a disinformation wholesaler at best, an inspired liar at worst, by none other than General Gehlen, the SS man who had sold American intelligence on his own network of spies. He was by that time the mainstay of West German intelligence and the newly formed CIA's best black knight. And he was believed.

But when it came to sorting the truth among butchers and their whores, Warfield was content to flip a coin. Gisela von Westrop and Reinhard Gehlen were two of a very sorry kind. At least her version of Müller's escape had the virtue of confluence with one other report which she could not have known about. Gehlen had no version at all. It was too bad for the conscience of Western civilization that Mother Hubbard had not been believed by CIG. Of course there was no telling what the man who accepted the report had believed, but Warfield thought he knew now.

BR was the personal sign of Helmut Becker. He was Bettina's father.

At 4:10 Warfield received a call from Ellen Pena. She had managed to obtain and intensify satellite transmissions of the Flint Hill RFD 4 area. With the information already entered into the computer, Warfield retrieved the photo map within seconds through the AUDRE system.

The area was heavily wooded and mountainous. Two secondary roads wound around the south face of the mountain, and tailing off from one was a tertiary road that followed a meandering creekbed for about two miles until it ended at the base of a steep ridge. When Warfield overlay the photo map on the most detailed rendition in scale that he could call up from the knowledge base, he found the road called Camelback. Leading off the road 1.4 miles from its beginning was a trail called Camelback.

He knew now without a doubt that Camelback Road was his target. Although Camelback Trail disappeared on the photo map twenty yards into the forest, he could see that it or an offshoot trail led to the top of the ridge. Up there was a clearing, a cabin, and at least one outbuilding. Warfield could see that no phone or utility lines crossed the face of the hill, but there could certainly be radio communications in the cabin.

It took them another hour to put themselves in the position to find out. The roads around Flint Hill were about as bad as they looked on the maps, and drifts of low-lying ground fog made them worse. Dawn was breaking when they found the gravel road called Camelback that ran alongside the creekbed. First light broke and then retreated in the shady lee of the mountain. By the time they reached the end of the road, darkness had come again. The late-model GM car was barely visible parked beside the footbridge that crossed the creek.

"I'll be damned," said Dixon. "And I still don't know what kind of car it is. You'd think those people would do something about that."

"Oldsmobile."

"If you say so."

As a matter of fact, Warfield could not really tell, but the engine was still warm, and in the soft earth near the lip of the creek he found a large footprint that had been made by a man wearing jogging shoes. Two hundred and fifty pounds, maybe more. Serge-sized prints.

In good light Warfield could have tracked him on cement. The ex-priest walked like a hillbilly on skis, splay-footed, heel-driving. He must have had a flashlight or he would have fallen on his face every five feet. The trail was rocky, snagged with roots, and when it reached the top of the first rise, as narrow as a man.

Or a woman. Warfield found two other sets of footprints on the trail in the spreading light that had begun to filter down the hill. They could have been made by two women or two small men. They preceded Serge's big tracks but by how much Warfield could not say. What gave him pause was that the earlier prints were made by tennis shoes.

No boots. Bettina had boots. Peggy Toth, if she lived here, would also use proper footwear. Dixon thought that the crescent-studded heel was definitely a man's because of the width. Two men, probably.

They worked up the hill more quickly. Serge's footprints were very fresh. One track made in the wet runoff from the cleft in the hillside still pooled slowly with water. The big man was no more than ten minutes ahead, probably less. Serge might be walking into a reunion—or an ambush.

The sun was up now but the light in the forest was still the light of shadow. They left the ferns and rhododendrons behind and came into the laurel and hemlock where it was higher and drier. The cabin was a mile and a quarter line-of-sight from the creekbed. They were climbing diagonally eastward. When they doubled back to the west no more than two hundred yards from the buildings on the shoulder of the summit, Dixon moved off-trail.

Warfield could not hear him six feet into the forest, and within ten feet could not see him, yet Dixon was moving fast. His specialty in Vietnam had been LURPs, long-range reconnaissance patrols, dogging the enemy for days and sometimes weeks; doing it without getting shot, mangled, or skinned alive; and coming back. He would reach the ridge at the same time as Warfield, and he would be coming in with the sun at his back.

Warfield could see the sunny clearing as a green golden glow seventy-five yards away near the top of the ridge. And then he moved off the trail too, toward the west. The underbrush was thick but low, the ground seamed with slabs of rock. Slinging the new HK 93, Warfield climbed a huge mossy boulder until he reached an ironwood tree that grew directly from its face. He climbed six feet of the ironwood to the massive trunk of an oak that had toppled by its roots into the dry water gap. Hand over hand up the barren but not quite dead branches, he reached the top of the crumbling Appalachian rock.

It was quiet atop the ridge. A smooth convection wind moved steadily across the summit. The sun was a strong clean presence. The trees and bushes were windswept and dwarfed. Warfield had no trouble advancing across the twelve-foot divide to the brow that overlooked the clearing. At the edge was a thick fringe of serviceberry. He approached the overlook on his stomach and parted the bushes. He would have been looking directly down into the clearing if the footprint had not caught his eye.

In fact it was the footprint with the crescent-studded heel. The base of the bushes had hidden it. Warfield looked back across the pebbly rock and sand that covered the bare parts of the ridge but saw nothing. If there were other footprints, they had been erased by the wind. That meant the track was old, a day old, perhaps more. It existed only because it had been sheltered. It had been put down in that spot by someone who had wanted to observe the clearing without being seen.

Warfield knew how bad that was. When he looked past the bushes into the clearing below, he understood that bad was not nearly good enough. The outhouse stood closest, backed up toward the overlook on sunken ground that had been trenched many times. The next building was a small barn that was now just a big shed. In front of both, at a distance of twenty yards, with good southerly exposure, lay the log cabin, a squat one-story chinked with cement and strung with antipest barbed wire. In the side yard were two things of approximately the same size and shape: a covered well, and a man kneeling on the ground as if in prayer.

The man was Serge Fenster.

He was not kneeling to pray. He was kneeling and puking. Warfield could hear the harsh sounds of it like an animal barking against the coming of night.

He moved down from the ridge at once, thinking that he had nothing to fear and everything to dread. The feeling of calm that touched every high wild place became instead the stillness of a cemetery. As soon as he cleared the elderberry brake at the bottom of the ridge, Warfield saw the carcass of the dog. It was a big golden retriever with daylight showing between the torso and the head.

But that was not everything, and Warfield knew it wouldn't be. He walked up the well-worn path from the outhouse to the side yard where Serge Fenster was indulging himself. The big man was on his hands and knees now. Fluids were still coming from his mouth and nose and eyes. He looked up at Warfield through the dense film.

"I wouldn't go in there."

They always said that. Usually, they were right.

In fact Warfield did not want to go into the cabin. He had the stomach but not the curiosity to look death in the face. He did not flinch when he saw the thing just inside the door. It was an eye. He knew that when the flies lifted from it before resettling in a dark greedy swarm.

As he entered the front main room, the flies lifted in a black cloud from the body that had been nailed to the plank table. In spite of all the blood and the barbed wire that had been strapped tight around her breasts and the butchery, the sheer butchery, that had been visited upon every inch of her flesh, Warfield felt a current of pure relief. The body was not Bettina's.

# PART THREE

# THE MEDICINE SHOW

# Blind Faith

WARFIELD was at a loss for what to think. Bettina might have been taken, or she might have gotten away. The fact that the dead woman, whom Serge identified as Peggy Toth, had been tortured seemed to indicate the latter, but that could not be taken for granted. Some people chose to ruin human bodies for their own pleasure, and other people, like Heinrich Müller, were not above spending blood to obscure the trail or simply to create authenticity with canned goods. Warfield wanted to believe that Bettina had escaped, and so he did.

Dixon finished his search of the perimeter and found nothing—no signs of flight, none of entry. Except for the lone footprint that Warfield had seen accidentally at the top of the ridge, the killers were phantoms in tennis shoes. The golden retriever, whose name had been Molson, might have given warning and been killed because of it, or he might have been annoying them at their work.

Though there was a sideband radio in the cabin, Warfield decided to wait until he was off the mountain before notifying headquarters of the disaster. He did not want to take a chance on the transmission being intercepted, and he did not want to be in the area when the local police arrived. He did want to allow Serge the opportunity to meditate on the error of his amateur ways.

When they reached the van, Serge began to talk. Not much persuasion had been required. Warfield had cuffed the ex-priest's hands behind his back and kicked him the full mile and a half down the trail, telling him that he was going to take him to a place more private than Camelback Ridge and fill him with enough drugs to cook the truth or his brains, whichever came first. The closer they got to the bottom of the hill, the more Serge believed the threat.

Even so, Serge began his monologue with some mild lies. He said that he had seen Bettina for the first time about two weeks ago. He and Sister George had been contacted by Ned Eglon, who had asked their help in finding a safe place to stow a fugitive. Eglon had not told them who Bettina was. He had said that she was a friend, and in great danger.

That was enough of course. They had known Eglon for several years, ever since Interfaith was organized. He had worked quietly behind the scenes for the cause even longer than that. It had been Eglon who recommended that the Sandinista government spend a good portion of their disposable income in hiring an American public relations firm to process their image. What other services he had rendered were highly valued in Managua, though unknown to Serge.

Yet there was a distinct line between advising a client, however discretely, and working undercover. The Fensters were surprised by Bettina's behavior, since it very quickly became clear that she knew quite a lot about the business of being on the run. Twice in the first three days she demanded to be moved because the security was not good enough. The third site, Camelback Ridge, seemed to satisfy her requirements. Only Father ("Nicaragua Libre") Manzini and Ned Eglon had known the location.

Manzini had not talked. He would never have broken security last night at Serge's insistence if not for the fact that Bettina had missed her last radio check. Now it seemed clear that Eglon must have given away the safe place. That was probably all the four-man team had been after. It was possible that they did not know that the photograph of Müller even existed.

Serge did not know anything about photographs. He assumed that the two deaths were related to Bettina's mission, whatever that had been. When Warfield suggested that her child might have something to do with the reason Bettina was being chased, Serge acted very surprised. He said he knew nothing about the boy.

But at least he had said it was a boy. Warfield understood all he needed to know about the child except for one important thing. He knew that would be slow in coming. They were at the bottom of the hill with the late morning sun filtering through the upper foliage as if through stained glass. The creek was a murmuring litany in the background; the only disturbance was the random pop of static on the open channel to headquarters.

"There's a chance that if you tell me the truth, Serge, I'll let you get back in that borrowed car and drive away. But I know you're lying about the contact with Bettina. Your wife was involved well before Bettina showed up here." Warfield paused because it was always best to space the interrogator's knowledge of untruth with his best guess. "And I know you're lying about the boy."

Serge looked at his short trousers and the knees and shins that were bruised and bleeding. "You're good at this," he said. "But, you know, I spent a week once with my ankles tied around my ears."

"And you didn't learn a thing."

"I learned that talking doesn't help anyone," he said. "Least of all the person who does the talking."

"It depends on who's doing the asking," said Warfield. "I'm going to tell you this one more time: my interest is in protecting Bettina. I can do that a whole lot better than people whose idea of security is to buy a big cuddly dog. It's shameful, what you people did here. No wonder Bettina kept moving. Did she even have a weapon?"

"There was a rifle in the cabin," said Serge. "At least I was told she had one. I didn't see it inside."

Warfield felt a spur of hope because there had been no rifle in the cabin. Although the two butchers might have taken it, Bettina had had the same chance. If she were armed with a long-range weapon in dense cover, they would not have found it easy to run her down. Perhaps the two men had tortured Peggy Toth in the hope of drawing Bettina back to the cabin.

"Was the boy with her?"

"Yes," said Serge.

That was good to know. Not only was Warfield chasing one less trail, but he could also understand why Bettina might have abandoned Peggy Toth. Bettina would protect the child first and last. She would have moved him completely out of danger, running, not looking back. She would not hear the screams of the woman who had sheltered her because she would be long gone. Her behavior might be considered callous, but it was what almost every professional would do. Warfield was counting on the likelihood that Serge did not know that. It was best he think that Bettina had been snatched.

"Who is the boy?"

"It's her child," said Serge as if any other alternative were offensive. "He's a good-looking boy. Healthy and very bright. His name is Esteben."

"After his father?"

"I wouldn't know," said Serge. "The English equivalent is Stephen. That's your name, isn't it?"

"That child is no relation of mine," said Warfield. "And Bettina's not running from me. I want to know his full name."

Serge looked around the slick stony soil at his feet as if he were searching for a place to lay his bones permanently. He scuffed the ground with one of his jogging shoes, which had been sliced nearly in half during his rapid descent. When he spoke, his voice glided away. "If they've got her . . ."

"She's as good as dead," said Warfield. "Like that one up on the hill. Maybe worse. And the boy is on his way back home. I want to know where that is."

"She should have stayed in Nicaragua," said Serge, as if he were interrupting a thought that had been long delayed. "It's the one place where she was safe. Cruz couldn't touch her there."

"You're talking about Esteben Cruz."

"Yes."

"Esteben Molenaur Cruz."

"That sounds plausible."

"Is he the father of the child?"

"Presumably."

Warfield took a step to the van. He opened the passenger's door and took from the map pouch a copy of the photograph that showed two men on a beach. Holding it before Serge's face, he asked for an identification.

"That's Esteben Cruz," he said. "The other I don't know."

Half an ID in this case was very good. It was more than the combined data banks of the United States government had chosen to provide. Warfield was almost sorry that he had handled such a valuable source so roughly. Serge had not recognized Müller, and he had not reacted to the name Molenaur, but that did not mean his knowledge of the subject was exhausted.

"I need everything you know about Cruz," said Warfield. "I have to get to him."

Serge gestured with one big shoulder. "Can I sit down?"

When Warfield nodded okay the ex-priest moved his bulk onto the deep step in the well of the van, causing the entire vehicle to list like a foundering ship. He began to talk without further preamble.

"Cruz would tell you he's Nicaraguan, but he's been living in Colombia since the day after the Triumph. He lived there before the revolution, as a matter of fact."

"Do you have any idea what he might have been doing back in San Juan del Sur?"

Serge shook his forty-pound head slowly. "It's a very wealthy family," he said. "They owned land all over Nicaragua. They had a huge coffee plantation outside Matagalpa, several farms near Leon, and a lot of property on the Pacific Coast. I heard that most of it was confiscated. The government was using new agrarian laws that restrict absentee ownership. Possibly he might have come back to contest the judgment."

"They'd let him do that?"

"Of course," said Serge. "The government is very careful of legalities. They would *not* let Cruz return to harass his wife. But they would allow him every opportunity to protect his rights."

"Even though his brother was killing Nicaraguans in the north?"

"I think you've mixed up cause and effect," said Serge. "The Central American aristocracy is sentimental about their ties to the land. Just because they have twenty million in the bank in Miami does not mean they want to lose a two hundred thousand dollar farm. Erich Cruz joined the counterrevolutionaries *because* the family's land was taken."

"What you're saying is that he joined the Contras not long ago."

"You should ask the CIA about this," said Serge. "They run that bloody show."

"I'm asking you."

"What can I tell you?" he said, shrugging like an armless bear, causing the entire van to waggle. "It's the same old story. You show your anticommunist card at the door, and they give you free run of the slaughterhouse. The Cruz family *is* very rich. Since the reduction in military aid by Congress, the counterrevolutionaries will take anything they can get. A hundred dollars will buy you a sack full of ears. A thousand makes you an officer. And if your brother is an arms dealer, presto, you're a guerrilla leader."

"Is that what Esteben Cruz does—deals arms?"

"That's what he's always done," said Serge. "Drugs. Arms. All the things that kill. I don't know details, so please don't ask."

Warfield wanted to ask someone because somewhere a file on Esteben Cruz existed that would gag any fastidious computer. Drugs and arms. Counterrevolution. Bettina had picked a stone winner to honor and obey. But she had probably not done much of either, if she ever intended it. Warfield did not think she had.

"When did Bettina leave Cruz?"

Serge allowed himself a moment for calculation. "It must have been eight months ago," he said. "About the time the Cruz family declared war on the government. If you're looking for a reason why she left him, that might be it."

"What was she doing in Nicaragua?"

"She came to my wife," said Serge. "Sister George is quite well known in Central America. Many people approach her for help. Al got Bettina a job in the ministry, working with the literacy program."

"The program wouldn't be right next door to State Security, would it?"

"Actually, it's in the next block," said Serge with all the sarcasm his situation would permit. "And actually, the government believes that their best security is an educated population. They reason—rightly—that only an ignorant citizen would welcome back tyranny."

Warfield was going to stop asking questions soon because he could not tolerate many more righteous speeches. But there was one more thing he had to know.

"Why did she leave Nicaragua?"

Serge seemed to smile faintly, although he might have been doing nothing more than grimacing in his handcuffs. He looked up the hill toward the path that led to the clearing at the base of the ridge—and to death.

"It was Ned," said Serge. "He heard that Bettina was in Nicaragua, and about a month ago he flew down to see her."

Warfield was not surprised to hear that, finally. He had misjudged Eglon's involvement all along, especially his degree of commitment; and he had not wanted to think about the relationship between Eglon and his ex-wife. After they were divorced, and even while she was living with Warfield, Bettina had kept a sometime connection with Ned, meeting him three or four times a year, discussing God knows what for periods of time that were not lengthy but that gave Warfield grounds for a jealousy he was not sure it was proper to claim. He had fought and subdued the feeling but for one lonesome time when she came back later than was perhaps proper, a little high, a little loose. Warfield had then given into the feeling in the only way he knew how, and when he had coaxed her onto her back, and they had done it (and she had seemed to know why they were doing it), he still did not know what she had done with Ned. Then. Later. Of course there had been a "later," and Warfield should have known.

"So Eglon persuaded her to return."

Serge said, "Yes."

"Were they planning to get back together again?"

"I know nothing about their personal priorities," said Serge, like a gentleman confessor. "They certainly had other concerns. Ned talked her into using whatever she had against Cruz. And she agreed to come back."

"Just in time to influence the congressional vote on Contra aid."

"Does it matter now?" he asked. "She and whatever she had are . . . gone."

"Missing."

"I hope you're right."

Warfield might have lectured the ex-priest on the virtues of blind faith in the devices of a professional if he had not heard the beat of the helicopter as it began to move up the narrow valley, homing on the signal from the van. That would be the sanitary unit from Meade and his ride out of this place.

# Tempest

WARFIELD was trying to decide whether to let Serge go or turn him over to the experts in the Behavioral Lab when the decision became clear. En route to headquarters, word was received that Mike Koricke's team had accomplished their mission. They had retrieved the file of Esteben Molenaur from the tapes stored at Bolling Air Force Base.

Warfield diverted the helicopter to Bolling, knowing that if the information contained in the tapes jibed with the things Serge had said, the big man would be seeing his kids soon. That was a risk Warfield was willing to take. Bettina might never contact the Catholic underground again, but if she did, he wanted her to know that he was looking, waiting. The rest would be up to her. As long as Serge could recognize his kids, the gamble might pay off.

As it happened, Serge was let go twenty-five minutes after they touched down. Waiting at Bolling was an oversized black van that housed Mike's team and a battery of communications gear. In good time Warfield saw to it that Serge was driven by one of the men directly to his dump-yard door, because the information that came up on the computer screen in the van tallied very well with the ex-priest's words. The file on Esteben Molenaur tallied precisely, except that there was much more. Whoever compiled it had done a thorough job of incorporating every possible source and no doubt a great deal of heavy link analysis.

Esteben Molenaur had been born in Cali, Colombia, thirty-seven years ago. That event had taken place in 1949, convenient to the end of the war and Heinrich Müller's reported arrival in South America. The father's name was Erich Molenaur. Mother: Maria Cruz. The family had been wealthy from its inception, and through the years it grew more money. Its interests were varied: a radio station, a bus line, a distillery, and extensive real estate holdings in Cali and in the Valle de Cauca to the northward.

Although the family enjoyed the kind of exclusive anonymity that is easier to obtain in Latin America than anywhere else, it was known that Erich Molenaur was a foreigner. His marriage into the large Cruz family had cemented his social connections, such as they were exercised. For the most part the Molenaurs lived a life of quiet seclusion on their estate outside the city of Cali.

Esteben Molenaur had been educated at schools in Switzerland and Spain. After completing his schooling abroad, Esteben worked for the Banco National de Paris as an investment analyst and in Spain for the weapons firm of Star Bonifacio Echeverria. In 1972 he returned home to Colombia, where he began a new career with the Colombian F-2, a special police unit concerned with internal security and narcotics. Banking, arms, intelligence: his apprenticeship was complete.

From the year 1975 onward, Esteben Molenaur had apparently devoted his life to the family businesses. He lived in Medellín, Colombia, and Nicaragua, where his younger brother Erich had moved several years previously. There was nothing to indicate that the Molenaurs were anything more than they seemed: a rich Latin American family with interests and residences in a number of different countries. In Somoza's Nicaragua they particularly flourished in spite of an incident in July, 1978, when a cocaine conversion lab was discovered on their property on the Islas de Maiz. The Molenaurs knew nothing of the factory, of course; indeed, the estate had been rented to a third party who could never be identified.

But the incident was embarrassing, even to men who owned so many parcels of land. They promised that it would never recur.

And it did not. The name of Molenaur was never again associated with the drug trade, though the family was supposed by at least one international agency to be a processor and shipper of cocaine from Colombia to larger markets in the United States and elsewhere. The import-export firm of Calico, S.A., incorporated in Switzerland, was thought to provide cover for narcotics shipments through its equally lethal but legitimate trade in all types of firearms.

Warfield had long ago stopped wondering why people with twenty million dollars took so many chances in the pursuit of twenty million more: it was a fact of life. In Latin America, the risk were lessened by the Godlike powers of the rich. The only inconvenience was a change in government, and the only catastrophe a shift to the confiscatory left. The wisest heads were people who scattered their assets throughout several countries. When the Triumph came to Nicaragua, upsetting many calculations, the Molenaurs moved their fungible assets out of the country. But rather than unload their real estate in Nicaragua at fire-sale prices, they chose to hang on.

The land reform program of the FSLN was apparently based on such miscalculations. Not only did the Sandinistas take property from the Molenaurs, but like most revolutionaries, the new government had a puritanical urge to suppress public nuisances such as a competing traffic in arms. Over a period of several years, the Molenaur family found themselves stripped of their lands and businesses in Nicaragua.

At that point, if not before, Esteben Molenaur became a Contra. He donated money to the cause. He donated his brother Erich, who had once attended military school. The Cruz Uno, as it was known, had garnered as much success as any Contra band. It was one of the few guerrilla operations that ventured into Nicaragua by miles rather than meters. Its specialty was the kidnappings and assassinations of political figures. And, yes, one of their major contributions to the war effort had been the assault on Totogalpa.

Esteben Molenaur had also expanded his dealings in the arms trade at about the same time. In addition to his office in Baranquilla, Colombia, he had established new locations in Veracruz, Mexico, and on Swan Island.

That last address was what Warfield had been looking for: it was a dead giveaway. Swan Island, which was claimed by both Honduras and the United States, was a large lump of guano between the Cayman Islands and the Central American mainland. For years it had been inhabited by none but CIA. There was no question that Calico, S.A., was being used as an arms conduit for Contra operations.

Warfield was not surprised by the association; it was natural, nearly inevitable. Molenaur's experience, his sympathies, and his knowledge of the area, especially the best smuggling routes, made him *de facto* a valuable acquisition. Even if his background were more sinister than it appeared, the priorities of the situation demanded a blind eye. Warfield knew that if he were in the same position, he would not have hesitated to recruit Esteben Molenaur.

The association also raised some interesting questions about Bettina. Could CIA have known about her relationship with Molenaur?

Yes.

Could they have been so slipshod as not to check?

Yes.

Would they have known and looked the other way if Molenaur were important to them?

Yes.

Would they have known and told him, causing a strain, and perhaps a breach, in the relationship?

Yes.

It was even possible that Bettina had been running not from Molenaur but from CIA when she fled to and from Nicaragua. Warfield thought that he knew why she had targeted Molenaur for love in the first place, but unless he accepted Serge's pat idealogical explanation, Warfield had no idea why she had left. Now that he could see Langley's big fin in the water, motivation was possible and multiple. There were a hundred different games that could be running.

The odds were also excellent that CIA had disappeared the Molenaur file from the interagency computer. That was Mike Koricke's opinion too, though he had not been able to determine exactly who had done the deed.

"I have the 'Date Last Changed,'" he said. "And the 'Changed By.' But I don't recognize the initials. We're running checks."

"It could be important to know, Mike."

"I'm doing my best," he said with a flare of irritation that reddened the left side of his face. Warfield had never seen that particular physiological response before in his life. It was as if only half the man, or half his emotional system, had the capability to react. The length of time that he had gone without sleep might have had something to do with it. Mike seemed to have lost ten pounds, but from where? He looked like a freeze-dried cadaver.

"I know you are, Mike. Turn this over to someone else. Go home and get some rest."

"Like hell," he said. "Sir."

Warfield could have said that he did not know what caused people to behave like that; but he knew. "All right," he said. "Let me know when you run him down."

"There's something else too," he said in a flat tone that might have come from exhaustion or something else. "I think it's significant."

Warfield was a little suspicious of bonuses that came in bunches. "So what is it?"

"There's another file on this man," he said. "I found the reference and the file number, but I can't get to it without your permission."

"Why not?"

"The information is stored in the new Beta computer," he said. "It's a special operational linkup between CIA and the National Security Council. Access is very strictly limited."

Warfield noted the reference to Beta at the same time as he saw the problem. Either Langley would have to be taken off, or the White House itself. He had not expected things to get this dicey this quickly. Who in hell was Molenaur to rate such a secrecy blanket?

"What's the possibility of reaching this subfile? Can you do it without being detected?"

"Of course," said Mike, as if he had been insulted again. "But it would be virtually impossible to do it within the machine. You'd have to go outside."

Warfield did not have to admit to being confused because he was sure that was obvious in his face. He had no clue as to how a theft would go outside to get inside.

"Do you want to explain what you just said?"

"It's really very simple."

Warfield said, "Go slow," because when they told you how simple it was, what they meant was how simple it was to them.

"You start with the fact that all electronic devices transmit a weak field of electromagnetic radiation," said Mike slowly, as if he were speaking to a dog. "Computer screens do. Even microchips do. Whenever a device emits a signal, that signal can be picked up. It's especially easy to lift from a computer screen, because each signal is unique. Once the information you want is brought up on an unsecured video screen, it's fair game. You don't need passwords or anything else. The user does all the work for you."

"How do you get the information you want onto the screen?"

"You ask," said Mike patiently. "You call up someone with access and have *them* review the information. Impersonate their boss—or someone in the office. They'd never suspect a thing because the information never leaves their screen. It's a totally undetectable theft."

"How would you intercept the signal?"

"With a Dillinger." Mike smiled shyly, showing teeth too big and heavy for the rest of his face. "An intercept device. You give me three hundred dollars and a ride to the nearest Radio Shack, I'll build you one in an hour or two. What you need basically is a television monitor and an antenna. The antenna picks up the signal, the TV translates it visually. We have a version at Meade that can intercept at distances up to a mile."

Warfield was having trouble with the idea because nothing could be that simple. "What you're telling me is that there's no such thing as a secure computer."

"That's obvious," he said. "Of course you can take preventative measures with your machines. You can insulate your computer rooms, like we do. You can insulate the buildings, like we do. Or you can stop the leakage from the individual machines. That's a very expensive way to solve the problem, so that's what the government does most of the time. You buy your machines already fitted with Tempest equipment. Tempest means Transient Electromagnetic Pulse Emanation

Standard. Tempest is a booming industry around D.C., because it doubles or triples the cost of something like an IBM PC."

"Does CIA have Tempest protection for the Beta?"

"For the machine, sure. But you've got to protect *every* screen, no matter where it is."

Warfield was thinking now of Howard Thunander and the history of keys—warded, radial, pin-tumbler—measure and countermeasure in the unending search for perfect security. That there was no such thing, but only attempts at it, seemed apt and in this case fortunate. That Mike had a notion of where an unsecured machine might be found seemed a forgone conclusion.

"You have a possibility in mind, don't you?"

"It's more than a possibility," said Mike firmly. "It's a cinch. My sister dates an NSC staffer. He's a new guy, very gung ho. Doesn't know one damned thing about computers, but he uses them in his work just the same. He probably thinks—if he thinks about it at all—that his office is well protected."

"But it's not."

Mike shook his head. "Do you want me to go ahead with this penetration?"

Warfield was glad that Mike had not asked for written authorization from higher up. "You go ahead with everything," he said. "Until I tell you to stop."

"One thing," said Mike. "Do you have to know this man's name?"

Warfield shook his head. He would never be sending the poor bastard a Christmas card. And he was beginning to think that for once in his life he already knew too much.

# The Sleeper

AFTER speaking with Mike Koricke, the last thing Warfield wanted to do was put in an appearance at headquarters. He sent the chopper back to Meade and caught a ride in Mike's van to NSA's downtown office, where he made a verbal report to the watch. His summary included as much detail as possible about the charnel house atop Camelback Ridge, and as little as possible about future directions, especially in regard to Mike's team.

The watch had two items to relay. The first was a call from Stretch Dixon in the surveillance van saying that he was within an hour of the city. The second was the result of Ralph Greenspan's attempt to trace the Colombian minister of defense named Esteben Cruz. The attempt had not been completely successful. Cruz was a member of a prominent and politically influential family. He had served two years as minister and another four years as the Colombian ambassador to France. He had a sister named Maria, but no record of her marriage could be obtained: Cruz was a very common name in Colombia and throughout Latin America.

But the reference was strong enough to increase Warfield's suspicions to a certainty. Molenaur's second son had been named Erich, after himself. The first son could have been named after Maria's brother Esteben. The practice was not uncommon. The name Cruz, so common, made for a familiar and ready cover to someone in need.

Warfield was thinking about those genealogical connections when the call that he had been hoping for came into the office. John Slaughter's high tenor voice, which was essentially at odds with his personality and body, spoke sweet words.

"Tulio Villazon," he said. "I have him."

"Where?"

"He entered the Colombian embassy three and a half minutes ago."

That was interesting, and less a coincidence than it seemed. "I didn't know you staked out embassies, John."

"I do this one," he said. "Twenty-four hours a day."

"I'll be there in ten minutes."

After leaving instructions with the watch to forward any calls from Stretch Dixon, Warfield commandeered a new Plymouth sedan from the pool in the Labor Department lot and headed up Massachusetts two minutes in front of his deadline.

The Colombian embassy was off Dupont Circle, one of the more elegant Victorian buildings in town. It was composed of the fanciful red brick so characteristic in many parts of the city, but trimmed in white stone at the borders, balconies, and front. A massive porte-cochere overhung the entrance with a nest of heavy ironwork. Everyone, including the guards, must have knocked off for *siesta,* because there was no action in the area except for normal pedestrian traffic and John Slaughter.

He sat in the back seat of a GM car. One of his plebes, a

man who introduced himself as Jim Turkle, occupied the driver's seat. He said that he was sure of the identification and that Villazon had been inside for fifteen minutes. No vehicles and only one person, a young woman, had left the premises.

"Now do you want to tell me what we're doing here?" said Slaughter. "I'm a deputy RD missing two staff meetings for a man I don't even have a warrant on."

"You didn't have to come, John."

"I didn't have to do a lot of things, Stephen."

"All right," said Warfield. "Tulio Villazon is one-fourth of a hatchet squad—and I do mean hatchet. They've killed two people so far."

"Then you're even."

"No," said Warfield. "We'll be even when I take him down and find out who he's working for."

"He works for Hector Aleria. I told you that last night."

"Maybe he's contracted out for a special job."

"You don't do that with Aleria," said Slaughter flatly. "He buys your services complete. In Colombia, that means he buys your soul—even if you don't have much of one left."

Warfield saw the contradiction, which was to say that he did not yet see the connection. He was sure there was one, if for no other reason than the predominance of Latin American drug traffickers on his list.

"Tell me something about Aleria's background," said Warfield. "Where does he come from?"

"Southwestern Colombia," said Slaughter, as if there were no such place. "The Valle de Cauca. That's known to some people as the Valle de Coca."

It was also a place where the Molenaur family had much land. Warfield could *feel* the connection arriving. "I thought most of the leaf came from farther south. Bolivia. Peru."

"It does," said Slaughter. "But there's good production in

Colombia. Aleria doesn't grow much on his own. He buys, he processes, he ships. He sells marijuana. He expedites heroin too."

"Does that still come through Argentina?"

"Daily," he said. "Young Hector's got the best French connection in the hemisphere."

"How does that work?"

"It works through blood," said Slaughter cryptically. "Aleria's mother is Colombian, but his father isn't even South American. The name Aleria might sound Spanish, but that's just because Spanish sounds like Italian, and Italian sounds a whole lot like Corsican. Old Antipas Aleria was one of those fellows who left Marseilles in a hurry after the war. One of those fearless pioneers in smack."

Slaughter paused in his narrative, but only to tease. He knew he was tracing the lines that Warfield wanted big and bold. The DEA man would make him ask for every piece of the puzzle, especially the last, tightest ones.

"How did a Corsican hood set himself up in Colombia?"

Slaughter smiled and said, "Love. Antipas was supposed to be one hell of a good-looking guy. That's usually enough for young women. He married into a prominent Colombian family and showed them how to be rich as well as prominent. His son grew up obscenely rich and influential. Hector went to school to learn modern business ethics. When he graduated, he added his father's drug connections to his mother's political connections, and pretty soon he was using the Cauca district as his warehouse, the Guajina district as his runway, and the Magdelena district as his wharf. Right now he's the biggest trafficker in Latin America, which is like saying—the world."

"And nobody can touch him."

"Stephen, watch my lips." Slaughter pointed to them. "Hector Aleria knows when a drug cop gets within twenty miles of his base. He owns the local police and the feds. I told you that one of his cousins is a general. I didn't tell you that another was a senator and a third—he's an uncle—used to be minister of defense."

And that, thought Warfield, was the final piece, a sliver of genealogy that locked in the borders. "Would the name of this minister of defense be Cruz?"

Slaughter did not reply at once because he was still groping along the parallel lines of his own thoughts. "It might have been," he said finally. "Just maybe."

"What would it take for you to be sure?"

"I'd have to be morc relaxed," he said. "That used to happen when my wife scratched my back."

Warfield had a back scratcher in the Plymouth: the file of Esteben Molenaur. He did not tell the DEA man about it, but when he motioned, Slaughter followed at a nonchalant distance. Warfield climbed into the Plymouth and took the first sheet of the two-part printout from the glove compartment. Then he unlocked the passenger's door and admitted Slaughter, handing him the sheet, which included nearly everything about Molenaur but his later exploits in his role as the Freedom Fighter's best friend.

Slaughter smiled like a hog at a free kitchen as he received the printout. He put his nose in it like a hog rooting for truffles. He did not divert his concentration for a second when Jim Turkle spoke over his radio from the GM product up the street.

"Bogey at five o'clock."

Sure enough. Tulio Villazon had appeared outside the embassy door. Warfield got a good look as Villazon passed up the street at four, three, and finally two o'clock. He was a compact man of slightly more than average height. He had black hair. His eyes were wide-set and badly centered, as if the skull had shrunk unevenly. Seeing him in three dimensions, Warfield had absolutely no doubt that Villazon was one of the four men who had killed Ned Eglon.

But the car that he entered midway up the block was neither the stolen Audi or the Chevrolet that had been posted as lookout in the street; the rounded box had to be a late-model Ford. Villazon started it up and pulled from the curb with much greater regard than he had shown for Eglon's front yard.

Without being ordered, Jim Turkle followed the Ford. While he was still moving across the four lanes, he was on the radio to the tandem car one block ahead that would form with Warfield's a moving screen. Nothing less than two outriders were needed, because traffic had started to thicken toward rush hour, and Villazon would be wary of a tail.

That was what Warfield thought. He was pleasantly surprised when Villazon proceeded up Massachusetts at the head of the parade without visible concern and without performing any basic countersurveillance maneuvers. The Ford turned north on Thirty-fourth Street and continued until it reached the Cleveland Park area. Quickly, Villazon swung off the street and into the driveway of a large, very strange-looking house that verged on a wooded lot.

The house must have been built before World War I, when eccentricity was permitted at the center of power. The roofs, of which there were several, flared like those of a Japanese temple. The modillions and the many gabled windows recalled New England. The stone porch belonged in Monterey. Yet the only thing that seemed entirely foreign was the figure of Tulio Villazon as he crossed the lawn, mounted the curving porch stairs, and knocked on the front door. He was immediately admitted to the house by a man Warfield could not see clearly.

Although he did not like doing it in Slaughter's presence on an open line, Warfield called back to headquarters and requested a rundown on the house, owner, current status, et cetera. He hoped that the watch understood that et cetera meant a full intercept blanket. Slaughter knew the procedure, of course, but he did not know the priority or the direction of the mission. Even after finishing his perusal of the Molenaur file, Warfield could tell that the DEA man had still not narrowed the parameters by much. He wanted to talk while they waited.

"This is the carnivore who had his file zapped from on high."

"My people retrieved the information from the backup tapes," said Warfield. "Another couple days and it would have been recycled into the ether."

"Looks like some of it has been already," said Slaughter. "This guy's life stops five years ago."

"We didn't get it all, John."

"CIA," said Slaughter, as if he were speaking the name of his most bitter rival, which was pretty much the case. Every DEA official would swear on the least provocation that the drug traffic flourished with the active connivance of CIA and State, who put foreign policy considerations above the welfare of their own citizens; who did so thoroughly, consistently, and everlastingly. Warfield saw no reason to disturb that perception.

"I think you're right, John. But I can't prove it yet. You could help me with an informed reading of that file."

"I stepped right into it, didn't I? I'm in a shithouse, but I'm not supposed to notice the smell." Slaughter snapped the printout with his finger, almost destroying the flimsy paper. "Okay," he said. "The thing that jumps right out of this is that you've got yourself a family trade. The Alerias marry into the Cruzes, so do the Molenaurs. They both own land in the Cauca Valley, which is a flat-out drug feif. The Molenaurs are probably transport experts from day one. They own a bus line. Every major trafficker in Latin America owns a bus line. That's how the stuff is transported intra-country. A distillery is also a good cover because you employ chemists and you buy a lot of chemicals, which you need for conversion. The radio station, on the other hand, might be legitimate."

"Anything else?"

"Well, Molenaur's banking experience is probably a key," he said. "Modern drug traffickers don't worry about getting caught with powder on the table. They're too sophisticated for that. They worry about how to transport and wash money. Knowledge and connections in the banking industry make that a lot easier, and Medellín is Colombia's banking center. This guy Molenaur was trained from the cradle on up. He goes to work for F-2 so he can learn the techniques used against traffickers. He also keeps a thick notebook of the guys who are best to bribe. Then there's the import-export business—the arms—but, hell, even you can see through that, Stephen."

"I did."

"This guy is a sleeper, grade A," said Slaughter. "I never heard of him until the other day. Of course his only mistake happened before I moved over to the Agency."

"I don't think he's made any since," said Warfield. "Not until he hired Tulio Villazon."

Slaughter agreed with a long shake of his head. "If Aleria would lend out one of his primary men, this is the guy he'd do it for."

"That's what I wanted to know, John. Thanks."

Slaughter gave a broad smile of acknowledgment. "I think there's another level here that you're not talking about, Stephen, but tell me one thing: Are you going to waste Villazon?"

"That depends."

Slaughter smiled again, bigger, broader. "You're going to waste him."

Actually, Warfield had thought of coming in through the front door and letting things happen. Villazon might not make it: that would be up to him. Warfield did not really care about Tulio or the rest of the team, but only about who was giving the orders. Once Warfield relieved that arbitrary pressure, the situation might become very manageable.

He knew that he was coming very close to the source, and a moment later, Warfield knew he had gotten too close. That became clear when he took the call from Amelia Worth at headquarters.

"I have two messages, Mariner. The first is from one Serge Fenster. He said to tell you that the wife and three kids are fine. You'll be hearing from them soon."

Warfield could not have hoped for better news, because Serge had only two kids. The third had to be a boy called Esteben, and if he was safe, then Bettina must be too.

"Roger, Banner. Awaiting part two."

"Part two is a negative on your request for et cetera."

"Say again, Banner."

"I repeat: negative, no, on your request for et cetera that address."

Warfield listened with passive fury to the dying spritz of interference on the two-way radio. When he spoke again, it was with quiet lidded calm. "Do you want to tell me why?"

Amelia's low voice returned with a shade of annoyance. "Be advised that the address we have is the private residence of General Andrew Hatcher."

Warfield did not reply. Although he knew the name of almost every general officer in the armed services, something did not register with that one. After a moment he clicked the mike twice to receipt for the transmission and dumped it onto the seat between him and John Slaughter. He looked at the milky blue eyes of the DEA man.

"Do you know this Hatcher?"

"Everybody knows him," said Slaughter. "Don't you read the papers?"

"No. I figure someone will tell me if there's a war."

"Well then, you should know this monkey," said Slaughter. "He starts wars."

And then Warfield did know the name. General Andrew Hatcher was the head of Double C, Citizens against Communism. He was a retired brigadier who had done yeoman work organizing and directing the fight against Marxist regimes all over the world. His front was sometimes known as Rent-A-War. The general's latest hobby was the Contra cause, if Warfield recalled correctly.

"Isn't Hatcher the one who runs that dog-and-pony show on the blue hair circuit?"

"It's more like a geek show," said Slaughter. "They carry a few fifteen year old Freedom Fighters around with them. Double amputees. These kids are worth a couple million a limb. More in Texas."

"Hatcher must have raised a hell of a lot of money," said Warfield. "And I'll bet he's very tight with CIA."

"The general walks in the front door," said Slaughter authoritatively. "You'd be surprised at the people in this town who take his calls."

"I wouldn't be surprised," said Warfield. "He's doing privately what the administration can't do publicly. They'll deal with anyone who can hurt the FSLN. What I don't understand is how Hatcher and CIA can operate practically uncovered with people like Molenaur and Villazon."

"Maybe it's not so sinister," said the DEA man without conviction. "You deal with Latin American facilitators, you sometimes find yourself dealing with the master facilitators—the drug types."

"But you don't think so."

"I think this administration doesn't give a damn for public opinion," he said. "In a crunch, they know they can PR anything to death. You and I are aware of how many times they've screwed up. But how many times have they been hurt by it?"

Never. Even Bettina's botched mission, as bad an intelligence gaffe as ever was, had been ridden out by good on-camera makeup and a whirlwind of political diversion. The only thing that suffered was the concept of intelligence itself. Warfield was convinced that there was such a thing; that it should be used with discretion and skill; that it could not be endlessly debased.

But it was clear, as clear as the lights coming on in General Hatcher's parlor, that Warfield's operation was going to be throttled. Everywhere the mission turned, it was running up against people who were just too powerful. CIA, NSC, and now the administration's stalking horse for Contra funding. Shiloh Parkins had tried to warn him of the heights. He had not believe she could be so right. If Warfield did not back off immediately, the operation would be shut down, and his career as well.

"John, I think I'm going to lose my job."

"That would be a shame, Stephen. You're the best there is at what you do."

# Hatcher

When Stretch Dixon rolled in with the surveillance van, Warfield told John Slaughter to go home. He did not tell the DEA man to be sure and cover himself with paper. Slaughter knew enough to realize that the sky was falling, and that the best defense was a ten-page report that put him in Baltimore for the afternoon.

Villazon was still inside the house. He had been there for half an hour. The length of his stay heightened General Hatcher's role from one of contact to one of complicity. This was no mere drop. This was a report to the station chief. That control was an erstwhile amateur and his asset a drug runner was more than Warfield wanted to absorb.

He did not realize how frustrated he had become by inactivity until he finished bringing Dixon up to date on the things that mattered. Even if Jack Brindisi kept his word, which was doubtful, he had no more than twenty-four hours left on the mission clock. There might be less for Bettina. Although the message had said she was safe, Warfield considered the source. His several calls to the Fenster residence had not been answered.

Dixon, who was unaware of the time element, did not think much of Warfield's tactics. "So all you want me to do is follow Villazon."

"Don't lose him, Stretch. He might turn out to be all we have."

"And you're going to—what did you say—*confront* this walking war machine?"

"I'm going to shake his tree," said Warfield. "Then I'm going to stand back and see how high the coconuts bounce."

"Stephen, that's the worst idea I ever heard in my life. It isn't even an idea."

"You want to hear Plan B?"

"No."

"It's where I follow Villazon and you confront the general."

"Plan A carries."

It went into operation eight minutes later when Villazon left the house and Dixon followed in the Plymouth. Warfield gave it another five minutes before he moved onto the porch. He used the doorbell, which was an old-fashioned crank-handle that rang like breaking glass through the house.

A woman answered the door. She was the sort who had approached sixty for fifteen years without discernible change. She had blue hair, great legs, and the demeanor of a professional secretary. She could have been that, or the general's lady, or both. Warfield knew that he could not mumble his way past her.

"I have a message from the DCI for General Hatcher."

Although the woman might have been surprised by the blips in procedure, she had no problem translating the initials of the director of Central Intelligence. Telling Warfield

"Come in, please," she took the name of Major Stevens and disappeared with it from the room through a doorway flanked by the same kind of pillars that graced the porch.

The furnishings in the room matched the eclectic nature of the house. The campaigns and outposts of the American military were represented like a collage. Oriental chests, a cuckoo clock, a Japanese tea table, a large carving of a Cambodian temple bird. Above the mantel were a Civil War saber, a long samurai blade, and a pair of short butterfly swords.

Warfield was examining the butterflies, which he knew how to use, when General Andrew Hatcher walked into the room like another fragment of empire. Though not a big man, nor an imposing one, the general conveyed authority with the suddenness of a desert billboard. He walked with an exaggerated lift to his stride, as if he were stepping over bodies. His face had the surface and character of a grenade. The haircut that he had first gotten at the Point was back in fashion through no fault of his own. The eyes were a very bright blue, so intense that they might have been insane.

"If you want, Major, I can show you how those work."

Warfield, who still had some good memories of the army, tried to hide his disdain for this human cartoon. He moved away from the butterfly swords with a respectful, "Yes, sir."

Hatcher took the double swords down from the wall and pried them apart. He unhooked them at the nose, taking one in each hand. "They're Chinese, major." He hefted the two blades like a merchant on the scent. "A perfect pair, perfectly balanced. I'm told that in the hands of a master there's no finer weapon at close quarters."

"Have you ever seen them used properly, sir?"

"No, I don't believe so."

Warfield held out his hand. When he took the grip of the first sword in his palm, he quickly engaged the nose of the second and jerked it from the general's hand. Releasing it in mid-air, Warfield caught the grip and with both swords bracketed the general's throat in a double thrust.

Hatcher did not flinch. He had had no time to react. When Warfield pulled the swords back, locking the noses with a high block and snapping the blades back together, the general took the occasion to breathe. He accepted his weapon back. The only thing that betrayed him were the blue eyes, which screamed. The voice was very public, very calm.

"When I bought these swords, I was told that only three men in the world knew how to use them well. Two were Oriental. The third was a major in the United States Army."

"Yes, sir."

"You're Stephen Warfield."

"Yes, sir."

Hatcher replaced the butterfly swords atop the mantel. He turned then and assumed the privileged place before the hearth, feet wide apart, hands at his hips, his body interposed between Warfield and those deadly pieces of steel.

"You served two tours in Vietnam," he said. "The first with an infantry company, the second with MACV. We might have crossed paths, you and I, and never known it."

"We have," said Warfield. "Now."

Hatcher read Warfield's tone correctly. The eyebrows that were as long as his hair moved close together. "You're not carrying a message from the DCI."

"No, sir."

"That's perfectly all right," said Hatcher. "I have time for any soldier who's fought the good fight."

Warfield was thinking that General Andrew Hatcher had a very pompous style, even for a military man; but of course he was not that any longer. He was part of the medicine show.

"I'm going to give you the benefit of the doubt, General,"

said Warfield in a level voice that could not be mistaken. "I'm going to assume that you really don't know what's going on in your organization. If I thought you did, I would have moved those two swords three centimeters to the left and right. I'd have severed your neck at the shoulders. I'd have had to kill the woman too, because she saw me. In other words, I'd have to behave exactly the way your own people behaved when they tortured and killed a defenseless woman less than two days ago. Prior to that they tortured and killed a reasonably defenseless man. I found both those messes, general. I'm here to tell you that there won't be any more."

The thing about a crew cut was that it did reveal a blush of embarrassment or a surge of anger to the roots of a man's skull. Hatcher turned red before he turned purple. The silvery-brown hair stood in violent relief like pig bristles. Generals as a rule did not react well to threats. Retired generals with CIA support and White House encouragement apparently had learned to master them to a finite extent.

"Major, I don't think you understand the . . ."

"I understand everything," said Warfield. "Including your priorities. You probably think you can ride this out because of your connections. You're wrong. Your friends will drop you when things become difficult. I can guarantee that they're going to be very difficult. I can promise you disgrace, General. Probably some jail time."

"This is absurd," he said.

"It's going to seem like that until the cell door swings shut," said Warfield. "You won't believe it's happening for a minute. And then you'll believe it for longer than you can imagine. All because your warped sense of patriotism leads you to deal with filthy butchering drug scum."

The general pointed. "I want you out of this house!"

"Incorrect response, general. You're supposed to ask what *I* want."

Hatcher dropped his finger quickly. He looked to the doorway as if expecting his outburst to have brought the woman back. When no one appeared, the general dropped his voice also.

"What do you want, Warfield?"

"This is an order, General. Tulio Villazon and his three companions will leave this country immediately. Tonight. In case you don't recall the name, he's the man who walked out of this house fifteen minutes ago."

The general did not acknowledge the order; he could not, really. "Is there anything else that you . . . wish?"

"Yes," said Warfield. "I want you to deliver a message to another of your friends. Tell Esteben Cruz that I have his son."

Warfield hoped that General Hatcher would be rattled just enough to reach for the nearest phone, which was atop a table by the window alcove in the room where they had met. That was the only chance for intercept. The laser-enhanced parabolics were extremely sensitive receivers; they could collect sonic vibrations from the window panes and translate them into speech simultaneously, but they could not penetrate walls or even heavy curtains. Though the general's curtains were heavy, they were not drawn.

And he did not draw them. The general remained in the room, pacing three times before the brightly lit window by the telephone. Warfield had a clear, brilliant view through the scope in the air vent. On the second pass he saw that Hatcher had reclaimed the butterfly swords from the mantel. Trying to duplicate the nose grab that Warfield had demonstrated, the general dropped one of the heavy swords to the floor.

Warfield heard the noise. It was a thump-clatter, distant but audible. He knew now that he could pick up conversation in the room. It would be better, much better, if he could move in closer. Every additional ten feet would improve the quality of the reception by ten percent, but he could not risk being seen. Only the cover of early night had allowed him to move the van within a hundred yards.

As far as he could see, General Hatcher had no visible security. That could change with one phone call, however. Though he was planning no direct moves on the general, Warfield did not want to lose his listening post. Hatcher was as high-level and unprotected as Warfield was likely to get. He did not expect the pressure that he had applied to result in panic. Consultation would do.

General Hatcher placed his call twelve minutes after Warfield left the house. The general used the alcove phone—an old rotary dial. Though the sensitivity of the receiver was not good enough to allow a digit count, Warfield felt virtually certain from the time lapse and the faint burr in thc headset that the call was local. At the most, local long distance.

Then, at the crucial moment, Hatcher moved away from the window. He picked up the phone in his hand and carried it directly across the room toward the pillars that flanked the hall. With his back turned to the window and due to his position in the room, most of the sound was absorbed down the length of the hallway. The only thing that Warfield received for the next forty-five seconds were garbled echoes.

But when Hatcher recrossed the room and stood directly in front of the window, he was good and readable. The salutations had ended, and his voice was impatient, irritated:

HATCHER: That's right. The son. The son! It used to rise in the east but not one damned thing works right after it passes through Russia.

Warfield guessed that they were talking about Esteben Cruz. It was nice to know they were all acquainted. The party on the other end took a fair length of time to complete his response before submitting to the general's lash again.

HATCHER: I don't give a Korean shit how important he is to you. He's compromising the integrity of this entire effort. You piss and moan about sterility codes. This is my reputation we're talking about. Either you take care of this or I'm going straight to the Man.

There was a short pause for rebuttal until the general came storming back.

HATCHER: Then I'll wake him up! Goddammit, you put a good story in front of him and he moves his head up and down just like a president. This is a helluva good story. Not pretty, but good.

There was another silence, much more lengthy, as Hatcher listened again. He took two steps and sat down on the edge of a chair, or chest, and hunched himself around the receiver. When he spoke, the sound of his voice was muted, incomprehensible to Warfield. There might have been several short exchanges between the two parties before Hatcher suddenly straightened up, turning, speaking loud and angrily.

HATCHER: Now you listen to me, Grady. I don't ever want to see that cross-eyed bastard again. It's bad enough we've got to deal with every *brigadista* we left on the beach, but at least they *care.* This one knows from nothing but blood money. He's a filthy murdering drug scum.

While Warfield listened to the silence as the other party responded, he filled in the context. They were no longer talking about Cruz. They were discussing Villazon, whose father had been abandoned at the Bay of Pigs. Warfield was also pleased that the general had adopted some of his own words to characterize the man. But the answer that Hatcher received was unclear from his next response.

HATCHER: Don't tell me about it! I do *not* want to know. Just get it done!

The general hung up. He did it hard, and when the carriage did not accept the receiver, he picked it up from the floor and did it again, hard. By and by he left the room.

So they were going to do something. Warfield took almost as much satisfaction from that as he had in listening to the private minutes of the general's life. That was the real man on the phone—the one who ordered up real things. Whether he had moved for retreat or assault was something that Warfield would find out soon.

# The Reach

JUST after Hatcher completed his call, Stretch Dixon reported that he had followed Tulio Villazon to an address in the Woodridge section of town. Actually, Dixon gave three addresses because of the open channel communications in the Plymouth. The last was the correct one.

Dixon also said that he could handle the surveillance alone, so Warfield spent a tedious fifteen minutes outside General Hatcher's house trying to run down the man called Grady. There were twenty-seven in the metropolitan phone book and nine more in the directory of government employees. None tripped recognition alarms. The man who Hatcher had called was important if not highly visible. His name should have jumped off the pages.

Nevertheless, Warfield ran the name through Vulcan and watched in a stupor as the screen belched possibilities. The most likely seemed to be a woman who worked for the Library of Congress, the least a civil engineer in the Parks Department. On their finest days the most they shared with people of real power was city water.

Warfield's mind kept turning instead to the one person who had first told him how high the reach would be. Shiloh Parkins would know Mr. Grady, or whatever pseudonym he happened to be wearing. Whether Warfield could coax the identity from her was another question. Thinking that he might as well try, he called the Parkins Foundation. When he got Shiloh on the line, she was very coy. She said that it was the busy time of the therapeutic day; that she couldn't get away for a drink; that it was incumbent upon her to keep the phone lines clear; but that if Warfield could stop by, she might be able to clear some time.

Warfield hated to leave Dixon on stakeout alone and deprived of sleep. He hated to give up his ear on General Hatcher. But Dixon was a model of endurance, and the general had not reappeared in his alcove window or anywhere else. Warfield, reluctantly he thought, said yes to Ms. Parkins's invitation.

On his way downtown, he received some indication of the direction things were taking at headquarters. Amelia Worth demanded a status report. When Warfield told her he had nothing to report, she asked him what the hell he was doing out there. He told her that he was going home for some badly needed rest.

He doubted if she believed any of it, but then Warfield did not care. When headquarters began to deny requests for intercept, they were one step from scrubbing the mission. If they had been fully cognizant of Mike Koricke's foray, they would have aborted already. Buying time and keeping the watch misinformed was Warfield's only option.

It was best that NSA knew nothing of the Parkins Foundation. Amelia would not have approved of a call on a courtesan any more than she liked Russian vodka. That they were the best of their respective lots would have made no impression on that keen but blinkered sensibility. And she would have been jealous.

In fact any woman would have been daunted by the sheer weight of Shiloh Parkins's sexual displacement. When she admitted Warfield to her inner sanctum again, he was again stunned by her beauty and by its changes. The pigtail was gone, unbound, the pale hair with metallic highlights feathering over her shoulders. The roomy white garment had been replaced by something in pink that stuck willfully everywhere. Her deep décolletage had dropped another impossible inch, and her voice was even more suggestive.

"You've done me a favor," she said. "Let me pour you a makeup drink."

That was all right. Shiloh had a bar in her ramified wall system, and she had nothing against Russian imports. She held the crystal goblet with the clear liquid in her palm, as if offering the apple.

Warfield took it. He took a drink like a bite.

Shiloh matched him by draining a cool inch of amber fluid of her own. The liquor worked its way into her body as if it were meant to be followed. "I was going to call you anyway," she said. "But I didn't know whether congratulations were in order or not."

"Concerning what?"

"Mister Gasqué," she said. "I've heard that you people receive your commendations in secret. The medals are kept in a safe."

"We don't receive decorations for pest control."

Shiloh laughed in a surprisingly natural, hearty trill. "God, that's cold-blooded," she said. "Wonderful."

"It's the truth," he said. "Not many people appreciate that."

Shiloh seemed to like his answer. She sat on the foreshortened sofa, which was very much like a love seat. Patting the cushion next to her, she bade Warfield sit at her left hand. His obedience put them thigh to thigh.

"The media reports were rather vague about our friend's demise," she said. "They seemed to think he was involved with drugs."

"He was," said Warfield. "Men like Gasqué are known as polycriminals. They're into literally anything that can turn a dime. It's nice in a way because when they blow themselves up we can drop any label around their neck."

"He blew *himself* up?"

"They always do."

"I was thinking—no, I was *hoping* that you'd killed him," she said with a sardonic smile. "I'm disappointed."

"Sorry," said Warfield. "Believe me, I'd have preferred him to stay alive just a while longer."

"So he could give you the answers you wanted."

Warfield nodded. He waited. It was clear that their conversation had come to the exact point where their previous interview had ended. Nothing was written that the same result could not obtain twice. He knew that Shiloh realized that too.

"You know, when I asked Stretch about you, he'd tell me only one thing: he said that you were the best counterespionage agent in the business. I don't even know what that means, Stephen. I don't think I want to know. But it answered most of my questions."

"It should have answered them all."

She tipped back the rest of her drink and placed it on a small table beside her. The table was jade. Her eyes, tonight, were almost green in the muted lighting.

"Perhaps," she said. "But I wanted to know something more—something personal. So I asked Stretch about that."

Warfield knew what was coming next, but he could not

think immediately of how to use it best. "He told you about Bettina."

"Yes."

"What did he say?"

"That when they refurbished the Statue of Liberty, they used you as a model for the torch."

Warfield recognized Dixon's voice in those words. He could also see the way out now. Shiloh Parkins, after all the Wharton School could accomplish, was still a woman.

"So you know everything about me."

"I know what puzzled me about you," she said. "You give the impression of a man who's romantically involved. And yet somehow isn't. It's curiously like mourning."

"Yes, it is."

"But I have the feeling it will be resolved soon."

"That depends a lot on you, Shiloh."

For a moment, she said nothing. Warfield finished his drink slowly, trying not to be completely overcome by the pink dress that was no more than an enhanced nakedness.

"You'd like to know the name of the man who sponsored Mister Gasqué," she said.

"Yes."

"But you haven't fulfilled your obligation," she said. "You said you'd find a man for me. You could have by now. Why haven't you?"

"I think you know."

"I may not."

But she did. The small distance between them had all but vanished and what was left was charged with lust so pure that every passing second seemed to contradict nature. And the seconds did pass. Neither the man nor the woman made the minor movements that would signal. At last awkwardness arose.

"You see what it is, Shiloh. We both know what's best."

Her voice was as heavy as his had been. "Are we really like that?"

"It seems."

She said, "Dammit."

"Let's go halfway," he said. "I know his name's Grady."

"But you don't know his last name?"

Last name? Suddenly Warfield realized that Shiloh had given him the key without surrendering her confidence. There was only one important man in Washington whose first name was Grady, and he was very important.

Warfield put his finger to his lips, signaling silence. Then he got to his feet. The kiss he gave to the lips he had closed was nothing like he had intended. But it was best.

One of the few things that could have pushed Warfield from Shiloh Parkins's side, and her image from his mind, was the name she had uttered. When he reached the van, Warfield fired up the computer terminal, but even before the information began to appear, he was seeing it in memory, the kind of bland recall that mounts aimlessly in every cell of the brain from the overspill of every media day.

Grady Souther was big. His position was listed as "special foreign policy advisor," but he was bigger than that. Although he had been kicking around Washington for twenty years, most administrations had been able to ignore him or find harmless posts for the man who was the grandson of a vice-president, the nephew of a United States senator, and the spiritual heir of Joe McCarthy. No one had ever thought to listen to him until the evangelical ravings against communism that he distributed through his chain of newspapers and radio and television stations were vindicated in Nicaragua.

Events had made the monomaniac a seer. Feted by every

right-wing organization, a hell of a fund-raiser, he was tapped as an honorary member of the new administration's transition team. Afterward, he was appointed to several jobs within government that called for idealogical correctness. National committeeman, speech writer, presidential troubleshooter—Grady Souther flourished. He was credited with inventing the phrase "Evil Empire," which had come to him in a dream. Because of his inspirational qualities, and his inexperience, which together comprised what was called "a fresh look," he was in 1982 named as special envoy to Central America.

What this meant in practical terms was that he implemented CIA policy and presided ceremonially over the militarization of the region. The first mercenary armies were hired. The weapons were requisitioned and stockpiled. The stateside training of indigenous troops began. Espionage assignments were handed out. In all these efforts Souther was one of the guiding lights, or cheerleaders. He had been the nominal head of Bettina's disastrous operation, though Warfield doubted that the man knew her name or what country her particular brand of work was designed to assist.

About eighteen months ago, after three inglorious years in the area, Souther had been recalled to Washington and named a foreign policy advisor. No reason had been given at the time. It was certainly not because he had called the cabinet of Costa Rica "a pack of crypto-Marxists" and the Nicaraguan head of state a "four-eyed spic." It was probably not because of the furor created by the mining of Nicaraguan harbors in violation of international law. If anything, it was due to the fact that he had been such a vigorous proponent of the invasion of Grenada. Souther's stock had risen steadily as the assault on the island became more and more of a public relations bonanza.

Grady Souther had gotten as big as any small-minded political appointee can get. He had a farm in Virginia, a wife in Palm Beach, and an office in the basement of the White House. He was sent on special missions to the Far East, South Africa, Israel, the Hague. And no doubt because they were his first love, he also kept a very close watch on the progress of the Contra armies.

When Warfield correlated the dates, Souther's return to Washington coincided very well with the reduction in military aid imposed on the Central American effort by Congress. This foreign policy advisor was obviously in contact and in league with General Hatcher's fund-raising efforts. He was also up to his rabbit ears in a lot of dirty work. He was pimping for murderers and dealing with drug-runners. Although Warfield did not think much of the company, he could imagine that it might be passed off as normal business relationship in Latin America, and even more normal in Latin American diplomacy.

What bothered him was that he could not think of any way to get at Grady Souther.

The man was just too big.

The beginning of a solution to Warfield's dilemma came in a roundabout way when he called Mike Koricke's van. Mike answered on the first tone, as if he had been awaiting contact.

"I've been trying to reach you, Mariner. Headquarters told me that you were at home."

"What do you have?"

"Beta access," he said in a voice that was deliberately low-keyed. "I penetrated the system twenty minutes ago."

"Where are you now?"

"At my sister's place," he said. "I've been working out of here since I lifted the password. I've got to tell you that I was feeling funny as hell sitting around Lafayette Park in a big black van."

Camped on the White House lawn for all practical purposes. With a full shudder, Warfield noted the address of Mike's sister in Rosslyn. It was right across the bridge in the first few yards in Virginia, a ten-minute drive from Foggy Bottom.

Warfield made it in less. It was just after nine o'clock when he arrived at the ten-story condominium apartment building across the Potomac River. The tall windows on the uppermost floor offered a grandiose nighttime tableau of the District. It seemed like another competing firmament out there, the darkness ditched in streets and water, the lights glowing in galaxies of petty stars.

They were not all petty of course. The brightest were often the ones that could not be seen. The basement of the White House was such a place. Langley another. Beta was the supersecret high-speed link between them, and the gangling young man in the aloha shirt had ripped it off as if it were a neighborhood liquor store. Warfield would have been appalled by the ghostliness of the theft if he had not been so curious to see the results.

"I hope you won't be disappointed," said Mike. "It's mostly a sequence of numbers. Of course they'd make perfect sense if you knew what they stood for."

Warfield was absolutely certain that he would not be disappointed. He sat on the edge of a Corbu chair with the nocturnal skyline behind him and watched as Mike set to work at his sister's PC. None of the equipment was from Radio Shack. Mike's sister, who worked for the Pentagon, had furnished the apartment in high-tech good taste. The only thing missing was her physical presence. Maybe she was out screwing that ambitious young NSC staffer. Well, so were they.

Very quickly the screen lit in four discrete columns of figures. The first column was easy to interpret—the figures were obviously dates. They began about eight months ago (about the time Bettina had left Esteben Molenaur for Nicaragua), and they continued up until the present, or nearly so. There were sixteen dates in all, but they did not appear at any regular interval. Instead, the dates grouped around distinct time periods. There were approximately four periods of heavy activity.

The second column was a series of six numbers in ascending order. Mike said that he did not know what they were for sure, but that they seemed to be the "key."

"The key?"

"The index to a record on file," he said very slowly. "Basically it's no different than any number that you'd assign to an invoice or payout." He paused and ran his hand across his face, scraping the stubble of beard that had the effect of making him appear still more gaunt. "Normally the key would appear first, but there's no reason why it can't be second or even last."

"Could it be a sterility code?"

"Sure," he said.

Warfield liked that possibility because he had heard General Hatcher raging about it. Sterility codes were used by CIA to disguise the origins of orders and sources of supply. Langley had so many cutouts and proprietaries that they sometimes confused themselves with their paper trails. The number meant that Esteben Molenaur was a link in this pipeline. Although Warfield had guessed that already, it was good to have the knowledge confirmed.

"What's your feeling about the third column, Mike?"

He emitted a nervous overrun of sound that might have been laughter. "Money," he said.

Warfield thought so too. Though there were no dollars

signs preceding the figures, there were decimal points, and two digits to the right of each one. CIA was always careful with the records of its cash, even when they were dealing with large amounts. And these were large. None of the amounts were for less than twenty-five thousand per unit. Most of them fell in the quarter- to half-million range. One read: 2 349 572.12.

The total amount came close to ten million of what Warfield supposed were dollars. That would buy a start at an army. Molenaur had to be not just an arms conduit for shipment of materiel to the Contras, but perhaps the primary one. He was indeed "important." Important and slimy, or they would never have gone to such lengths to conceal his identity.

Warfield did not have to ask what kind of story the last column of figures told. The numbers were all the same, five digits and two letters all in a row: 386 41 SR. The SR could very well stand for Grady Souther.

"If the third column is cash disbursements, then the last must be a bank account."

"The laundry mark," said Mike. "Provided that it's dirty."

Warfield would have bet all the clean money he had in the world on that chance. There was a very good reason why this file had been segregated within the Beta system. Though Congress had forbidden military aid to the Contras, private contributions, such as those solicited by General Hatcher, were permitted as long as they were not funneled through government agencies. But everyone with more than a fifth-grade sense of intrigue knew that the law was being circumvented. This file, when matched against CIA codes, would provide the proof.

If Warfield had wished for leverage against Langley, Hatcher, and Souther, he could not have found better. He had them down and he had them dirty.

"I want a copy of this file, Mike. When you submit your report, don't leave that fact out—or anything else. Tell exactly what you did—on my orders. That'll clear you."

Mike accepted the out with graceful exhaustion. Like a driven stake, he lowered himself into the chair that Warfield had vacated. "What are you going to do with it, sir?"

"Call me Stephen. And you don't want to know."

"I understand," he said. "Stephen."

"You can do me a favor if you take your time submitting the report," said Warfield. "Tomorrow morning would be just fine."

"I'll be lucky if I'm awake by then. You can count on tomorrow afternoon, Stephen."

# Sold Short

WHEN Warfield checked in with Stretch Dixon, he found that Tulio Villazon had gone mobile. He and three other men had left the Woodridge section heading north. Unless they were making for the Baltimore-Washington International Airport, Dixon did not think they were leaving the country.

Neither did Warfield. He had not expected that his order to General Hatcher, and its relay to Grady Souther, would result in compliance. His aim had been to flush out Esteben Molenaur and his local operation. That was happening.

While Warfield was crossing over to the parkway, Dixon called in an update. He said that the car with the four Latins had turned off the highway at Laurel. They had made their way to a house on Chantilly Road, if you could believe that.

Warfield had a little problem with the information, because he did not know why the four men would be going to his house now. They were looking for him, of course. But why go there when they had no idea when he would return? Were they planning to stake out the house for hours, days?

That was doubtful. It was much more likely that they had been told Warfield would be there. Seen that way, the answer became clear. Someone at headquarters had passed on his location. Wanting to know very much who that was, Warfield contacted the watch, which had changed over. Ellen Pena was back at the controls.

"Where do you have my location, Banner?"

"You're at home, Mariner."

"Who else knows that?"

The line went silent for half a minute before Ellen's voice returned. "We logged two requests for your terminus and ETA. The first was Mike Koricke. The second DIRNSA."

DIRNSA. That was the answer. An enemy could have spent weeks trying to suborn information from NSA, but a friend, a highly placed one, would simply call the director of NSA and inquire politely. The director, who probably did not even know the details of Warfield's operation, might answer what would seem to be a reasonable request. If the friend were high enough, DIRNSA might answer a request that was less than reasonable. Obviously, he had.

And Grady Souther was high enough. He was so high and mighty that he would not worry about the request being traced back to him. Everyone was on the same side after all. The death of one government employee might be cause for hard feelings, but these things could be worked out. By next year DIRNSA would be moving on to another post with NATO or JCS. The directorship of NSA was one of the best stepping-stones in the hierarchy of the U.S. armed forces, if a man's record at that post were reasonably clean and free of controversy.

Warfield tried not to be bitter. Being objective was best. The four-man team was probably not planning to kill him, as they had not been planning to kill Ned Eglon. They would want to ask questions, first and foremost where the boy, the son of Esteben Molenaur, was hidden. Pity Warfield when he could not answer in the allotted time. The team would have to make another bloody mess.

But this time the blood would be their own.

Warfield had acquired the house and land on Chantilly Road about two and a half years ago when, on the advice of a mathematician at NSA, he had sold short one of the highest flying stocks in the memory of man during the greatest bull market in history. Certainly he would never have done it if he had not been half crazy over Bettina's disappearance, but he had done it with all the money and margin available to him, and he had watched—he had marveled—as the stock crashed from a high of eighty to a low of four and five-eighths, and then he had taken the nearly one hundred thousand dollars in profit and put a good down payment on a home that would remove him from the reach of landlords forever.

Like Warfield, the property was not stylish. The house had a basement that smelled of sulfurous mud and rooms that angled like a forecastle. Everything that was not antiquated, like the plumbing, wiring, and heating plant, was detached, like the garage and part of the porch. But he had not bought the place for its possibilities. He had spent the money for the land, ten acres, and also for the buffer of adjacent land, another twenty-five acres that belonged to a horse farm farther up the road. The combination meant that Warfield had no near neighbors, which was the object.

The solitude was a blessing every day, and on this day a feast. Before the last turn on the way home, parked three-quarters up the hill, stood the Plymouth that Stretch Dixon had been driving. Warfield, who had been running without lights along the two miles of Chantilly Road, pulled in front of the car and shut down his van. After removing the necessary equipment, he got out, stood on the side of the road, and waited.

The sound of rocks clicking together came from the hillside, probably from the stony, grassy bald at the summit. The noise was practically inaudible under the steady rhythm of the nighttime cicadas. Warfield would not have heard it if he had not been listening very closely—and he did not hear it again.

Dixon lay in the deep grass at the top of the hill, invisible from a distance of more than ten feet. He heard and acknowledged Warfield's coming by tipping the half-shuttered night-glasses from his face and passing them over. Without any other greeting, he pointed down the far side of the hill into the valley.

"One in the thicket past the big oak tree," he said. "Two drifted down toward the house."

"I thought there were four, Stretch."

"I lost the last one," he said without apology. "Maybe he's down along that line of little bushes by the garage."

"I'll find him."

Dixon nodded. "What do you want me to do?"

"Disappear."

"Which way?"

"Ten miles in any direction."

The whites of Dixon's eyes narrowed perceptibly in the darkness. "I can help, Stephen."

"Not this time."

"We're into the Tarzan mode, is that it?"

"It's my jungle, Stretch."

"Falling down goddamn house," he said. "Biggest mosquitoes in the state of Maryland. You should turn this place into a summer camp for ghetto kids. Show them they're better off where they are."

That was the longest speech of criticism Warfield had ever

heard from Dixon, and it was the last thing Warfield heard from him that night, because Capitol Detection was already removing itself from the case, gliding crabwise down the side of the hill, gradually rising to full height as he neared the berm of the road. Entering the Plymouth without the faintest click of metal, easing the car out of gear, Dixon backed it down the blind turn to the bottom of the hill and out of sight. Warfield never heard the engine start.

Then it was quiet except for the cicadas and the low distant rumble of bullfrogs in the pond on the nearby farm. No moon, no streetlights, scattered stars. Warfield studied the house with the night glasses but saw no one. The two men might have been around back or in cover at several different places. Or they were inside.

The man that Dixon thought might be along the line of bushes by the garage was not there. Warfield swept every visible inch of ground between those rank boxwood bushes, searching for the shapes of shoes or the hint of a shadow. He found nothing.

But the window at the rear right-hand side of the garage showed a sign. It was no more than a dim changing pattern, but it was at the right height for a man, and the topmost part was of a distinctly lighter shade. Although he could not confirm the shape as a man's, Warfield marked it probable because of the way the garage window looked onto the house obliquely. Not a bad post for an ambush.

The team was taking no chances. The man in the thicket down past the oak tree had a rifle with an elaborate scope. He was plainly visible from the top of the hill but not from the road where he was expecting his target to appear. If they were going to try to take Warfield alive, this man would be their insurance against things getting out of hand. If they were going for a quick kill, he would be the designated hitter. In either case, he was the one who would have to go down first.

Warfield chose the SIG 9 mm and the knife. He would have liked a rifle but he could not afford to be burdened. He could make no noise, because the team would be alert for intrusion; he could give them no profile, show no shadow, because he was probably not the only one with night glasses. That meant a long belly-crawl from the base of the hill to the thicket.

It took a full half-hour to get in close. They always say a man knows his land like the back of his hand, but Warfield was not sure that he would have recognized his hand among a dozen similar ones, and he found plenty of unpleasant surprises on his own property. Broken glass all around the fence posts between his land and the horse farm. Thick shoals of rocks in the dry creek bed that rattled like castanets with any heedless movement. Sand spurs, fleas, incredibly big and hungry mosquitoes, and within twenty feet of the thicket, a convenient fringe of waist-high cover that he knew too late was poison ivy.

The man with the rifle still did not know it. He sat in the middle of the huge shining leaves, some as big as sea-turtle shells, looking pleasantly bemused. His left arm rested on a rock about three feet high. The rifle nested over that arm and his lap. He wore a baseball cap with the bill turned backwards and held in his mouth an unlit cigar.

That was good, because at night in the open air at very close quarters a man's best line of defense was often his sense of smell. This man would have none. Warfield used that edge to work as slowly as possible around to the left rear, where the man's vision was partly blocked by the big rock and the reversed bill of the cap. Warfield could have touched him sixty seconds before he finally made the move, but he worked so close that when he brought the knife to the back of the man's neck he had leverage as well.

"Your choice, friend."

The man did not hesitate. He dropped straight onto his back, clearing the knife with a piece of his forearm, and at the same time he tried to tumble into a lifting kick. By that time he was dying. The knife was hilt-deep into his throat, striking through flesh into the ground. The kick stiffened harmlessly over Warfield's right shoulder. The rifle scraped once against the rock and dropped silently to the ground.

Warfield was unconcerned about the small noise because the distance to the house was a good fifty yards. He was unconcerned about the man's quick spastic death because somewhere other and better life was being born. The surprise about this one was that the man had lived to be so old.

He was about fifty. Warfield could not recognize him positively as one of the team at Eglon's, but he fit the general profile. Latin, about five ten, one eighty-five, with a small scar that rose from the right upper lip toward the nostril. The scar, his age, and the fact that he had had some training in hand-to-hand almost guaranteed that his identity could be traced eventually.

Right now Warfield was just glad to have the rifle. It was a Mannlicher with a decent Trijicon infrared scope that with luck had not been knocked from true in the skirmish. The man was also armed with a full-sized .45 in a padded ballistic-fiber hip holster. That was interesting because the item was standard issue in the U.S. armed forces. It might mean nothing. Or it might say something about the source of supply.

Warfield spent time propping the man back up against the rock. Although he did not think the figure could be seen with precision from the house, he did not want to take the chance. Thoroughness usually produced results, and in this case it produced an added bonus when Warfield found the palm-sized two-way radio on the ground beside the bleeding rock. He should have known it: this team was always well equipped. They would have emergency communications, and they might have scheduled check-in times.

The discovery made Warfield pick up the pace just a bit. He had been planning to back out the way he had come, but now he decided to risk a more direct approach. There was a bower of pin cherry trees to the left of the house that would screen anyone coming in from that direction. If Warfield could cross the fifteen yards of open ground without being seen, he could take advantage of the natural cover almost all the way up to the beginning of the driveway.

Moving with the rifle made the going much harder, but Warfield did not want to be caught without a long-range answer at that point. Undoubtedly the other members of the team had convertible automatic weapons. They might be under instructions to take him alive if possible. When they discovered they could not do that, Chantilly Road would become a killing ground.

The crossing took ten minutes. The scrub grass was just high enough to hedge his width and just patchy enough not to indent a clear trail behind him. No cars with lights came up the road while Warfield was exposed. No one used the radio. He slipped into the drainage ditch on the far side of the driveway by the cherry trees knowing that he had not been seen. Now the problems were all on their side.

They had several. If Warfield did not lay himself wide open, the man in the garage was useless. If the other two were outside, they were dead meat in the dark for a stalker whose presence they did not suspect. If they were inside, they might live a little longer. Warfield wanted to take one of them alive, but he was not committed to the idea.

He worked his way down to the far end of the ditch, checking the ground in four-meter overlaps all the way to the low pile of rubble that was his stone fence. There was nothing in the area. No one was along the hundred-foot length of the fence or on the hillside beyond. Unless there was another man posted at very long range, that meant the two men were inside the house. And one in the garage.

Warfield moved back a few yards toward the house. He moved the rifle onto a comfortable benchrest atop the stones and put the scope on the garage window. He got movement right away. A man. His face was not blacked nor was he dressed in black. His shirt was light, showing like high haze behind the dirty windowpanes. That was what Warfield had seen from the top of the hill with the night glasses, and that was what he closed down on in the scope. He could take the opening any time.

And then a voice said: "Tulio?"

The answer, deep, unaccented: "All clear."

"Omar?"

"No problem."

"Raoul?"

Raoul did not answer. His soul was hurtling through space and his radio was in Warfield's pocket.

"Raoul?" The voice was more insistent, a little tense, with maybe a splinter of panic in it.

Warfield could have tried to impersonate Raoul, and in some situations it might have worked, but not in this one. Found out, Warfield had only one move left, and he took it. He notched the scope down four inches under the head of light-colored hair and fired.

No time for damage assessment. The .30 calibre magnum shell traveling at several thousand feet per second blew apart the whole window and anything directly behind it. Warfield spun away and scrabbled hard down the length of the stone wall until he reached the hillside, then it was up and over, rolling into cover behind a basswood tree hung with a thick base of creeper. Using the tree as a shield, Warfield back-crawled fifteen feet farther up the hill to a fender of big rocks. From that position, he had a controlling field of fire onto the house.

They had to come out, and they had no idea what they were coming out into. As he was working around to the thicket, Warfield had spotted their car two hundred yards up the road by the gate to Red Askew's lower pasture. They would make for the vehicle, directly or indirectly, very soon. One shot might mean a firecracker to Red or his boys. More than a couple meant the phone, the cops.

Warfield could have started punching out the windows one by one, but he did not want the law either. He did not want his position revealed. His fondest desire was to terminate the life of one more inglorious butcher quickly and catch the last intact and keep him that way for the minutes or hours it would take to scrape information from what he surely called his brain.

Instead, there was a squawk in Warfield's pocket. Tulio Villazon's voice, the one that had lately called "All clear," came through the two-way radio in quick bursts.

"Hey, man, you all alone out there?"

Warfield did not reply.

"Hey, man, we can work this out."

Warfield thought he saw a movement at the window in what he sometimes called his music room. He trained the scope on the window but saw nothing beyond loose shapes that might have been the curtains.

"Twenty-five thousand apiece," said Villazon, like a talking ratchet. "Fifty thousand dollars. You let us walk."

There was no money, and even Villazon did not believe in

the last part; but after a moment, Warfield decided to test the airwaves. "Throw your weapons out the front door."

Warfield put the scope against the back door, and just as he brought it to bear the Dutch screen door swung out but not wide and a man dove and rolled across the patch of pigweed and flagstone called the patio. He stopped against the assortment of brick called the barbecue pit. Warfield had a shot but did not take it because he wanted them both outside at the same time.

But the second man stayed home. That was the smart one. He waited until his partner lurched from beside the barbecue pit and made a low quick zigzag toward the drainage ditch. When he was halfway there, at maximum exposure, the screen door flicked open again and the second man threw himself onto the patio.

Warfield did not want to do it but he went for the easy shot. Ten feet from the ditch the first man threw his countermoves to the wind and ran straight, flat out. He gathered himself for the headlong dive, and when he was just about to leave his feet, Warfield fired.

The impact rammed him into the open ditch. There was no doubt that he was hit, hit hard, because the human body does not do what the mind cannot imagine, and no mind can imagine the force and velocity of such a projectile striking home, intercepting blood and will, obliterating bone, pinning all the fine muscle and meat to the suddenness of the earth like a dried and weightless specimen.

That left one, and that should have been a manageable number. Warfield held the high ground and he had good reach with his weapon. In almost every direction the man chose to run, he was covered and as good as down. In every direction but one.

He could come on straight ahead—straight up the hill toward Warfield. Having seen the flash from the rifle, he could with his AR-15 put out enough fire to keep Warfield pinned behind the rocks until he got within range to finish. He could do it pumping, screaming, and firing if he had the nerve for the job—and he did.

Warfield had moved off the man in the ditch. He had swung his sights back toward the patio when he saw without the aid of the scope the dark figure vaulting the barbecue pit, veering for the big doghouse that had been sitting on the first terrace of the hillside unused for years, and coming round the other side, opening up on full automatic, the rounds already crashing off the rocks, bracketing almost perfectly the single shot that he had seen in the dark.

He was screaming *"Chingada!"* and Warfield was thinking that he had never fucked this man's mother but that he had to counter the assault immediately and with surprise. With force. Without thought of taking the man alive because it never worked if the intent was unequal. If one was berserk for the kill and the other unsure.

Warfield spun out from behind the rocks and hit the ground. He brought the SIG 210-2 right onto the flaming muzzle of the automatic rifle and fired three times, right, center, right.

For a second the firing continued, but it was high and suddenly higher, wild, ripping through the leaves of the basswood tree until everything stopped dead. Silence rushed into Warfield's deafened ears like a new god, powerful, invisible, real. And then he heard the man.

He was making weird peeping, shrieking cries that were not human. Dogs made sounds like that when two tons of automobile smashed their bodies and put them mercifully into shock.

As quickly and carefully as he could, Warfield approached the man lying flat on the ground. One leg was twisted and pinned under him, as if he had been blown backward by the impact of the bullets. The AR-15 was at his side but both hands were clasped to his belly, holding in the pain and the slivers of intestine that showed through the bottom of the shirt. He had been hit twice in the abdomen and once higher.

Esteben Molenaur was dying. He was the man who had appeared in the photograph taken on the beach. He was the hunter of his child and the hunter-killer of his wife. He was the cutout whose identity half the administration seemed bent on protecting at a cost that was ridiculous.

And then he was none of those things because he was as dead as the grass on which he lay in Warfield's backyard.

# Vulture

WARFIELD retrieved the van from down the road and with it he retrieved the four men. They were all dead. Tulio Villazon had been gone before he hit the ditch. The man posted in the garage had bled all over the spare refrigerator and the lawn mower. Warfield hosed down the garage, collected as many spent cartridges as he could find, and turned the sprinklers on the back lawn.

Five minutes later the Laurel police stopped by, but they were only making a courtesy call. Warfield told them that there had been shooting. A possum, he said, had been into his garbage every night for a month until this night when he walked into an ambush. It turned out that there had been a whole family involved in the nocturnal raids. Warfield did not know if he had gotten them all, but if there were any left, they were surely discouraged.

By the time he wound up his discussion of small-game shooting, noting his preferred weapon, the Remington .223 XP-100, and his favorite load, 26.0 grains of Hodgdon H335 with the fifty-two-grain Speer 1035 hollow points, the two young cops were thinking about nothing but turning their shift. Warfield never got to the part about how many times he and their chief had shot skeet at the Arundel Club together.

And he was glad when they turned around in his driveway and drove out Chantilly Road to the state highway instead of making the longer pass that would have brought them to the car parked down by the gate. After they were good and gone, Warfield went after the car, which was the Ford that Tulio Villazon had driven earlier in the day, and brought it back into his driveway. He pulled the four bodies out of the van, photographed them, and packed them logwise into the trunk and back seat of the Ford. Then he ran their images into the AUDRE system.

There were no surprises on Tulio Villazon, who died, as he had lived, sucking mud. And there was nothing at all on the man in the garage, who had very little face left to identify.

But the older man, the cigar-chewing sniper, had a history. His name was Raoul Llaneza. He was a Cuban, a veteran of the Bay of Pigs, who like many of the old *brigadistas* had never given up the active life. The FBI had a warrant outstanding on him for complicity in the bombing of a Cuban airliner in the mid-seventies; but of course if they had really wanted him they could have gone to his employers at Langley.

Warfield was not expecting much, if anything, to appear when he ran Esteben Molenaur's photograph. He had no criminal record and no criminal activities that would surface as a result of his association with Hatcher. A thorough photographic search had been done by headquarters staff with the picture taken on the beach. But since AUDRE was such a new system and its knowledge base was constantly expanding, Warfield tried one more time.

And scored. The man whose file matched the picture was named Omar Mahdrani. He was a Jordanian national living in England with a passport that showed recent and frequent trips between London, Washington, and Teheran. His pattern of movement had been flagged by Customs Service and referred to the State Department unit that had jurisdiction in counterterrorism. The feeling apparently had been that Mahdrani fit the profile of a potential hijacker. The information had hit Customs' computer almost three months ago but had not been linked to the AUDRE system until this week.

Warfield could not quite believe his luck, and he was not sure he could call it that because the file also displayed a recent charge for homosexual solicitation in Washington. Another inconsistency. The new input did serious damage to Molenaur's macho image and possibly to Bettina's self-esteem. Thinking that the data seemed more like confusion, Warfield ran the photograph through the machine again. He hoped for a more coherent result, but the response stayed the same. Esteben Molenaur had been reincarnated as a gay Omar Mahdrani.

Then Vulcan came through, rumbling and chattering like a good information-smith. More data on Omar Mahdrani—and very significant. Approximately nine months ago, NSA had been requested to provide intercepts on all communications that originated from Mahdrani's home and office. The request had come from CIA. No additional data was available through Vulcan.

Warfield was more than intrigued now. Information on Molenaur, probably on the order of half a ton, had been sitting at the Puzzle Palace all the time he had been busting his hump on this mission. And although the request from CIA for intercept was fairly routine, why would they be monitoring someone who was obviously one of their own? There was only one way to find out.

"I have you back on duty, Mariner," said Ellen Pena.

"This is priority, Banner. I need a look at the intercept file on a man named Omar Mahdrani."

"Stand by."

Warfield waited a tense four minutes until Ellen's voice returned. "Mariner, your request is denied. This file is Eyes Only DIRNSA and DAD."

"People are shooting at me, Banner."

She said, "Duck."

That was an answer. Warfield knew it was probably the best he was going to get. "Proceeding to duck," he said. "Meanwhile, I need to know who originated the request for intercept."

"CIA," she said.

"I know that, Banner. Give me a name."

She told him to stand by again. When Ellen's voice came back, it was cloaked like a Mexican bandit's. "Regarding your request for segmented information, be advised we have Subject Knowledge Intercept on Mahdrani as of December 2, 1985, instituted by Restricted Interdepartmental Group member Adam P. Merrycroft."

For several moments Warfield tottered on the verge of disbelief and revelation. Merrycroft. Adam "United Fruit" Merrycroft. He had been Bettina's CIA control in El Salvador. He had been station chief to Grady Souther's special envoy. And he had lifted Mahdrani-Molenaur's communications with the subject's foreknowledge, which meant that they were working together to intercept third parties.

"Banner, do we have dissemination on this intercept?"

"We have consumer copies to MT at CIA and SR at NSC."

The White House and Langley again. Souther and Merrycroft. The symmetry was perfect. Souther had been promoted back to Washington. Merrycroft had been demoted to the same place. Of course he should have been sacked or sent off to run ratlines in Togo; but this was CIA, where you could kill a man, chop him in pieces, and mail him to his wife, but you could not rescind his membership in the Yale Club.

Boola-boola. To the tables down at Clyde's. What was the idea of competence when measured against the possibility that a senior government official might lose his dinner partner? They would put Merrycroft at a desk for a while, until the stink blew off him, and then he would be back in business, assigned to this new RIG.

It had happened before. A younger Merrycroft had been one of those involved in the planning of JM/WAVE, the operation that came to be known as the Bay of Pigs. Nowadays it was fashionable to say that President Kennedy's refusal to provide full air support doomed the invasion. But what about those advisors, like Merrycroft, who assured Kennedy that once the landing was made the Cuban people would rise up and throw off their chains? In fact almost none of them had. They may not have loved Castro but they loved us considerably less. They liked us running their government and lives about as much as the Nicaraguans did.

It only made sense that Merrycroft would be leading the way this second time around. Removed from the war zone, given a new mission, he would recruit old *brigadistas* like Raoul Llaneza, and he would accept garbage like Tulio Villazon, whose father had been at *Bahia de Cochinos.* Probably the man with no face was a Cuban too, an alumnus. CIA was using them all over Latin America because they were Spanish-speaking and committed. They did things that men like Merrycroft wanted done but could not order. In El Salvador they liased with the death squads. In Honduras they translated assassination manuals. In southern Nicaragua they conducted the campaign that destroyed Eden Pastora, the FSLN renegade who was the only viable Contra leader.

But a man did not invite them home to dinner. They smoked big foul cigars and spat on the floor and were apt to tell stories like the one about the fellow they strung up to the rafters in the barn, and how they tied the bucket to his testicles, and how every couple of minutes they added another good-sized stone to the bucket, and after six or eight hours, you just would not believe the things that *maricone communista* started to say.

. That favored method of interrogation made Warfield think of Roderigo Diaz, the boy-guerrilla who had recanted his testimony and shamed them all. They must have tied a washtub to his balls and let Merrycroft sit in it. Diaz had paid the price. Bettina and Section Turnkey had. Only Merrycroft had not.

Warfield should have seen through this business long ago, but he had not because every time he thought of it he saw those filthy pictures of Bettina and Diaz. He hated the sight so much that he could not think. He had never asked himself *why* the pictures were made. They could never have been used against Diaz because he would not have cared if they showed him naked and bucking with Joan of Arc. No, the pictures could only be used against Bettina, Warfield, and NSA.

"Banner, do we have backup numbers and addresses for priority dissemination to MT and SR?"

"Affirmative, Mariner. Stand by."

While Warfield waited, he called up through Vulcan all the information in the data base on the press conference of Roderigo Diaz. That boy had said a lot. No one had really been listening, least of all Warfield. He had never thought what Diaz had to say was important, or the truth. The boy had raved about the Marxist millenium and the diabolism of

CIA until even the leftist press became bored. But Diaz had said some very interesting things. Before being taken away, he had given every detail of his fall.

Warfield read and reread the various eye-witness accounts of the session until he had absorbed, arranged, and analyzed every component, until he found the possibilities he wanted and fit them part by part into a coherent system. When he was finished, he drove to the house of a friend in Rockville, where he stayed just long enough to put some unstoppable gears in place; then he wheeled back onto the beltway and down into the city with the first address that had been relayed by the watch.

While he was still in transit on the Cabin John, Warfield heard a broadcast come through the radio in the Ford: *Zopilote* Leader to *Zopilote* Zulu. No one answered the net call because the network no longer existed. They were dead weight putting an incredible drag on the car's six-cylinder engine. But it was useful to know that Vulture Leader was still up at this hour, and worried, trying to raise the team. Warfield knew it was Merrycroft when he pulled to the curb across the street from the house in Georgetown and a second, more frantic call nearly knocked him out of the front seat with its close powerful transmitter.

Warfield snapped off the receiver before it woke the neighborhood. The street was a quiet cozy one lit by gas lamps that spread archaic light over cobblestone sidewalks and brick houses. The buildings were all 2.5 stories high, windows ornamentally shuttered, doors brightly enamelled. James Monroe might have walked the neighborhood of an evening, composing his Doctrine for the ages.

Warfield left the car and crossed directly to the house. There was a wrought-iron fence and a walkway of cobblestone that led through an unlocked gate into a garden in the back. A walled garden. Warfield appreciated its charm almost as much as he liked the privacy. Working with a glass cutter and suction cup, he had the kitchen door open in forty-five seconds.

It was a bachelor's kitchen with a blender to shave ice for drinks and a coffee grinder to provide the fixings to sober up. The kitchen smelled like coffee and the front drawing room like rum. Merrycroft was in neither. His spirit, such as it was, held forth in the furnishings and bric-a-brac as old as the house itself. Unlike Eglon's antiques, these were inherited. There had been Merrycrofts in Georgetown when it was a nasty tobacco port on the Potomac. If Warfield had anything to say about it, the line was at its end.

He was about to move up the long staircase that led off the foyer—not a passage he liked—when the sound of footsteps descending changed his mind. The tread was distant, indicating that the man was coming down from that short third floor. No doubt the radio was up there. Warfield waited at the bottom of the staircase until the footsteps sounded directly above his head and began to come down the last flight.

Adam Merrycroft's tread was tired. He hesitated on the last steps and then came directly into the room, head bowed, unaware of anything but his private thoughts. Warfield wanted to get inside that twisted head, because it guarded almost everything he wanted confirmed. It was a strange head, as odd in the interior as on the face. Merrycroft had the hair and complexion that people called Black Irish, he had a nose that the world likes to think of as Polish, and a jaw so weak and overshot that no self-respecting nationality would claim it. He was about fifty-five, and he seemed both youthful and aged, as if he could not decide which way to go. Not until he looked up at Warfield after almost tramping on his shoes did the decision seem plain.

"Good evening, Vulture."

He said, "What? Who are you?" But he knew before he spoke. Merrycroft had known for some time that his operation had gone wrong, and he should have been alert to danger. That he was not said about all that needed to be known. He was typical CIA, imagining that no one would ever call him to account. Merrycroft was a high-level bureaucrat at one government agency as his brother and brother-in-law were at others. None were culpable. What need would such an obscure, scholarly man have for security?

But Vulture had a bit of a need. Warfield threw him against the bannister and shook him down to the ankles, where he found a neat palm-sized .45. Roland Gasqué's weapon of choice. Warfield took it and spun Merrycroft onto his flowery little couch. He tossed him a set of handcuffs. Merrycroft cranked them on as if he knew how.

"Feel safe now, Mariner?"

"I just want you to get used to them," he said. "You still have your fingers free. Use them to dial Grady Souther. Get him here."

Merrycroft pushed a length of bone into his jaw with an effort that must have cost some physical strain. "Do you really think I can do that?"

"He'll come," said Warfield. "Tell him your life depends on it. And hurry up. We have a lot of things to talk about."

Merrycroft made the call. He did it after Warfield told him the location of his team and how they were disposed. Merrycroft seemed to take the news more personally than seemed to be proper. The left side of his face luffed like a sail set too close to the wind, and he looked away toward the antique model train on his reeded mantel as if he were gazing on a lost adventurous youth. All his Cubans gone, and no hope of sending a man down to Havana to buy them back with medical supplies. His brigade was no more. That it had never been worth a damn was something he could not admit. No one ever had.

But he pulled himself together and got "G.S." out of bed and told him enough to get him moving but not enough to aggravate Warfield. Merrycroft knew the situation was very serious and he knew why. He had not survived to be a middle-aged civil servant by saying things that would threaten his life. But there was no telling how many men that prim mouth had put to death with its coffee and rum.

"Grady won't be arriving for a while," he said with the high sauntering voice that was one reason why the intelligence community knew him as United Fruit. "His farm is halfway to Leesburg."

"That's all right. We're not going anywhere."

Merrycroft yawned, bringing the backs of both hands up awkwardly before his face. "But I'm so tired," he said. "Too tired to care."

"Is this the part where you tell me that I'd better go ahead and shoot you?"

"It should be."

He was getting bolder already. The comment held a sardonic bite that was meant to rearrange the relationship a bit. Warfield decided it was time to put it back on keel.

"Roderigo Diaz said it in front of a few billion people, including you, and he meant it. He said a lot of things that should have been listened to. I finally did."

"Bravo, Mariner."

"The most interesting thing he said was that his unit never had a penny that didn't come from you." Warfield watched Merrycroft's face, but there was no luff this time; just a little ripple in the eyes. "He said the money came from CIA, but he meant you, Vulture. You were CIA in El Salvador. You and your Cubans."

He smiled with that mouth as slit as Heinrich Müller's. "If you're asking questions, perhaps you'd like to know that the Company had no assets in El Salvador until I arrived. *Nothing.* The station had been shut down in the mid-seventies as an economy measure."

"I'm not asking questions," said Warfield. "I know what happened to Bettina. I should have known a long time ago, because the fact is that you couldn't infiltrate a Marxist cell in El Salvador if you had assets on every streetcorner and Miguel Mármol in your pocket. But your career was on the line—a lot of pressure coming from Washington—and you had to produce something. So you rigged a cell. You did what CIA always does—you went out and bought what you needed. They had to be authentic revolutionaries, though. Real live Reds. Real terrorist activities. They must have taken you for plenty. You probably financed half a real revolution setting up a phony one."

Merrycroft was listening closely; he might have been editing. "Would you have me deny the first part?" he said. "Or the last?"

"Try denying that all you needed to complete the setup was an innocent," said Warfield. "You couldn't use your own people. You needed someone from outside—someone with credibility. That was Bettina. She probably pegged you for a fool from the beginning, but she took her work very seriously. She went into the cell and didn't come out because she knew it was too dangerous to keep a man like you informed. When she finally did tell you what was going on, it scared the hell out of you. The cell was doing very well with your money. Bettina told you exactly how successful they were. She told you the cell should be closed out, because it was too effective.

"You didn't have any objection to that of course, as long as you got what you wanted. You told her to go back in and target one man. Establish a relationship—as binding as possible. She had a month to accomplish that, which was plenty of time, given her talents. Once the proper level of emotional attachment had been formed, she would notify you and the cell would be destroyed. All but one man. His name could have been anything but it happened to be Roderigo Diaz."

Warfield cleared a little space in time for Merrycroft to react, but the tall man with the face and body of an extinct bird did not. He seemed as immune to Warfield's cutting delivery as he was to any kind of truth. That was his strength. It was the one thing he shared with every competent man in his trade.

"Diaz got the full course. The Treasury Police worked him over in the places where it didn't show, and when he was softened up they brought in his woman and explained in detail the things that would happen to her if he chose not to cooperate. Roderigo had a thing for Bettina. He had no idea that God hadn't sent her to him. So he said yes. He said hell yes, if only they'd let the woman alone. And of course they went him one better. They told him if he memorized the script, they'd give him the woman *back*.

"And when he did, they did. The police stopped beating on him, and they took him to a nice house and gave him the woman and he gave them the words: Syria, Lybia, Cuba, Nicaragua. They were easy to remember. When Diaz was ready for prime time, you showed up and told him how it would be—the States, the press conferences, *Nightline, Today.* Roderigo Diaz would be a first-class propaganda weapon directed toward the only audience that mattered—the American public. The woman would be the guarantee of his good performance.

"But when you sent him north, you took the ground out from under him. He knew that he couldn't fly through the air without one of your planes to carry him, and he knew he couldn't walk away from the urinal without one of your men shaking him down. It was going to be like that forever. For as long as he lived. And he probably figured out how long that would be—until he wasn't useful any more. So he chose the spot where he wanted to die—in front of the biggest audience that any unsuccessful guerrilla ever had. Diaz was a brave boy. If things go the wrong way down there—and they probably will with people like you on the job—Roderigo's going to have a statue in the *Plaza Barrios* some day."

Merrycroft had listened with an affected boredom that could not entirely mask the insult to what he would call his pride. He began to say something with a thread of emotion in it, but suddenly checked himself when the left side of his face began to twitch again with a loss of motor control. Merrycroft fought against the tic, mastered it, and spoke in a very dry tone.

"That's an interesting theory, Mariner."

"It's not a theory," said Warfield. "It's a choice between believing you or Diaz. And that's no contest, Vulture."

# The Black Chamber

THERE were many paintings on Merrycroft's walls, and one of them was done in the manner of Degas, depicting a ballerina at rest, her legs apart, her leotards turned down to her calves, her most private parts exposed and exaggerated. The statement was more lewd than erotic. It told Warfield something about the man who would buy it and hang it next to the very traditional and chaste portrait of a woman who was probably his mother.

"When did you decide to make those pictures of Bettina and Diaz? That was the smartest thing you've done in your life, so I can't believe you planned it. I think there was another reason. You wanted to look at her—at them. I'll bet if I went through this house, I'd find a whole trunk full of things like that."

To prove that he was unflappable, Merrycroft crossed one leg over the other and looped his fettered hands across his bony knees. "You're too crude, Mariner. Furthermore, you have no imagination."

"We all have glands, Vulture. You have a way of honoring

yours that's a little more peculiar than most. There's a supermarket of smut on every third corner in this town, but that doesn't do the job. The whole psychological element is missing when you can buy it off the shelf. It's too easy, too accessible. And not nearly dirty enough. It only gets that way when you know the people involved, and you know they're working out something a whole lot more complicated than sex. They're working it out for you in a private place where love and politics and death are all mingled. That's the real black chamber. That's your damned filthy mind."

"So you understand the dynamic," he said with irony that turned back on itself all the way to candor. "I'm surprised."

"Don't be too quick at that," said Warfield. "Because I also understand that compromising photographs always have another use—blackmail. You knew that Bettina might tumble to the truth about your setup, so you took out insurance with the pictures. You arranged it so that Diaz would seem like her protégé from the beginning. If anything went wrong, she'd end up looking like a traitor. On the other hand, you'd look like nothing but what you are—an incompetent. To someone with good connections, that's pretty much like saying he's a gentleman. Being successful means you're too serious about your work."

"You should ask Allendé about that," said Merrycroft blithely. "Chile was a very serious business. Fatal to many, including the great red leader."

"You weren't giving the orders there, Vulture. That's the difference."

"No," he said quickly, seriously. "The difference was that *we* controlled the operation. Everything was back-channel through the Company. Not even our embassy knew. That's why it worked—perfect security, perfect execution."

"Or greater incompetence on the other side."

"I wish you'd stop using that word," he said in his largest, laziest voice. "You're bitter. That's understandable. You had a good thing going with Turnkey. But surely you realize that it was never intended to be anything more than a stopgap. Turnkey was redundant for at least two years before the bell tolled."

"We survived because we were efficient," said Warfield. "That's one test CIA never had to pass. All you people were ever good at was buying stooges and smearing the stooge's enemies. You smeared us with one set of dirty pictures. The only thing that surprises me is that you didn't get rid of Bettina when you had the chance. But you probably figured you owned her by then."

It was Merrycroft's turn to touch on what he knew was a very dangerous subject. Remaining silent was an option, but not a good one. When he spoke, his voice was very flat and careful. "She's a persuasive young woman," he said. "Very persuasive."

"You mean she offered you something more tempting than herself," said Warfield without emotion. "I wondered how she managed to disappear completely. But there are a lot of places to hide when the people who are supposed to be looking for you aren't looking at all. Bettina showed up one day with this good-looking guy at her elbow. Arms dealer, very anti-Red, knows all about washing money and smuggling into Central America. You know that you can use the education and the training. You've been looking for someone like Molenaur for six months *before* Congress cuts off military aid to the Contras." Warfield waited for Merrycroft to respond but got back nothing. "How am I doing, Vulture?"

"Your point of view is skewed," he said. "You seem to forget that the mission of the intelligence services is to protect the interest of this nation. The officer who doesn't understand that is brain dead."

"I understand that you've been doing everything you can to stretch the law to fit your conception of the public interest," said Warfield. "The current law, that is. And now another vote is coming up on restoring aid, and it looks like you can win. There's probably only one thing that can stop the momentum—a scandal. Bettina provides the potential for that when she leaves her husband. It seems she forgot to tell you one little thing about Molenaur: that his father is Heinrich Müller."

In fact Warfield did not know if Müller was alive in Colombia, dead in Berlin, or burning in hell, but the mention of that name had shaken Merrycroft. His skull seemed to recede, leaving wattles of slack skin. The weak jaw that held the folds of heavy skin drooped like the gullet of every flesh-eating bird.

"Suddenly, the blackmailed becomes the blackmailer," said Warfield. "She's set you up perfectly. She turns your own weapon back onto you. It's one thing to have the Sandinistas calling us Nazis, but everyone knows that's just a *word*. You're the man who makes it *real*. You've got to be the damned biggest fool in the history of your damned foolish agency—and you know it. You're worried, of course, but you don't absolutely panic until you find out that Bettina's headed for home. That's when all the long knives come out, isn't it, Vulture?"

Merrycroft shrugged but did not protest the reading because no other was really possible.

"Bettina leaves Nicaragua," said Warfield. "Suddenly the threat is very real. You try to cover every avenue of approach she might take—me, Eglon, the Interfaith Coalition. You might have done all right too, except for those Cubans. They think they're still on the beach. They're still waiting for that universal uprising and the air support—and they're being led by a man who's personally involved in the outcome of the mission. Molenaur stops being a conduit and becomes a father. He wants to save his son and murder his wife. It isn't very long before other people who stand in his way are being killed. Everything's out of control. The only way to bring it back in hand is to kill more people. At least that was the only solution you could find. You and Grady."

Warfield mentioned that name because he heard the car in the street outside the house. He had not heard it running but he heard the absence of noise when it shut down. The door clicked closed like a purse—an expensive car. The footsteps they heard belonged to a heavy man sure of his destination in the night. He took the first three steps up onto the terrace. Warfield waited for him to take the next two of four up to the front door before opening it.

The chesty man standing in the spill of yellow light on the steps was the administration's chief foreign policy advisor, and he could have been more: Grady Souther could have been president in the face. His thick blond hair had whitened at the temples and his jowls had expanded, but basically he was the same man who had devoted his life to the service of what was once called the radical right. His nose was slightly pugged, his forehead strong, his jaw prowlike and combative. The teeth, the eyes, and the complexion were all a shade brighter than his age should have allowed.

"Come in, sir."

Souther's hand had been raised to the level of his cheek in order to knock; he used it now to point at Warfield. "The only place I'll go with you, son, is after Kodiak bear."

Warfield stepped aside and held the door open for Souther. "You'll want to join this discussion," he said. "Adam and I were just talking about Omar Mahdrani—or Esteben Molenaur—whichever you prefer."

The mention of those names was magical. Souther

dropped his hand as if it were useless weight. He took the last step and a half and sidled through the doorway without turning his back to Warfield. Seeing Merrycroft in handcuffs on the couch, he balked too late. The door had shut behind him and Warfield showed him the little .45.

"Who are you?"

"I'm called Mariner, and I'm with NSA."

He said, "No Such Agency," and laughed for effect. "You're going to get your budget cut for this."

"That's been done already," said Warfield. "Now go over there and sit down with Adam."

He did that with comfortable reluctance, knowing his way around the house but not the situation. He sat, patted Merrycroft on the knee, and turned his distinguished media face toward Warfield.

"Okay, *compadre.* Shoot."

Warfield would have liked that. People as dumb as Grady Souther in positions of power should have prices on their heads. The ancient Carthaginians crucified blundering leaders, but this democracy had no such useful devices.

"I'd advise you to treat this matter as if your life was at stake," said Warfield. "It is. General Hatcher realized that right away."

Souther knew now who his antagonist was, but he adjusted his attitude by degrees. "Andrew Hatcher is a very good man," he said. "A patriot. A hero. If I was on a conventional battlefield, I'd want him driving my spearhead right up the enemy's gut. But he doesn't understand guerrilla warfare. He didn't understand it in Vietnam and he doesn't understand it in Washington. He does not know that if you don't give a damn for your dignity, you can't lose a fight in this town. Frankly, Mr. Warfield, I don't think you understand that either."

"I understand it," said Warfield. "But you're an amateur at

the game. You don't even have the sense to cover your tracks when dealing with maniacs like Roland Gasqué."

Souther was not phased by the introduction of that name. "Question is: Do I know that man?"

"You seem to know every foul ball and mercenary in the Western Hemisphere," said Warfield. "You know the players, but not their capabilities. You sent Gasqué and Dupard after me. They're dead. You sent the Vulture team after me. They're dead. You've run out of killers."

Souther looked at Merrycroft for confirmation. He got back a very short nod that seemed to induce a new sobriety. The handsome head moved itself to a new camera angle, a practised one that gave him more jaw than five Merrycrofts and more authority than a monument.

"If you're talking about resources, be assured this government has them."

"But you can't touch most of them," said Warfield. "Or you would have from the beginning. You two are way off the reservation. Everything you've done has been outside channels. Everyone you've used has been a free-lance deniable. It's because what you're doing is against the law—and you know it. Even so, you left a trail. You didn't recognize the first basic principle of espionage. Adam here forgot it. You never learned it."

"You're going to tell me what that is," said Souther viciously.

"Three words." Warfield held up fingers. "*Nothing is secure.* I know all about Molenaur. I know that he was also called Omar Mahdrani. I know what he did for you. And I know how to tie him hand and foot to you because I know about that secret Beta account."

Warfield had been expecting a significant reaction to his words, but what went on in Souther's mind as it translated to his face was a metamorphosis of huge proportions. The planes of the monument all but lost internal support. His mouth opened and his tongue filled that natural gap as if it were blown loose. He seemed to speak from reflex.

"You can't know," he said. "You can't know *that*."

"Three hundred eighty-six forty-one SR."

Souther looked with the same blasted expression to Merrycroft, because when things like this had happened to him before, he had always had CIA personnel to consult. But his helpmeet gave no succor. Merrycroft looked at virtually the only bare patch of plaster on his crowded walls.

With all room for maneuvering gone, with his mind reduced to a blankness deeper than usual, Souther addressed Warfield with a plea that quavered with emotion. "I don't suppose it would do any good to tell you that you have no idea what's at stake here," he said. "Absolutely none."

"If you want to explain yourself, Grady, I'll listen."

Souther wanted to do all things but that. He started to speak, but the divide between the truth and expedience was too large. "No," he said. "I can't do that."

"Then listen to me," said Warfield. "You have until ten o'clock this morning to submit your resignation from this government. That goes for both of you. Six hours. If I don't have those documents in hand by that time, I'll release all the information I have to the Senate Foreign Relations Committee—and the press."

Warfield was sure he had the perfect box for Souther and Merrycroft, but two seconds after he left the house doubt set in like the false light of dawn from the east. The Ford with the bodies in it was gone from its parking place across the street. And a big sedan was moving down the street toward him.

He had tired legs, Merrycroft's .45, and a moment to decide. Fatigue almost rushed him up the cobblestones to the next clump of antique houses and an alleyway that he hoped led to the adjacent street. Anger almost drove him to draw down on that pale gray sedan. Familiarity finally caused him to hold his ground. Warfield recognized the car. Though it had no vanity plate or bunting, the big sedan was the one that had been assigned, perpetual and new, to the deputy assistant director of NSA, Jack Brindisi.

The car stopped in the street alongside Warfield. One of the smoked black windows rolled down and a voice that was cavernous but clear emerged from the depths. "Get in, Stephen."

Warfield hesitated. He saw an outrider come into the street from the left in an older black sedan. He heard a car start up to the right. Those were the several facets of Jack's invitation. There might be more. Warfield finally moved to the car because he thought it was safer inside than out.

Jack sat in the back seat alone, looking alert and hard-eyed. He was dressed, as always, for Gorbachev's funeral—dark suit, pewter tie, black shoes and socks. Warfield slipped onto the seat beside him, wondering not how he had come to be in the street—anyone with access to the watch and half a mind could have known that—but how long he had been there. For sure they were not hanging around. The driver, wide Matt Anders, sped the car out of the street quickly.

"How did you know I hadn't gone to Souther's place instead?"

"You're a professional, Stephen. I guessed that you'd neutralize your opposite number first. When I saw Grady's car in the street, I knew I'd guessed correctly."

"What else did you guess?"

"That you'd leave them alive," he said.

"Why would I do that?"

"Because you're a hunter," he said. "You wouldn't kill unless you needed the meat."

"I was hungry, Jack. But they promised they'd be good."

"Good, I think, is a relative term."

"You're right," said Warfield. "I told them I'd sink the Contra vote unless they resigned their positions. Now I'm telling you in case you think it can be stopped. I've got automatic triggers in place that will activate unless *I* take them out."

Jack's voice remained at the same toneless level of inquiry, but his delivery lacked confidence. "The press?"

"Foreign and domestic."

Jack looked out the side window at the streets of the old town that had been named not for our first president but for one of our first kings. The yearning for the old summary powers was strong in the Federal City, and strongest here at the core. The empire needed bread, circuses, and gladiators who would fall on their swords at the command. What it got instead was snake oil, mercenaries who could not shoot straight, and the press. Threatening NSA with public disclosure was like threatening God with His image. Jack was looking for a firing squad in those quaint streets, but he saw only the specter of the six o'clock news.

"I understand your anger, Stephen. You think I withheld information that could have helped you. But believe me, I knew nothing about Molenaur. I had no idea he was the man called Mahdrani who we were monitoring. In any case, the product we were receiving from him dried up about two weeks ago. I didn't connect the shortfall with Bettina's reappearance, because I had no reason to make the connection." Jack turned to Warfield again. "You should also understand that if I had known, I would never have permitted this investigation to begin."

"Nice people you'd protect," said Warfield. "Calling them the scum of the earth would be doing plain dirt a disservice. The higher it goes, the uglier it gets."

"That's irrelevant," he said with strange conviction.

"Tell me what that means."

Because the DAD disliked incoherence, even his own, he paused to reformulate his thoughts. "It means that there's another level to this matter you know nothing about. I talked to Mike Koricke, and he told me about the Beta account in Molenaur's name. You've been operating on the assumption that the money was diverted from Hatcher's operation to the Contras and augmented along the way."

"I know it, Jack. Not even Grady Souther is stupid enough to run clean money through a laundry."

"Oh, the money is dirty all right. There's never been dirtier money on the face of this earth than the funds in that account."

Souther and Merrycroft had said, without saying, nearly the same thing. Warfield was beginning to wonder if he really wanted to know what was behind the last door. But finally he did, because Bettina was behind it too.

"You're going to have to tell me, Jack."

"What will that buy?"

"Consideration."

That was not enough but it was vague, and Jack was incapable of sustained haggling with subordinates. He took a moment to weigh the weak offer and another to gauge whatever trust had survived the years. Then he spoke calmly and precisely.

"Nine months ago I was requested to provide intercept on a group of men," he said. "Mahdrani was one of them. He was aware of the surveillance, which overlapped among the others. They were mostly arms dealers who were facilitating the transfer of sophisticated weapons overseas—primarily antitank and antiaircraft missiles—in exchange for payment into a Swiss account. Those monies were transferred to a bank in the Cayman Islands, chiefly through Mahdrani, and finally to the Contras. The operation was very sensitive. It was conducted through NSC with CIA support, as you know."

Jack stopped talking at that peculiar place, and Warfield could not understand why. Selling weapons to raise money for the Contras was illegal; but so was nearly every other method that passed through channels. There was still something the DAD would not let out.

"What the hell, Jack, are they selling them to the Russians?"

"Worse," he said.

The DAD had no sense of humor. None. He watched the faces of others to cue in his own laughter. He had never made a witting joke that Warfield had ever heard. His face right now was grim.

"Who's buying the hardware, Jack?"

He said, "The Iranians."

As the big sedan slid quietly, pneumatically, onto Pennsylvania Avenue at M, Warfield felt the helm slipping. He felt that he might be insane. He might be dreaming, but his dreams were more rational than this. Even his nightmares of Kabkan, which always included the face of that young Iranian airman and the muzzle of the M-16 adhesive-taped to the base of John Slaughter's skull, carried more reasonable content.

"Jack, you can do better. That's the craziest thing I've ever heard."

"I am completely serious," he said. "They're selling weapons to the fundamentalist government in exchange for money and the promise of help in freeing some of our hostages in Lebanon."

"What influence do the Iranians have in Lebanon?"

"Quite a lot," said Jack. "Apparently it's the pro-Iranian groups that are holding most of the hostages."

They had taken hostages at Kabkan, the station that was also known as Trackman II. It was the most vital listening post on the Russians that we had, and NSA personnel had remained on station in spite of Khoumeni's coup and common sense until the Iranian airmen there mutinied. When John Slaughter went in to negotiate for the release of the technicians, they had taken him hostage too. Warfield might have been next, but when he saw that rifle taped to Slaughter's skull, he also saw that the safety was on, and he had killed the dim-witted kid who was holding it with one perfectly pronated blow, gotten Slaughter out, and sent back the message that these people could only be dealt with in force.

But the embassy, after consultation, said no. Eventually they ponied up two hundred thousand dollars a head to every bloody kidnapper at Kabkan for the release of NSA's people. Eight months later, the same embassy staff was being held hostage by even more senseless fanatics. The American public had been treated to a spectacle of humiliation that had lasted longer than some wars. And they had never really known why.

"Doesn't the administration realize what's going to happen?" said Warfield. "Kabkan led to the taking of the embassy. The Iranians will have the hostages released—and then they'll take more. And more. Who in hell is making decisions like this?"

Jack's voice was low, a whispery tiredness that was as close to pain as it was to exhaustion. "I think perhaps it's Grady."

*"What?"*

"So you see the difficulties," he said with unconcealed scorn. "Grady has help of course. CIA is providing counsel and back-channel liaison. One of the hostages is their station chief in Beirut. They want him out at any cost."

Warfield saw more than difficulties. He saw undisguised

catastrophe for himself, NSA, and the country. This latest cycle of blackmail would do more than embarrass an administration: it would destroy every vestige of sane foreign policy. And then Warfield saw something else.

"Grady can't be making decisions like this himself. Someone higher up has to have approved."

Jack said, "Yes."

Yes? Warfield stared straight ahead down Pennsylvania Avenue. Real dawn was beginning to break but it was hard to tell through the thick smoked glass that surrounded them on every side and even to the front. The world was darker than it should have been.

"No one's really in charge. Is that what you're trying to tell me, Jack?"

"I didn't say that exactly."

"You never say anything exactly. Try."

Jack phrased his answer with great deliberation and frightening care. "He can still be talked to. His concentration is not good, but his mind is reasonably clear. I can reach him."

Warfield sat waiting for more words until he realized there would be none. "Good God."

"We are truly in His hands," said the DAD. "And in yours."

The big gray sedan pulled up to the curb in front of the guardhouse that stood before the white Irish Palladian mansion at 1600 Pennsylvania Avenue. Jack rapped three times on the thick window that separated the front seat from the back. Anders turned and nodded. He hit parade rest behind the wheel but did not shut down the engine.

"What do you want from me, Jack?"

"You mustn't release your information," he said. "I think you can see that clearly. The entire government would be paralyzed. We can't allow that to happen for the fourth time in less than twenty years."

"I should have killed them," said Warfield. "No wonder you were just sitting out there in the street. You were hoping I would."

"It might have been better," said the DAD. "Cleaner."

Was that what they had learned in the years since Vietnam: that some things were dirtier than death? Warfield had no answer, but he was making a list. At the head were conspicuous consumption, mercenary armies, and dealing with any kind of blackmailers.

"It's going to come out, Jack. You can't keep something like that a secret forever."

"I know," said the DAD. "But it must not come from us. I can promise that you and Bettina will be safe. I can also promise that Grady's days are numbered. Give me six weeks."

"Long enough to make sure the Contra vote passes."

"Yes," he said. "That's our leverage."

Warfield could see that it was and that it had always been. He could also see that few worse bargains were ever struck between two men who called themselves honest. Warfield nodded. He did it without thinking.

The DAD breathed relief that should have clouded the translucent windows of the sedan to the point of sightlessness. "I've accepted your resignation of course," he said. "But you'll find six months severance pay in your bank account. I was thinking you might want to visit South America. We'll talk when you get back."

Warfield could not believe it. He had just been told to go and find Heinrich Müller and not to return until he did. The worst part was that he knew he would go.

"That would be one hell of a diversion, Jack. That might get us Turnkey back."

"More, I think."

He was probably right. When it came to bureaucratic Indian poker, Jack could bluff and call with the best. The restoration of his tactical unit would be like giving him back the three balls he had been born with.

"You want Müller alive, I suppose."

"Alive but comatose would be ideal."

"All right," said Warfield. "I'll think about it."

The DAD smiled because he had won. He tapped the glass between the seats twice and the thick window rolled down. "I'll be going inside for a while," he told Anders. "Please drive Mr. Warfield to twenty-eight twenty-nine Sixteenth Street. He has a date with a young lady."

# Stephen

THE address that Jack had given led to the front entrance of the Mexican embassy. The building of buff-colored stone was done in the English Palladian style. It had been commissioned in the days before taxes and ruinous heating bills, by the wife of a treasury secretary who had given it to her husband for Christmas, 1911. Much grander than its neighborhood, the security was therefore professional and thorough even at such an early hour. Warfield entered the building unarmed.

A guard took Warfield's name and escorted him into the main anteroom. With incredible dignity he bore himself to the upper floors by way of a staircase dominated by a del Rio mural three stories high. The anteroom itself was impressive, with high decorative ceilings and a fireplace that was no less than baronial. The woodwork seemed gilded in gold, the walls painted green and gold, papered between the wainscotting by gold and white floral patterns. It looked more French than Mexican, more Old World than New.

Like Bettina.

He had no idea how he was going to react but as she came

down the sweeping staircase in a cheap housecoat flung over a bedsheet nightgown all he could think was that he wanted to buy her better. He wanted to do everything of no consequence, which was everything that she despised, because what she looked good in was anything. Warfield felt awkward, unsure. He knew he was unwashed. She stepped off the staircase onto the large golden rug, and the knowledge that they shared the same plane in space drove him to her so hard and completely that he had no comprehension of the passage. He had his face in her hair and his hands on her body. They were burrowing and murmuring and fitting in every forgotten place. Years flew away into the vaulted ceilings. It was impossible that he would ever let her go.

"How long can you stay?"

It had taken her forty-five minutes to ask that question, which was eight hours less than it would have taken any other woman. Warfield did not like the new short haircut that fell across her brow in a limp clump but he was getting used to it. The missing mole at the corner of her mouth made him feel absent-minded. He kept wanting to reach into his back pocket; he didn't know why.

"For a while," he said. "I promised Jack I'd stay out of his way—which means out of the country as soon as possible."

She tossed her head once—her gesture of acceptance—and the forelock bobbed likeably on her brow. "He's changed," she said. "We only spoke for a minute, but I was surprised by his attitude. He was . . . considerate. Almost charming."

"He's scared to death."

"I didn't think that was possible," she said with a smile. "He runs this country, doesn't he?"

"We'd be better off if he did," said Warfield. "We've got some people with their fingers on the buttons who are very scary. Your friend Merrycroft is right up where the air is thin. It's made him completely crazy."

"He's a truly evil man, Stephen. He's more evil because he appears to be harmless."

She seemed to have said what she wanted, but Warfield needed to hear the rest, the unsaid that had put the little, almost invisible tracks of sadness into her face. He might have been imagining that; it might have been the way the morning sun fell through the tall windows behind them, spreading a faint brocade of light and shadow.

"Is that what you thought when you went down there—that he was harmless?"

"No," she said. "But I thought we were all on the same side. I wasn't naive about anything but that. I had good background on the politics and history. I knew about the repression and the death squads and the fact that fourteen families own every acre of good land in the country and that what we were doing was making it safe for them to exploit their own people again. I was prepared for all of it, and I did my job. I didn't see the bodies in the ditches and I didn't hear the screams at night because I knew I was getting *out* of there. I was some kind of supertourist. I had a ticket home."

"A lot of people felt that way in Vietnam," said Warfield. "It's okay unless it kills you."

"I sometimes think it did," she said. "I would have done *anything* to get out of there. I did *everything* that Merrycroft asked, even though I knew his methods were slipshod and unprofessional. The first time we met for briefing he took me to the Café Benito at the Presidente. I couldn't believe it. Here we were sitting in the most conspicuous place in the capital. Later I learned that he went there every day to play squash. The morning round-robin. I was his second appointment. The first was a young woman who came to plead for her brother's life—and he hit on her too."

Warfield was not going to ask if Merrycroft's overtures succeeded with either woman. He was afraid that the answer might drive him back to that house in Georgetown and plain, if justified, murder.

"Why didn't you come back, Bettina? You could have worked things out."

"I thought that's what I was doing," she said. "I knew I couldn't face you, or Jack, or any of the others. I'd lost my ticket home. When you start to think like that, your mentality changes. You'll do anything just to have revenge."

"I'd say you got it," said Warfield. "You set Merrycroft up with the sweetest double cross I've ever seen."

Although he had paid her a genuine compliment, Bettina shook her head fiercely, as if she were angry. Her voice was near to anger. "I meant it to be," she said. "My only regret is that so many people—some of them innocent—had to die."

"That's always the risk," said Warfield. "You had to know that from the minute you left Molenaur. Why did you wait so long to do it? Why did you leave him when you did?"

"I had no choice," she said with a very strong sense of resignation. "About nine months ago, I was cut out. Esteben began traveling overseas using a new passport. Suddenly, he wasn't telling me anything. Neither was Adam. I became paranoid very quickly. If there was something they didn't want me to know, it meant that I was untrustworthy. We were living in Baranquilla in a very spooky house with a lot of very spooky Colombians around. I knew I was being watched by the household staff and by two men whenever I left the house. So I ran."

Warfield did not want to tell Bettina why she had been cut out. He was happy to know that she did not understand the importance of that move. She had misread it, perhaps for the best.

"Is that when you went over to the Nicaraguans?"

"*Went over?*" Bettina scoffed and shook her head but did not laugh. "I'm sorry, Stephen, but you just don't know how absurd that sounds. It's true that I was debriefed by Nicaraguan intelligence when I came to Managua. In fact I volunteered to talk to them so they'd let me stay in-country. There were two men—one Cuban—both younger than us. I didn't understand for a while that I was talking to the stars of their Foreign Intelligence Section. They were the ones responsible for devising a strategy to deal with the U.S. And do you know how they did it? They read an article in *Covert Action* by Phil Agee. He predicted how CIA would go about trying to subvert their revolution. Step by step. So these two men received medals for knowing how to read English, because they haven't been wrong yet. CIA never varies its pattern. What worked in Iran to put the Shah in power, and in Guatemala to get rid of Arbenz, must be infallible, even if it failed in a hundred other places. They never learn a thing."

"I'll go along with that," he said. "Even Sister George is smarter than CIA."

"And much sweeter."

"I never saw that side of the lady."

"She was very good to me," said Bettina with a humility that was almost disturbing. "She made the time I spent in Nicaragua worthwhile."

"And you were going to pay her back by springing the information on Molenaur's father at the right time."

She shrugged. "That was the plan."

"It would have worked," said Warfield. "But they knew you were coming."

"Yes," she said tersely. "I don't know how."

"Try Eglon's partner. He's Cuban."

"It's always someone," she said. "I should never have come back. But I thought I was doing something . . . right."

"Maybe you were."

She had not expected that admission. It seemed to give her encouragement. "You know, there's a grand tragedy in the making down there, and it's not just the Contra war. This administration doesn't know what it's *do*ing. There are villages in Guatemala and Honduras where the only gun is a fifty-year-old pistol buried in someone's back yard. And they're pumping the latest automatic weapons into the area by the hundreds of thousands. They're making every man with a grievance a potential guerrilla leader. The results will be felt for the next fifty years. Or forever."

"You may be right," said Warfield, because she probably was. "But this vote will pass. Molenaur's no threat dead. He's just another casualty. If his brother lives out the week, I'll be surprised."

Bettina knew that. She had known it because Jack had told her. Perhaps she had known it from the moment she picked up the phone to call Warfield because she knew then that her husband had to kill her, or himself, whichever came first. It was a death machine that she had set in motion, and she regretted it now.

"I'm sorry that I involved you at all, Stephen. You've got better things to do than spend your time visiting political refugees."

"The important thing is that you'll be safe here."

She nodded tentatively, conditionally, it seemed. "I had a talk with the ambassador last night," she said. "He assured me that I could stay as long as necessary. But I don't know, really. The Mexicans are walking a fine line between the U.S. and the Nicaraguans. If too much pressure is applied, they might not be able to resist."

"You don't have to worry about that."

Bettina looked at him in the way she always used to do—as if he knew things that others did not and could not. In that little shadow play of mystery and trust their love had lived and grown and might be mended.

"Are you sure, Stephen?"

"I guarantee it."

The maid's room looked out through barred windows across the rear courtyard directly into the slums that backed so many of the buildings on Sixteenth. The sun had topped the walls and sprung color wherever it could. Warfield felt a trickle of sweat run down his back; it stopped, meandered, reversed course. Her hand. Her touch was as feathery and calm as her voice.

"It was one of the last things my father ever told me," she said. "A bedtime story for a grown-up child who had just joined NSA. He said that if someone wanted to make a name in the intelligence services, he should find Heinrich Müller. It would mark the end of an era, and the beginning of a better."

"From Kronos into Zeus."

"My father always called him Kronos," she said. "That's what I called him too. I had a file on him with all the information from my father and all the published material that was available. I was going to find Kronos. But I never imagined how easy it would be."

Warfield turned to face Bettina. The room was still night-cool but her body glistened with moisture. They were not and had never been cautious lovers.

"Easy?"

"Time consuming—but easy," she said. "I contacted Eugenio Heitzman, the man who originally filed the FBI report from Argentina. He was alive four years ago, and as far as I know, he's still alive. I asked him if he'd ever followed up on Kronos. He said yes and no. Although no one had seen

Kronos again in Argentina, about two years after his arrival in Buenos Aires, he transferred his funds to a bank in Medellín, Colombia. That was all Heitzman knew, but it was very interesting. He'd never told that to the FBI of course, because by that time they were out of jurisdiction."

"I never thought of going at it that way," said Warfield. "You have a very logical mind."

"German and methodical," she said. "Before we got together, I used to date a CSA. Remember?"

"The Bostonian from G Group," he said. "I do remember."

She smiled and cleared a space for him on the narrow bed with the dog-eared mattress and the bright dark blood stain exactly in the center. It had been the wrong time but nothing could have kept them from it.

"Asa knew all about computers," she said. "He did a lot of analysis for me. At least that's what he liked to call it. In reality he was reaming the Colombian bank accounts. That took a while. Most records going back as far as the forties don't hit computers except for tax purposes, and the Colombian IRS is a little spacy. But there weren't that many people with the bank who had assets in the millions. I narrowed the list without too much trouble by making some inquiries of my own. I excluded the families who'd been rich forever, and the ones that were very recent."

"It came down to two names," said Warfield. "Molenaur and Aleria."

When Bettina was surprised, the hauteur that seemed so much a part of her beauty gave way to a younger, more childlike configuration. No one would have noticed it but Warfield.

"That's very close," she said. "How did you know?"

"Genealogy. But go on."

"There wasn't much more detective work," she said. "But it took me the longest time to do the simplest thing—refer to a dictionary. I was in El Salvador at the time—in the university library. A few seconds later, I knew I had something in Erich Molenaur."

"That still seems too simple," said Warfield. "A man like Müller just wouldn't go for light cover."

"I thought that too," she said. "But, you know, there's a basic arrogance about so many of the Nazi fugitives. It's almost as if they want to be found out—to be recognized. It's not because of guilt. It's because they were powerful men once. Incredibly powerful. Gods in terms of the power over life and death. Eichmann did everything but advertise in the papers. Mengele was more brazen. His family had a business in Bavaria, with branches in Brazil and Argentina. Mengele lived all over South America. When his father died in 1959, he flew home to Gunzberg for the funeral."

"Makes you wonder about the Israelis."

"Yes, it does," she said. "But they're very sensitive to possible reprisals against the Jewish populations in Central and South America. They also have such a large weapons trade in the area that they can't afford to offend their best customers. I know for a fact that Esteben had extensive dealings with them."

"The son of the head of the Gestapo."

"Yes."

"You're positive it's Müller."

"I have no reasonable doubt," she said. "I had very little when I married Esteben. I've seen his father five times—in Colombia and once in San Juan del Sur—and there's no question in my mind. You'd have to get close to really understand. It's his eyes. No man has ever had eyes like that. He's eighty-five—eighty-six now—but time stopped for him at some place. He's still the hunter. He should be the most nervous prey in the world. And he's not."

"What's his estate like?"

"A fortress," she said.

Warfield moved his hand over her body. He cruised in the

luxury of it. "I want to know everything about it," he said. "Every wall, every window, every generator, every room, every piece of furniture."

"No, Stephen."

"Yes," he said. "I'm going after Müller. That's the one chance to put everything right."

"It won't work," she said. "I've only been to the estate once, but I can tell you the security is impenetrable."

Warfield spanned the narrow bed with his arms. He lay his body against hers and kissed her lips. Speaking softly, nudging her legs apart, he said, "Nothing is impenetrable."

After a moment, she began to laugh, and it was the first time for that.

About seven-thirty, while they were having breakfast at the long brass-topped table in the kitchen, the child came down. He was usually not a late riser, Bettina said, but the last few days had shattered every pretense of routine in his young life. Yet children were adaptable, and she thought that he had actually enjoyed the business of being on the run. At Camelback Ridge he had been the perfect soldier.

The thing about Esteben, or Stephen, was that he was a mess. Warfield had seldom seen a child so ill-favored. He had a nose like Tip O'Neill and a fleshy mouth that pouted as a matter of course. His eyes, some unlucky combination of blue and brown, might generously have been called hazel. His body was ungainly and his neck belonged in the outdoor section of a zoo. Warfield was so shocked by the malformation, and baffled at its origin, that he could not speak. Desperately he searched his mind for some echo or cliché that might save him. And then he remembered what that lying rogue priest had once said.

"He's a good-looking boy, Bettina."

When she smiled proudly, Warfield's black heart broke.

He knew then where that sense of resignation and humility and sadness in her had its source. She was a beautiful woman still. Esteben Molenaur had been a handsome man. Bettina had labored long and brought forth a curiosity. He looked even worse with Rice Krispies up his nose.

"I understand why Molenaur would want the boy back," he said, though in truth he did not.

"His father wanted Esteben more than you know," she said. "Men always want most what they can't have."

Again Warfield did not know what to say. Bettina's parents had fought over her for years, and it seemed unreasonable but somehow inevitable that the pattern should repeat in the next generation, like an alienation in the genes. That seemed infinitely sad too.

"It's a good thing Molenaur's dead," said Warfield. "He might have tried to come after the boy through the courts."

"No," she said. "He wouldn't do that. His only chance was to kidnap Esteben."

"You seem sure."

"An American court would never strip a mother of her son and award custody to a father who was a known homosexual," she said. "Never."

Warfield heard what she said clearly, and he remembered that little item in the Mahdrani file that had seemed so inappropriate. It still seemed that way.

"I think I'm missing something here, Bettina."

She shook her head with woeful and patient good nature. "Stephen, why would Esteben Molenaur marry me? He could have had his pick of any beautiful woman in Latin America. Beautiful *and* rich. But that wasn't what he needed. His only interest in a wife was for window-dressing. I made him a man. I didn't interfere with his life-style. He knew I wouldn't. I was never supposed to."

"Then the boy isn't his."

"He's mine," she said.

"But why would Molenaur want him back so badly?"

"He loved him in his way," she said as if that were possible. "He was not a particularly good father, but he loved the idea of having a son. An heir, you know. When I took Esteben away, I took not only a son but the evidence of his manhood and the continuance of his line. He killed to get them back. He was man enough for that."

Yes. Warfield did not forget the way Molenaur had charged his position, firing indiscriminately, calling him a motherfucker. And now the son, who was done with inhaling the cereal, bore down on Warfield. He had spotted a competitor and he moved in fast, slapping playfully at first, then swinging from the heels. Esteben had a good right hook. Roundhouse but good. He paid no attention to the conversation that progressed between this stranger and his mother because he was intent on breaching Warfield's defense, which consisted of soft hooking crane-hands, almost impenetrable.

"He's active," said Warfield. "Bright. You can see that."

"He gets it from me," she said with a possessive but coy smile. "The rest is from his father. The mouth. The ears. You can't tell about the nose because that's the last thing to take final shape."

It was for sure the boy did not resemble Molenaur, who had thin lips and relatively normal ears. The things that grew from the sides of young Esteben's head were huge and nearly lobeless. They looked more like Warfield's.

"How old is this child, Bettina?"

"I wondered when you'd ask," she said, smiling. "He's three and a half. He'll be four in December."

Warfield nodded and began to count it out but he knew before he started that the calculation was far beyond simple mathematics. Four years and three months ago he and Bettina had been living in sin just across the street from the Clay.